# Roses
# Don't Have
# to be Red

Jen Atkinson

Ink & Quill Publishers

Henderson, NV
2018

*Roses Don't Have to be Red*
Jen Atkinson
Copyright © 2018
All Rights Reserved

Line/Content Editor: Denice Whirmore
Interior Design & Formatting: Jo Wilkins
Cover: Richard Draude

ISBN: 978-1-941271-24-7/Paperback
ISBN: 978-1-941271-39-1/E-Book


1. Fiction/Romance/Contemporary
2. Fiction/Romance/Family Life
3. Fiction/Romance/General

www.iqpublishers.com
Published and Printed in the United States


10 9 8 7 6 5 4 3 2 1

For

Kris, Becky, and Greg
Samantha Blake is blessed enough
to have two sisters who are her best friends,
they love her and believe in her.
And I am just as lucky.

Greg is especially lucky because he has
three sisters who love and adore him.

Also for

Samantha
My dear friend who was the first to read
and love this story, long before anyone else.
Thank you for believing in me then, and now!

# Acknowledgement

*I* believe everyone has a gift, and all gifts are in a process of development. Some are just starting out, and some are far along their way. Wherever mine is, I feel so blessed to be able to share my gift of writing. So, thank you to a loving Heavenly Father who blessed me with a gift and an opportunity to share it.

I need to thank my editor, Denice for all her work, for having faith in what I've written, while helping to improve it. And to Jo my publisher for all she does and for making it happen!

I'm so grateful for good friends, who I feel are always cheering me on! Fara, Kim, Gina, Sam, Amy, you are always some of the first to buy, and read, and share, and support me! And I feel so blessed to have you on my team!

To Heidi, my friend, who has read multiple stages of each of my books and who invests herself in them almost as if they were her own, thank you. I feel so blessed and humbled by the amount of faith and effort you are willing to put into my dream.

Penny, Jay and Cowboy Donuts, thanks for always letting me debut a book with a fun space, donuts, and friends. You are so dear to me.

To Marc and his fantastic UPS store, thank you for caring so much to perfect my business cards, book marks and signs. And for always getting excited about my next project—you are such a great friend and support!

Thank you to Mrs. Haider, one of my 8th grade teachers… years and years later you asked my mom when my first novel would be out. That simple question, made me sit down and plunk out what had been swirling in my brain for a good year, and is now known as Roses Don't Have to be Red.

A great big thanks for all the love and support from my wonderful in-laws, Ron and Kathy. I'm forever thankful to be a part of your family.

I had these wonderful parents who would smile and nod when as a child I would say I'm going to my room to write a book. So many little things you did or said gave me confidence. Thank you, Mom and Dad! My mom believed I could do anything. Anything! I don't know why, but she did and I had to borrow from her abundance of faith more than once. I am so grateful to have been raised by such a beautiful human being.

Thank you to my dear siblings, Beck, Kris, and Greg. You remind me of our mother, and when I feel so desperate for her, I am grateful I have you.

Thank you to my sweet little family. To Jeff, your thoughtfulness and love as you read my work means so much to me — I can't fully explain. You are an amazing support and I feel so thankful I have you. To my ever growing children, Tim, Landon, Seth, and Sydney, I wish time would slow down just a touch. I want you little, a little longer, though, I see all the God given gifts you have, and I'm thrilled to see what you'll do in this life. You each have something beautiful to offer.

And to you, my reader, thank you for reading this book and cheering me on. I am grateful beyond words.

# Roses Don't Have to be Red

# Chapter 1

## 27 Years and 7 Months
## and Oh So Single

Grabbing tools and paperwork from the employee room bench, I shoved them into my old backpack. "Eve, can you believe that Angela Bell?"

"What do you mean?" Eve scowled, her pretty face scrunched with wrinkles. "Hey, those are mine."

Ignoring her, I jammed the protective eye gear and face mask sitting next to her into my worn bag.

"Sam—Sam, hey—Sa-manth-a!"

"What?" I paused mid-shove and faced her glare.

"Those. Are. Mine." Standing, hands on her hips, she rolled her eyes at me.

"Oh, right. Sorry." I took the last few items out of my ancient, middle school pack and set them next to her.

"What's with you?"

"What's with me? I slammed my fist against the metal bench, a clang sounding throughout our work changing room. "Did you really just ask that? Were you not at the same retirement luncheon as me?"

"Come on. Angela was fine."

"Fine?" Hissing out a breath, I cocked an eyebrow.

Sure, Angela was eighteen and sure when you're eighteen you're supposed to be a little stupid. I still can't believe they asked her to speak—I mean, just because she's Ray's niece.

"It was Ray's day," I said. "*His* retirement. All she did was

1

announce her engagement!"

"She said she loved Ray, too."

I took off my boots, tossing them into my locker. Flipping the strands from my falling-out ponytail away from my face, I looked up at her. "Only because he introduced them! And did you hear what else she said? *I've been waiting my whole life for this.*" I couldn't help the high inflection my voice took when mimicking Angela, or the gag reflex that came each time I thought about it.

Eve pushed my shoulder and whipped her head from side-to-side. "Come on, Sam, shut up. Her family runs this place, and she's a sweet kid. You don't want to lose your job because your volume level is stuck on high and you hold a grudge against anyone who gets married before age twenty-five."

"I do not hold grudges." I kept my volume on high. "I couldn't care less. It's Ray I'm thinking about." She's right though, I needed to lower my voice. I couldn't lose my job over *Angela Bell*. Finding a place to work in this remote area without commuting to Jackson or Idaho meant only a handful of options, my option--Bell's Lumber Mill.

Leaning down, she whispered, "Is this about Angela…or is this about *you*?"

"Me? Ha!" But my voice did that stupid high pitched thing again—making me sound guilty. I slid into my street shoes and stood, following Eve out. "We've got to get out of this town Eve."

"I happen to like the Valley," she said.

And I did too.

Star Valley was a small community deep in Wyoming, far from anything and anyone else. Several tiny towns made up what we called the Valley. And Eve was right. It was a good place. A good place, with good people, people who married young and worked hard; people who filled their homes with children and values. I was lucky to have grown up here. But as a *single* twenty-seven year old woman, Star Valley was like my own personal *Happy Valley Hell.*

"I hope you like being single," I mumbled under my breath. I regretted it the minute I said it. Eve was a whole year older than me. She hadn't grown up here, but somehow she fit right in.

And she seemed fine with the fact that she wasn't married — or dating — and that her prospects were nil.

She turned and peeked at me, walking into the sunshine. "I didn't catch that."

Sunday. Family dinner night. I still itched with irritation about Ray's retirement party two days earlier. Now, I would have to endure *Nana.*

Unbuttoning my coat, I opened Dad's closet and hung it inside. My night to cook, I arrived early. Maybe I could avoid confrontation if I appeared hard at work.

"Samantha, remind me, what is your age now?" said Nana the super spy — I never even heard her coming.

"Twenty-three, Nan." The closet door still blocked my view of the little silver-haired fox.

Nana cleared her throat — a scolding sound, and started in on me. "Let's see, I am eighty-one, so that would make you…" Nana paused for a moment. "Samantha Blake, don't you lie to your Nana."

Closing the closet door, I faced her. Placing my hands on her shoulders, I stared ahead with a clear view right over the little lady's head. "Nana, you are a very intelligent woman, you know perfectly well that I am twenty-seven-years old." She asked me the same question last week — and I know the woman's memory hadn't gone yet.

"Why would you lie to your grandmother?" She shook her head, and folded her hands together, laying them against the skirt of her floral dress.

"Nana! You know how old I am."

She glared at me, the wrinkles around her eyes creasing.

Blowing a sigh through my lips, I hung my head. "I need to cook."

"You are right, Samantha. I do know how old you are. You are three years older than your mother when she married. You have a birthday coming. Soon you will be single and twenty-eight years — "

"Ellen." Dad trotted down the stairs. "Samantha knows this.

You reminding her will not change the situation."

"What situation?" I turned, flipping my brown ponytail into my eyes, my hands on my hips. Did he really think *this* was rescuing me? My two-day irritation flared. "There isn't a situation. Being single is *not* a situation!"

"It is when your almost thirty," Nana said, her eyes as wide as shot glasses.

Covering my face with my hands, I muffled through my fingers. "No! It's not."

"What's going on? Situation?" My oldest sister walked into the room. Elizabeth, married Eric at twenty-three, right after serving two years in the Peace Corps. Mother of two with one on the way — yes, she is a superhero.

"Samantha refuses to marry." Nana's flamboyant hands flew through the air with her shocking news.

"Oh." Liza sighed. "*That* situation."

"Pu!" I folded my arms. "I *refuse*? Oh, that's it, Nana. I am just so stubborn, I refuse." I forced a laugh at her ridiculous assumption. "Whom would you have me marry, Nana?"

My younger sister plopped on the couch, just in time to hear my speech. "What about Robert?" Amanda, my baby sister, married her high school sweetheart at just nineteen. Two years ago she and her husband Max adopted their first child.

"Robert? Who the heck is Robert?" I'm so glad the whole family made the time to analyze my life — again.

"There is no reason for language, missy," Nana said, shaking a finger at me.

"You know." Amanda ignored Nana and bounced her eyebrows at me. "*Robert,* Junior year?"

Blinking, I stepped over to the couch where Amanda sat and bent down. I whispered, hoping only she could hear me. "Prom Robert?"

"Yes. He moved back west, he's in Jackson. I saw him in the grocery store."

"Really?" I sat beside her, my body sinking into the couch. "I haven't seen him in years." The boy did look good in a tux, and he gave me my first real kiss.

"I know!" Amanda sat up straighter and clapped her hands together. "And he is still so cute."

"Who's cute?" Max walked in carrying little Jillian.

Amanda winked at her husband. "The catch we're setting Sam up with."

"Ah, sorry Sam." Max sighed.

Scooting passed me, he kissed his wife hello. I smiled at the sight of my little sister with her husband and child. I loved my family—*Fiercely*—which is why I've never left the Valley. But watching their lives move on while mine stood still, had taken its toll. I wanted to move on, I wanted what they had, but I just didn't know how to get my hands on it.

"Samantha, I've had the most wonderful idea." Nana appeared in front of me, her arms opened wide. "I will find you a husband."

"Ohhhh, no you don't." I stood and started into the kitchen. "Nope. No thank you, Nan."

Shuffling after me, she said, "Of course I will. Your sisters can help me. Your mother would have wanted—"

"Nana, I know. But if Mom was alive today, do you really think her answer would be to have you, my Nana, search every corner of the state until you've found me a man?" I threw an apron over my head and pulled the pork roast from Dad's refrigerator.

"As a matter of fact, I do." Where did this woman get her energy? "It really shouldn't be that difficult. You've got her long brown hair and big brown eyes. She was always a looker. Besides, she would want you to be happy, Samantha."

"Who says I'm not happy?" I beat the meat with a tenderizer. But I could see it in Nana's victory smile. I had already lost this fight.

After a long night with my family, I left my sisters to do the dishes and came home to my quiet, house. Already in my pj's, I lay on my bed. Picking up my phone, I texted Eve.

Me: Eve, maybe we should move.
Eve: In? Together? You're my best friend, Sam,

> but I'm too old for a roommate.
> Me: No, like out of town.
> Eve: Is this about Angela Bell? I'm not moving
>     because your panties are all in a bunch
>     over an eighteen year old getting married.
>     I love you, Samantha, now get over it.

Opening a half gallon of ice cream, I plopped onto my couch—the couch I picked out, without help from anyone. Only my opinion mattered. I flipped through the channels on my smart T.V. The television I bought myself with my overtime pay—I didn't have to ask another soul to buy myself that prize.

My insides hurt. My independent thoughts not all that comforting. My head pounded, and all I wanted was a hug from my mother. Feeling like crap always had me pining for Mom, but she couldn't rescue me. Mom married Dad at twenty-four. Did Nana give her this much trouble? Probably not, by twenty-five she had Elizabeth. By twenty-seven, she had me, and at twenty-nine she was done with Amanda. She earned a degree in Chemistry, something I know nothing about. She never entered a career, but who could with everything else she accomplished? She worked harder than any woman I've ever known. But mostly, she loved her family—with every word, with every action, she loved us.

I wanted the chance to do the same—didn't I?

When I turned sixteen, Mom got sick. Test after test, and then the diagnoses. Colon cancer. She went from being sick, to being a patient, to no longer resembling herself. And then she died. One night, after almost a year of fighting, she asked Dad to gather us all around her. She told us each goodbye. Two hours later the world became a little less beautiful, and life would never, ever be the same.

How did she know? How did she know what to do with her life? How did she know what to study and whom to marry and how to live? How did she know she would leave us when she did?

And why didn't I inherit any of that know-how?

It wasn't even nine o'clock. Still, I trudged my pathetic self into my bedroom, using my cell as a flashlight to guide my way.

I dropped it on the night stand and fell into bed.

I hadn't shut my eyes yet when the phone started to sing. Picking it up, I looked at the screen. Nana. Sighing, I shut my eyes, and for a small second thought about ignoring the call. "Hello, Nana."

"Samantha, I am serious about helping you find a mate. Keep Friday open, you'll have a date." My semi-crazy, Dr. Seuss grandmother wouldn't rest until I had a ring on my finger.

"Why don't you just get online like everyone else today?" Eve asked when I told her about my apparent *situation*.

"Well, that's great for some people, but I'm not one of them," I said, yelling above the noisy machines in the shop.

"You'd rather have *Nana* setting you up?" She yelled back, adjusting her safety goggles.

"That's not what I said." I pushed my protective eye gear up off the bridge of my nose. "I'm just not a person who can feel sparks through a computer screen."

Laughing at me, Eve pulled another strip of wood through the router.

"Why don't you take your own advice?"

Smiling, she said, "Maybe I will." But I didn't believe her.

Holding my head, I shut my eyes. "We are going to end up old maids who work together, live together, shop together, clean together, eat together—"

"No we're not," she said, shutting down the router. "I don't like you *that* much. Besides, I already told you I won't move in with you."

7

# Chapter 2
## Blind Date #1

What a long week. Nana called me every day, reminding me when and where to meet my date. I wouldn't be forgetting anytime soon—she'd made sure of that. Cello's, seven o'clock. I would meet *Martin* at the small, local, sit down restaurant—the only one in town where you didn't seat yourself.

So, at 6:45 I slipped into my best jeans and readjusted my work-day ponytail, ready to meet Nana's fix-up. Confession—I was a little excited. I hadn't been on a real date in a year—okay, fifteen months. But who was counting?

Jittery, I walked over to the hostess. "Hi, I'm meeting someone. His name is Martin."

"Ah yes, Mr. Benet. Right this way."

Following the girl through the sea of tables, we stopped and she directed me to a table near the back.

Turning to the table at my left, a *boy* sat in Martin's chair. His blonde hair stood up in back with the front gelled to a crunch and combed to the side. His oversized suit and too long tie clearly belonged to someone else. "Oh, miss?" I tapped her arm, stopping her before she left me there babysitting. "I think you must be mistaken."

"No mistake." Her lips parted, cracking into a crooked grin.

*Mr. Benet?* Is he even out of high school yet?

Stepping over to the table, I cleared my throat—announcing my arrival. Maybe he wouldn't see me… or hear me… maybe I could sneak out and—

"Samantha?" His voice cracked, and he stared at me as if unsure.

Why did I make any sound at all? "Ahh—" I could lie...

Crossing his arms over his child-size chest, he grinned, his braces glittering in the fluorescent lights. "You're older than the picture your grandmother gave me, but then she said you would be."

"Oh, ha ha. Yes, it's me." She gave him a picture? My cheeks burned hot, I needed a cold drink and possibly restraints so that I wouldn't be arrested for harming an eighty-year-old woman. "You must be Martin?" I said, my fingers crossed behind my back with insane hope that this was just a huge misunderstanding. Waiting for an answer I already knew, I bit my lip, tearing off small pieces of attached skin.

Slicking his already gelled hair back with his palm, he stood. "Yes. I am so happy to finally meet you. Your grandmother has been telling me about you for a while now. You and I both played the tuba in high school."

"Really?" I said through a weak laugh, falling into the chair beside me. "When was that exactly—high school?"

Sitting, he crossed his legs, his hands clasped on top of his knee. "Your grandmother is a wonderful lady. She really loves her family."

Biting my ripped up lip, I breathed. In through the nose. Out through the mouth. "She does." Flipping through the menu, I clenched my jaw. "So, what do you do Martin?"

"I'm so glad you feel comfortable calling me Martin." He rested his elbows on the table top.

Squinting, I looked at him in utter confusion.

"Last month, I earned my Eagle Scout. This month, Dad gave me quite the promotion at work. From now on I'll be wearing suits and ties, if you know what I mean." He tugged at the collar on his too big suit coat. "It's kind of a big deal. People usually refer to me as *Mr. Benet.*"

"You just got your Eagle Scout?" My menu slipped through my fingers and onto the ground. "Isn't that something you earn before you turn eighteen? How *old* are you, Martin?"

10

"My project was a pretty big deal. I did a coat drive. Maybe you read about it in the Valley Times?"

Managing to shake my head no, I stared across the table at the skinny, pimpled boy. Could I go to jail for this blind date?

"I collected forty-five coats for the homeless—"

With my palms pressed against the table, I leaned in closer to him. "Your age Martin, how old are you?"

"Of course, we don't have that many homeless in the Valley, but my Dad's having them shipped to—"

"Martin!" I slapped the table top. "So help me—tell me how old you are this minute!"

"All right, okay. Although, I should tell you, I think it's superficial to—"

A growling noise I'd never heard myself make before left my throa,t and he flinched.

"Eighteen, I'm eighteen. My birthday was two days ago."

"Two days!" I stood, then sat, then stood again. *What the*—

"Don't go," he said, reaching over and pulling me down by my sleeve.

"Did my grandmother tell you how old I am?" I fell back into my seat.

He grinned and waved off my concern. "Oh that. Don't worry, Samantha. Mrs. Michelson has been clueing me in for months. I know you're thirty. It really doesn't bother me. I've always been more mature than other guys my age. But we won't be able to take our time with this." He pointed to me, to himself and then back to me again.

Closing my opened mouth, I gathered what I could of my composure. I spoke—trying to sound like my fourth grade gym teacher. "First of all, *buddy*, I am NOT thirty yet. Secondly, we will not have to rush anything, because there isn't going to be a *this*." I copied his pointy-pointy motion. "Okay? Okay. Now, since I'm here and hungry, I will let you buy me dinner, but that's it. Got it?"

"**N**ana!" I didn't wait to drive home before yelling at my elderly grandmother. "What in the world were you thinking? He is eighteen years old."

"What does age matter?  Besides, twenty-seven years is quite young."

"Why, Nana, that is probably the sweetest thing you've ever said to me. You're right, twenty-seven is young, but it is indeed too old for a boy just eighteen."

"Well, I was trying to find you a catch, dearie.  Any boy your age and unmarried must have something wrong with him."

Laying my head against my steering wheel, I moaned. "Then tell me Nana, what is wrong with me?"

## *Chapter 3*
### *27 Years and 10 Months*

The next three months I refused to speak to Nana about more blind dates. Martin Benet's braced face haunted my dreams. How could Nana set me up with him? A *boy*. Is that really who she saw me spending my life with? Don't get me wrong, there was nothing wrong with Martin Benet—I'm sure he would be a great match for someone his own age. But even without the age issue, he just wasn't my type. So, I chose to drown in wondering what could be wrong with me.

Sitting on the metal bench next to Eve, I tapped my pen on the edge of my seat, making a small clanging noise to the beat of a song I couldn't name, waiting for our morning work meeting to start. Angela Bell—no, Angela Cash now, stood to motivate us. Her new husband took her hand to help her stand on the work stool.

Leaning in, Eve whispered in my ear. "Are we going to start talking about moving again?"

"No, I'm done with that." What was the use? I'd never left the Valley, not even when Mom died—I couldn't leave Dad and Amanda. When Amanda got married, I insisted I still needed to be close—for Dad, and my sisters, too. I'm not completely pathetic. Eventually, I moved out, got a place of my own—two whole years ago. And my two bedroom, one bath rental house sat two entire blocks from Dad's. Yeah, Eve had nothing to worry about. I wasn't going anywhere.

"Okay. Just thought I'd make sure. I need to know when I should start collecting boxes."

"Ha. Ha." I rolled my eyes, my head bent, so only she could hear me. "Like you'd follow me."

"You're right. I wouldn't."

I contorted my face at Eve, sticking out my tongue and crossing my eyes. Ignoring me, she focused on Angela's speech.

"We work hard," Angela said, "for the ones we love and the love of our community."

Looking at Eve, I pointed my finger down my throat, a soundless gag at Angela's words. Turning back, I pretended to re-tighten my ponytail.

Angela hopped down from the chair and the crowd stood, ready for the work day.

Facing Eve, I gave her my uber dreamy eyes and puckered my lips at her.

The palm of her hand flattened overtop my face, while she stared past me.

Walking around to each of us, Angela passed out red and white heart covered thank you notes. I didn't go to her wedding reception or get her a gift—which earned me a scolding from Eve, but I still got a kissy-face thank you.

"I thought you were over this Angela thing." Eve bent down to tie her boots.

"I am."

Her brows rose on her forehead, and she shook her head at me.

*F*eeling at home in my father's kitchen, I placed an apron over my head. A peace washed over me like it always did when I entered a kitchen. The world may not have a place for me, but this kitchen did. When Mom died, I coped by cooking for Dad and Amanda. My dream of going to culinary school may be long gone, but it still felt natural and right whenever I stood in front of a hot stove. Spreading out a variety of spices I'd brought from home, I ran my hand along the counter. Nana walked into the kitchen, and I kissed her cheek hello. "How are you, Nana?"

"Hair pulled back again?" She shook her head.

"What's wrong with my hair?" I tugged on the end of my ponytail. "This is a very sanitary way to wear your hair when cooking." I didn't mention it had been pulled back all day, but then I didn't really need to. I almost always wore my hair back — easy and efficient.

"It isn't suitable for catching a husband though."

Ignoring her, I pounded the chicken with my tenderizer until my hand hurt. Between Nana and Angela Bell, I might need therapy. But how can you tell the woman who helped raise you to zip it?

Bringing the meat bat into the air, with both of my fists wrapped around it — Angela, Nana, husband hair, kissy-thank yous —

"The bird is already dead, Samantha." Placing her hands on her hips, she stared at me, her eyes knowing. "What is the matter?"

"I think I'm ready for another date, Nana." Maybe I'd gone crazy to let the woman at it again, but doing nothing made me just as crazy.

Clapping her hands together, she sped walked to my side. "I knew this would happen sooner or later. I've already been planning! I've got the perfect match."

"Nana, do you know who Robert George is?" As long as she was looking — couldn't she look toward my old prom date?

"No, I do not." With her hands on her hips, she continued. "But, I do know —"

"He was my prom date, junior year. He moved back east right after prom, but he's back." I had spent too much time wondering about prom Robert since Amanda mentioned him. But I was more chicken than the bird in front of me to do anything about it. "Do you think you could look him up?"

"Did you really just ask our eighty-one-year old grandmother to find your old boyfriend for you?" Elizabeth stood in the doorway, her hands on her hips reminding me of Nana. But Robert wasn't my old boyfriend, he was just one date. One really great date.

15

"Oh, hey Liza," Heat filled my cheeks and I averted my eyes. "I just thought, since she is so gung ho about finding me a date, she could—"

"Samantha, you are a grown woman," Liza said, treating me like I was a little girl. "Look up Rob yourself."

"Almost a thirty year old woman," Nana said.

Ignoring Nana, I glared at my sister. Yes, maybe it had been a childish request, but she wasn't in my shoes. She had no idea what it felt like to be me. She left home before Mom died. She didn't have the guilt keeping her here.

Folding her arms, she glared back. "You are very capable of finding yourself a date."

Tapping her pointer finger to her lips, Nana hummed. "I would have to disagree with that, dear."

I wanted to glare at Nana, but Liza wasn't done with me. "Why are you having our Nana, or anyone for that matter, find you a date?"

"Hey!" I pointed at Nana. "This was her idea." I blamed Nana. I actually pointed, accusing my eighty-one-year old grandmother. I threw my hands up in the air. "Because, Liza! Okay? *Because*. We live in this tiny town where no man over the age of twenty is single. That's why. I can't find a date. It's been over a year since I was last asked out."

"Whose fault is that? There *are* single people here, but how would you know any of them? You work, and then you go home and spend time with your T.V. You can't get asked out when you never leave your house, Sam."

## Blind Date #2

Despite Liza's scolding, I let Nana fix me up again. Todd had graduated from *college* in chemical engineering. She said he was the son of a good friend who lived and worked in a town that neighbored ours in the Valley.

Nana instructed me to wait just inside of Piggy Iggy's Pizza—a kid's place in another town in the Valley. Only fifteen minutes from work, I planned to do as Nana requested and let my hair down, but I didn't have time to go home and fix up any sort of hairdo. So, I just readjusted the ponytail and called it good. Still, Amanda loaned me a shirt that I kept in my work locker so I at least had something nice to wear.

I chose to think cute rather than creepy that Todd wanted to meet at a kid's restaurant. In my head I pictured us playing the race car game, side-by-side in the bucket seats. Smiling at the thought, I covered my mouth. I was getting ahead of myself and letting my silly head run away.

Walking inside, I stood next to the front doors. Looking around the establishment, I didn't see a guy sitting alone—so I assumed he hadn't arrived yet. I jumped out of the way as a small child ran by, feeling the eyes of suspicious parents on my face as I stood there, an almost thirty year old woman without a child at my side. Children laughed and ran throughout the place. A mother raced by, chasing down her escaping toddler. Bells and whistles rang from various machines. Children laughed and cried and screamed out with glee. Was every child in Star Valley here? A giggling little girl stopped my rising nerves. My niece and two nephews loved this place. And just like that, with one laughing girl, the ridiculous unease in my gut left. I smiled, breathing out a calming breath, glad I let Nana into my non-existent dating life.

This would work, it would be right—as soon as I found Todd. Checking my watch, it was ten minutes after our meeting time and still no Todd. "I don't know what is worse, getting stood up or dating a boy scout." I glanced at my watch again, twelve minutes after. Looking up, I stood nose to nose with Piggy Iggy's clown, Iggster. "Oh, hello." Stepping backward, I bumped into the door. "You frightened me a bit."

"Sorry, miss. No reason to be scared. Clowns are here to make you smile." The red nose and rainbow wig bobbed with laughter.

"Aha." I forced a laugh, but not much came out. His white face made my skin crawl, and I wished he would go find a child to give nightmares to.

Rocking his head side-to-side, he didn't leave. "Are you by chance, Samantha?"

Catching my breath at the sound of my name, I stopped

avoiding his stare and made contact with the black circles around his eyes. Did I know this Iggster? "Yes, ah, I am." Or—yes, he must know why Todd's late!

"Oh boy!" He jumped in the air, laughing like a character out of a Saturday morning cartoon.

One of his big red shoes came down on my foot. "Ouch!" I backed away but my spine already lay flat against the closed door.

"I'm Todd." He held out a white gloved hand, twice the size of his regular hand. "Sorry I'm late, but my shift ran long."

Coughing, I poked his protruding, stuffed belly. "You—you're Todd? You?"

"Uh-huh." His belly rocked with the confirmation.

"Ah. Oh. So, do you volunteer here or something?" Volunteer work—yeah, volunteering is good, and honorable, and non-freaky.

"If they *pay* their volunteers, then yes!" Chuckling, he held his overstuffed sides.

Okay, so he wasn't exactly in a tux…we weren't exactly at prom, and he wasn't a volunteer. Still, working with kids in his spare time… I could get on board with that. "Wow, I'm surprised you have time to date, work as a chemical engineer and clown around." I tried to laugh at my stupid joke, but I couldn't. My insides squirmed, screaming at me to run away!

"What was that?" he asked over a sobbing child scuttling by.

"I said I'm surprised you have time to date." I yelled, but kept my distance from his white face.

"Let's sit down." He held out his gloved hand for me to take and follow after him.

Patting the glove, I motioned him along without holding his hand. Following Todd through loud video game music, flashing lights and crowds of children, I sat at a table near the back. Holding up a gloved white finger, he gestured for me to wait. Todd skipped off to the drink station, his oversized red shoes clomping along the tiled floor. My pulse raced. I watched him balance our cups on his wide palms. Todd held out his hands, and I took the drinks, setting them on our table top. The back table at least meant less noise ringing through my ears. We wouldn't have to yell to hear one another.

"I think it's really great that you take the time to work here." He must love kids—right?

"Oh, I wouldn't have it any other way. The kids are great. The boss is the best. In fact he just gave me a raise. I'm up to $10.50 an hour now."

Laughing at his joke, I tore my gaze from the polka dots covering his chest. "That's great! Really bringing home the bacon, huh? So, how often do you do this?" So, he wore a clown costume on our date. So, he was—*is* a clown. So what? Right? The date could only get better, couldn't it? Let's get awkward and a little strange out of the way—right off the bat. I could move on from here.

I'm up to thirty-six hours a week." Holding the sides of his drink with both hands, he sipped from the straw.

"That many? When do you find time for your *real* job?"

Setting his drink down, he crossed his arms, laying them over his fat belly. "This is my real job." The disgust in his voice threw my *it can only get better* theory right out the window.

*Nana, what have you done?* "Oh, I thought you were a Chemical Engineer." I sucked in a shaky breath and held my rickety knees still with the tips of my fingers. *This could not be happening.* Explanation. Explanation! Let the man give an explanation.

"That's what my father likes to tell people." Rolling his eyes, Todd shook his head, his wig staying perfectly in place. "I do have a degree, but my true passion has always been in the clown arts."

"Clown arts?" My skin crawled with invisible ants, making me want to scratch every bare section. Tremors moved throughout my body, from my head to my toes.

Nodding, Todd continued to talk about the art of clowning for over half an hour. It wasn't until a little boy came by and wanted Todd to make him a balloon monkey that he shut up. The boy left and he immediately started back in.

The tornado going on inside of me couldn't let him. This had to end. "I'm sorry. I am going to have to leave."

"We haven't even ordered our pizza. Do you have to work in the morning?" he asked, his clown nose crooked on his white

19

face.

I could think of only one way to get out of this, only one way he would just let me leave—brutal honesty. "Todd, I have a confession."

He scooted his chair in closer, his fake stomach folding over the top of the table. Staring at me with wide eyes, his red nose inches from my face.

"When I was seven years old I went to a neighbor boy's birthday party. A clown jumped out of the bushes and scared me to death. I poured my pop down his pants and pushed him down. I have never been able to look at clowns the same. I'm sorry. This just isn't going to work."

Jutting from his seat, Todd's chair fell backward. His wig lopped to one side, he pointed at me. "How dare you. Clowns make people laugh, we make people happy."

Shaking my head, I'd had my fill of the wonder of clowning. "You're scary. Lose the wig and white face."

Todd's hand flew up to his colorful wigged head. "You're crazy. Clown hater."

Standing, I stared up at him. "I am not the crazy one." Picking up my Styrofoam cup, I was ready to escape this nightmare Nana called a date.

Todd protectively held to his oversized pants and flung his own drink right in my face. "Did you know we have a support group for abused clowns?"

I gasped. Ice and lemonade ran down the inside of my shirt. My body shook and cubes fell from my clothes to the ground. With the sleeve of my shirt, I wiped his drink from my forehead and cheeks. "I was just leaving. I'm not seven anymore."

*Blind Date #3*

Yes, as insane as it may sound, there was a third blind date. Nana's description—a very attractive young man with a great job—for sure this time. Nana wanted me dating a clown as much as I did. She explained that this time she had been to his place of employment, Valley Credit Union—which is maybe why

I allowed a third setup to occur.

I couldn't imagine a banker throwing his drink on me.

Getting off work early, I pulled into Idaho Falls and at six o'clock on the dot. I walked into Willie's Miniature Golf to meet *Jeremy*.

Crossing the green, I entered the small building to rent my club and ball—the spot where Nana had told me to meet him. One man leaned against the counter. One. But he couldn't—no, he could not be my date. My second cousin, Jeremy Michelson, stare back at me, his eyes mimicking the wide disbelief of my own. The club fell from his hands, clinking to the ground.

Turning on my heels, I escaped through the door, somehow managing to keep my gagging to a minimum. "Nana!" I screamed into my cell. I had a two hour drive to ream her out. How could she? What was she thinking? What was I thinking? This wasn't working.

"Samantha, he is my brother's grandson. That makes you second cousins once removed or something to that effect. Certainly not close enough to be considered a relation."

Wringing the steering wheel with my hands until my knuckles lost all their color, I yelled at my eighty-one-year-old grandmother. "That's it, Nana! We're through. I will find my own dates from now on."

## Chapter 4
### *28 Years and 1 Months*

*T*hree dates in six months, that's not too bad. And they weren't that awful. The Boy Scout was really very nice and my cousin is quite the catch.

"What is wrong with you?" Eve asked. My blank stare must have given my thoughts away.

I zipped my work jumper and looked at Eve's pretty face. I couldn't lie to Eve. She was my best friend. "I am trying to convince myself that my dating life is normal and healthy."

Her eyebrows rose to an abnormal high place on her forehead. "Sam, nothing is normal or healthy about that."

"Yeah, I know." I hung my head. Stomping my foot up on the workbench, I tied the laces of my boot. "What about you? When was the last time you went out?" I asked, turning things around on her.

"Hmm, with you last week." Her blue eyes sparkled as she teased me.

Eve, I'm serious. I can't remember the last time you told me you went on a date."

"Probably because I haven't dated in a while." How could she smile while she said that?

"Well, that's sad." Why wasn't she more irritated?

"It's not as sad as what you've been doing, Sam." She brushed her dark blonde hair from her shoulder. "You do realize that there are plenty of people on this planet who don't get married until that ripe ol' age of thirty—right?" She shook her head at

23

me. "Besides, I'm happy. I love my job. I go skiing every other Saturday. I just bought a house. So, don't try dragging me down into your wallowing world."

She was amazing, and I was pathetic.

Working in a crowded, loud warehouse, we didn't talk anymore. Eight hours later, my insides molded together like warm, icky jell-o. I'm a jerk. A *single* jerk. A discontent, single jerk. "Eve, I'm sorry for what I said. I know you're happy, and I'm glad."

Shaking her head at me, Eve smiled, showing off her perfect, straight teeth. "Don't apologize. I just want you to be happy, too."

"Eve!" Angela Bell—err, Cash stood behind us. "Samantha. I have something to say—"

Oh, I hated it when she started a sentence like that.

"William and I are going to be parents! Isn't it a miracle?"

Moving next to me, Eve linked her arm with mine and pinched my side. "Ouch!" Yelping, I wiggled away from her. Her eyes went wide, warning me, and I bit my lip.

"That's really wonderful, Angela." Eve patted Angela's shoulder.

The girl bounced away, her blonde curls bobbing behind her.

"She is going to be a mother? She's a baby. A child in a woman-size body." My cheeks burned. At least she would get fat.

"Okay, so she's a little young. Still, her age doesn't declare her ready or not, Sam. She is happily married. Maybe she *is* ready."

"You can't be serious!"

"Shush." She held her finger to her lips and looked past me for any sign that Angela had heard us.

And what's with the pinching?" I shoved her shoulder.

"You would have said something stupid."

"Ah—" My mouth dropped open. "That is—"

Sitting down, she pulled me onto the bench beside her. "Samantha, you are almost thirty years old, do not make me shush you again."

## Blind Date #4

$N$ow, I'm not completely crazy. Nana wasn't the only matchmaker in the family. Max had single friends in neighboring towns, and my little sister had an itch to meddle in—or help, my situation too. Plus, she promised to keep a look out for Robert.

Aaron had married young. Eight years and three kids later, they divorced.

Sitting in my sister's home where I'd spent hours with her and little Jill, where I'd eaten dinner countless times and laughed until water spewed from my nose—sitting here with my family, in what could be another home to me—made this time, this blind date feel different. Feel right.

The doorbell rang, and I jumped to my feet. Amanda waved her hand, her blonde head bobbing a silent, *play it cool*. My sister had insisted on loaning me another outfit. She tried combing out my ponytail bump after work, but it was no use, so she gave me a fancy twist on the back of my head. She tried to talk me into eyeliner, but I knew she'd poke my eye out.

Opening the door, a tall, well built, handsome *man* stood in front of me. Not a boy or a clown or a cousin, but a man. My sister had taste. This was a definite improvement.

*Thank you, Amanda.*

"Samantha." Aaron grinned. "I'm so happy to meet you."

"Me too—to meet you," I said, swimming in his big green eyes. He must be perfect.

"Hey, man," Max said. He and Aaron shook hands and then Max turned to me. "Amanda needs your help. She isn't sure how to julienne—err something. She said you'd know."

"Oh, okay. Sure." I gave Aaron a small non-eyeliner flutter before skipping off to the kitchen. Holding up a knife in one hand and a potato in the other, Amanda looked from one to the other, biting her lower lip. "Oh, good. Sam, how do I—"

"Give me that." I took the knife and potato from her and went to work. "How have I never met him before?" I could swim in those eyes.

Amanda smiled, then tapped me on the head with her wooden spoon. "He was married, remember?"

"Oh, right." So maybe he wasn't perfect. He had a flaw — one. "You never really told me what happened there."

"As he is in the dining room waiting for dinner, this isn't really the time to explain." She waved her hands at me. "Keep cutting! But I'm glad you like him."

"He is perfect."

Setting her hand on my wrist, she stopped my cutting motion. "Whoa, sister. Don't do that, to him or yourself. No man is perfect. You need to remember Aaron was married. He has a past. He and Jamie were both at fault in their marriage. Not to mention you *just* met him."

"Yeah. Okay." I nodded, still thinking about those green eyes.

Finishing my task, I followed Amanda out into the living room.

"Jamie said our baby girl is walking." Aaron clapped his hands, talking to Max. "I can't believe it. Melissa, walking! I'm missing everything."

"Wow, already?" Max laughed, his dark eyes on Aaron. "Jillian didn't start walking until she was 13 months. You guys are going to have your hands full with that one."

"Jamie can handle it." Aaron sighed and didn't seem to notice me, his date, had returned. "She is great with those girls."

Max crossed one leg over the other, setting his ankle on his knee. "How are you and Jamie getting along?"

"Max!" Amanda squealed, her hands pinching her hips. "Can you help me in the kitchen? Please!"

Poor Max stood, his eyebrows knit together, staring at his wife and wondering, I'm certain, at what he'd done wrong.

Taking Max's seat next to Aaron, I crossed my arms, my anxious nerves rising with the quiet.

"So," he said. "You ever been married?"

"Ah—" I scanned the living room carpet. "Nope."

"It's great. Well, hard, but really great, too." He smiled, and somehow it wasn't as perfect as I'd remembered. Still, he had potential. At least he wasn't my cousin.

26

"I've heard it can be difficult," I said, not knowing what else to say. Why would he say that? What should I respond with?

"Oh, yeah, it can be—especially when you work three jobs and never see your wife."

"Wow, you have three jobs?" I asked, begging to change the subject.

"Yes, I do."

"What are they? Why so many?" My hands knotted together in my lap. *Please, please, please new topic.*

"Well, Jamie—uh, that's my wife—"

Err, wasn't she his ex-wife? And did I say perfect before? His green eyes had started to resemble baby poop.

"I wanted to give her a big house, a new car, you know? I tried to earn enough money to make that happen for her. I guess she didn't appreciate it."

I couldn't help it. I had to state the obvious. This poopy-eyed man couldn't see it. "What's a nice house and car worth if you don't have the one you love around to share it with?"

Aaron stared at me, his poop-green eyes darting back and forth. How much would the light bulb in his head sting once it turned on?

"You're right. You're absolutely right!"

"Guess it's not that difficult after all." Laying my back flat against the couch, I faced forward, not wanting to stare at Aaron's face any longer.

"I didn't even know what I had." He stopped.

Staring up at the popcorn finish on Amanda's ceiling, I groaned. "Until it was gone." *I was hoping for a date, not a counseling session.* I'd yell at Amanda later.

"You're right, Sandy." He gave my shoulder a pat.

I brushed his hand away. "It's Samantha."

"Max, Amanda!" He yelled, standing up and rubbing his hands together.

The two hurried into the room, a hot pad covering Amanda's right hand. "What's going on?"

"Sandy," he said, pointing at me, "just helped me realize what I need to do. I am going to quit one of my jobs and beg Jamie to take me back."

He was so not as cute as I thought.

"What did you say to him?" Amanda said in hushed tones, nudging my side.

"I. . . I. . . I don't know."

Walking over to Max, Aaron hugged his friend. Then slapping my shoulder, he smiled, looking disgustingly dreamy. "Thanks, and don't worry, a lot of women are single at thirty."

Dancing out to his car, the three of us stood in the doorway watching him.

"Well, that could have been awkward." Amanda's tone rang with sarcasm. Gaping at me from the corner of her eye, she forced a giant grin that wrinkled her face in all the wrong places.

Biting my cheek, I blew out a puff of air. I was cursed.

"He really is a great guy. It's just—"

Turning, I walked back into the house, not waiting to hear how great the man I just chased away happened to be.

"Where are you going?" Amanda hollered from the doorway.

"To look up cousin Jeremy's phone number."

## Chapter 5
### 28 Years and 4 Months

"I don't think you should give up," Nana said, sitting down to Sunday dinner.

"Yeah, Sam." Amanda reached for my hand. Done feeling guilty for my 'counseling session' date, she'd joined Nana's team of, get back on that saddle. "Just because you've had a couple bad experiences—"

"A couple?" I dropped my fork. More like a mountain of nightmares. I had been too embarrassed to tell my sisters about the man who showed up on my doorstep—a gift from Nana. He offered me daisies and *Madams Aging Cream*. Maybe I shouldn't have been so offended. He sells the miracle potion. Still, I shut the door in his face.

"And they sound more like something from a Stephen King novel." Liza cradled her new baby daughter, Isabelle. Her dark hair fell onto the blanket covering the infant and she hushed the baby in sing song tones.

Coughing, Eric adjusted in his seat next to my sister. "We started out with a nightmare and ended up okay." He kept his eyes locked on his plate, shoveling mashed potatoes and peas together with his fork.

"What are you saying?" Liza stared at him her eyebrows raised.

"Just that maybe, sometimes it's worth facing a nightmare to get what you want."

Nana clinked her water glass to Eric's. "Bravo."

*E*ric's words stuck with me throughout the next week. So, my past few dates hadn't been ideal. Wouldn't Amanda and Liza go through a few nightmares to find their Max and Eric? I knew they would.

My sisters' lives weren't perfect. Between job searching and infertility, their families had struggled, but they also had direction. I wasn't naïve. Getting married may not make my life easier, but wouldn't it make it better?

So, when Nana told me she had a date lined up for me, I didn't argue. I didn't reject her on the spot. I listened. She set it up for Friday—she said, because neither of us would have to work the next day. "He'll treat you right, my dear. You can count on it."

Promising Nana to leave work early and wash my hair, I hung up the phone. I could wear my hair down—I didn't because of work and pure ease.

Pulling up to my little house, I sighed. I should be more excited. Weren't people usually excited to go out? Closing my eyes, I lay my head back against the seat of the car. Blowing out a puff of air, I opened the car door. Sure, I wasn't bouncing in my seat over the evening, but I showed up. Like Eric said, I would stick to it. Face the nightmares—and pray one day I'd wake up to something right.

Flipping on the lights to my dark living room, I screamed and jumped back, hitting the closed front door. The jarring blow knocked me to the ground.

"I told you we should have turned the lights on," Liza said, reaching out a hand to help me up.

Amanda and Nana sat on my couch. "Well, that would spoil the surprise, now wouldn't it?" Nana stood and walked over to me.

"Oh, you surprised me." I held my heart, my pulse ran crazy. "What are you doing here?"

"We're here to help you get ready." Amanda wrapped her arm around Nana's shoulders, as if they were a team.

Scrunching my nose, I couldn't think of anything more horrible at the moment. The three of them dressing me, primping me—blah.

"Oh, get over it." Liza grabbed my hand, pulling me after her. "Get in the shower. We're going through your closet."

"Wha—no. I mean, I wasn't going to shower, I was just going to stick my head in the sink and wash my hair." Talk about nightmares—Nana picking out my clothes. And going through my closet? No, if she found that one mistake I bought back in 2014—no, that wouldn't do. "Seriously, I can dress myself."

"Seriously?" Amanda looked horrified. "You smell like sawdust and sweat. Ew. You *have* to shower." Pushing on my back, she forced me into the bathroom. Swatting my butt, she laughed. "You thought the men were nightmares, what about you—not exactly a daydream Miss Lumber Mill."

"Hey!" I looked back at them—offended by my sister insinuating I could be the nightmare.

Nana threw a towel, hitting me in the face and Liza shut the door.

With my hand on the knob, I stood there trying to scheme how I could overtake the three of them. Nana may be eighty-one-years and ninety-five pounds, but the woman had spunk. She might be the hardest one to wrestle.

"I don't hear the water running!" Liza yelled through the door.

"Argh." Tearing off my shirt, I threw it to the floor. "I don't hear the—" I mocked Liza's bossy tone. Throwing all of my clothes onto the tiled ground as if they were the ones who offended me, I stomped into the bathtub. Ripping the shower curtain closed, the material tore, leaving a gaping hole. I didn't care. I let the water run anyway. I sat in the steam and heat until the water had gone lukewarm. They were trying to help. And I needed help—my way wasn't working. I couldn't be mad at them—not really. I was frustrated, which mades me feel like a child. Only, as a child, Mom had been there to help me fix my problem. Now, I could be as frustrated as humanly possible, and Mom wasn't here to help me. Nana tried—like she always did. She stepped into our lives in a major way when Mom passed—my other mother, but not Mom.

Turning off the water, the silence and the steam enfolded me.

31

Taking a deep breath, I dried myself and wrapped one towel around my body and the other around my long brown strands — ready to meet the masses. They were here to help — and after I let go of my pride and independence, I would love them for it.

My clothes laid out on the bed, situated just right. The disapproving look on Nana's face told me she'd found my little red 2014 blunder. My sister's just smiled. "We'll let you get dressed," Liza said.

They hadn't done a bad job — not really. And none of it belonged to Amanda. The pencil skirt and blouse had both sat in my closet untouched — for who knows how long.

Sitting in front of my tiny bathroom mirror with Nana, Amanda and Liza each crammed around me, I let them work me over. Liza twisted and pulled at my newly showered hair. Amanda applied powder and gloss and goop — none of which I owned. And Nana gave orders. She directed, criticized and applauded all that they did.

Standing, I studied myself in the mirror. It wasn't terrible. Makeup — I didn't do makeup — what's the point? But… I looked… good. Like me, only on girly juice. The green blouse and black pencil skirt didn't look half bad on me either. I couldn't remember wearing either — but then I didn't really have a reason to. Liza pulled my hair back — but it didn't look like it usually did. She twisted and shaped it up on top of my head, and for the first time in my life, I had sexy hair. Nana stood back admiring their work, black pumps in her hand. She set them on the ground, and I didn't even need her to tell me to step into them.

### Blind Date #5 — # 6 if you count the surprise salesman

*H*oping the drive to Jackson hadn't messed up my hair or wrinkled my skirt, I stepped out of my little Honda. I had never looked so ready to meet someone special. My excitement levels spiked. Shivering, I walked through the front doors of Vitali's. *I can't believe I'm here.* Mom had taken me into Jackson several times growing up, and we always walked by the fancy Italian restaurant. I would press my nose against the glass and try as hard as I could to see the wonder inside.

Taking a deep breath, I pushed into the dim lighting of a quiet, quaint dining room. A brighter light at the other end of the room showcased a long wall map of Italy. Small spot lights shone down on the detailed drawing. There weren't booths or awkward cubicles separating the seating, but small wooden tables for two. The dimness and the setup of the room made each table feel secluded. A small crystal vase with a single rose bud sat in the center of each table.

My heart raced. My toes pinched at the front of my shoes, and my skin tingled with the strangeness of meeting someone I didn't know in such a romantic place. I couldn't decide if the feeling signaled terror or excitement.

Walking to the hostess, my feet wobbled in my heels, my green blouse shimmered whenever a light hit it. The happy inside me left me feeling like I had walked into someone else's  life. The quiet hostess led me to a spot near the map. More private than the other tables in the room, it had to be the best seat in the house. What had my date paid to get us such an elite spot? Up close, the details of the painted map of Italy became clear.  Trimmed in gold, small golden dots marked certain cities on the massive piece of art.

"Mr. Vitali will be right with you," the hostess said.

My high heel tipped to the side and my foot gave out under me. I plopped into my seat and gulped. "What?" I hushed my clumsy surprise. "Mr. Vitali? Why?"

"Because, Henry Vitali is your date, Miss." She shook her head, but smiled at me.

I had been so worried about myself, I hadn't thought to ask Nana for more details about my date—even his name, and she never offered this time. *Henry Vitali*. The heir to Vitali's?

I crossed my legs, staring at my skirt. Setting my foot back to the ground, I tapped my heels on the wooden floor. Biting the inside of my cheek, my nerves more anxious now, I reached out to the rose bud, pricking my finger on a thorn. "Ow!" I whispered and brought my bleeding thumb to my lips.

"Here," a man said behind me. Taking my hand, the older

man folded my thumb into a white linen napkin. Still holding my hand in his, he bent and kissed the back of my hand. "Samantha," he said, his dark eyes looking into mine. He was very handsome — for a grandfather. The wrinkles around his eyes and the mixture of gray and brown in his thick head of hair made me think of Mom's crush on Sean Connery.

"Henry?"

He nodded, his kind, gentle smile like a peace offering. I didn't even consider scolding him as I had the Boy Scout.

"Your grandmother speaks very highly of you."

"Well, that's nice to hear. She has something other than *she isn't married yet* to say about me?" I laughed and Henry joined me. Yes, he was older, but my nerves calmed, as if I sat across from Dad.

"Yes," he said, sitting down. "Much more. You're right though, her only complaint is that you're thirty and unmarried."

Smiling, I repressed the urge to roll my eyes. I didn't correct Henry. My mother always taught me to respect my elders and I'm sure he didn't know better. "So, Henry, tell me about yourself." This may not be the love connection I hoped for, but I would do my best to enjoy myself — Henry would be great company. "Do you own Vitali's or is that just an incredible, crazy coincidence?"

"I do own Vitali's. My parents started the business after they traveled over from Italy in 1942. They didn't have any money or any job opportunities, just looking for a better life. Mom started cooking out of our house and selling to the locals — just enough for us to get by, while Dad did every kind of odd job you can think of. Mother's food was in higher demand than they could provide. Eventually, when funds allowed, they started a small restaurant — that turned into… this." He gestured around the room.

"That's amazing." I could listen to Henry talk all day. The tone of his voice and the way he made everything sound interesting — like a child at Grandpa's feet, listening to good ol' day stories.

"It is, isn't it?" Smiling, his eyes watered and sparkled in the moisture. "Samantha, why don't you tell me about you? You're young, attractive, intelligent, why the dating troubles?"

"You really get to the point, don't you?"

"Well, it's just that when your grandmother forced me into this, I asked myself—when a thirty year old woman agrees to date a sixty-four year old man, I wonder what's going on in her head?"

"Oh, Henry." Of course she'd forced him into this! "I didn't realize I had agreed to date a sixty-four year old man. My grandmother didn't mention our age difference, but please believe me when I say you are a breath of fresh air."

"Have the others been that bad?" He crossed his arms and laughed.

"Uhh, yes. But that doesn't diminish your goodness. You are a wonderful date." I grinned, already feeling like we were friends. "I do think you would have more success with someone else, at least when it comes to love."

Smiling, he took my hand. "You remind me of my youngest daughter."

"She's thirty and unmarried too?"

"No, she is honest, gracious, and kind."

Flushing at his compliments, I diverted my eyes to the ground.

Our sweet, father-daughter like moment was interrupted by a hushed, unfamiliar voice, "Sam? Sammy Blake?"

Turning in my seat, I tried to make out through the dimness who had said my name—my old name, my nickname from years before. A man stood in front me, but his face wasn't clear.

"How are you?" he asked, the inflection in his voice telling me he knew me. Of course he knew me—he'd called me *Sammy*. I stood to see him better, using the light from the map to help me. His face had aged a bit, as had mine, but it only made him more attractive.

"Robert George!" My voice was too loud in the quiet room and I covered my mouth. I had thought of Rob a hundred times since Amanda mentioned him six months ago. I couldn't believe he stood before me. "You're here!"

"Yeah, it's been a while." His hand waved up and down toward me and my gratitude to my sisters for dressing me and slathering me with makeup magnified. "You're all grown up."

"Yep." I put my hands on my hips, hoping I looked like Amanda in her feminine stance. "You too." Would it be inappropriate to ask out my old prom date in front of my current date?

"Are you here with your husband?" He asked, looking past me at Henry.

"Oh! Um, no." Scanning down Robert for his left hand, I saw no ring on his finger. Motioning to Henry, I introduced them. "Robert, this is Henry Vitali."

Henry stood and shook Robert's hand. "Just a friend," he said, winking at me.

"Yeah." I smiled back at Henry. "Ah, no, I'm not married," I said for the first time in my life with joy.

Then a young beautiful blonde walked up behind Robert, slipping her hand into his. Turning, his eyes lit up when they caught her face—I had never seen eyes like that look at me before. His blue eyes had an on button, and she was the switch. The world slowed down—like fate forced me to take it all in. *Suffer and do it slowly.* I watched him clutch to her hand and kiss her cheek.

"This is Jane, my fiancée."

Nodding and more nodding … It's all I could do. Finding my voice, I mumbled. "Jane. Fiancée. Hi."

"This is Samantha, an old friend from high school." Robert's flashlight eyeballs searched until they found Jane's face again.

Jane spoke—but I don't know what she said. Watching them wave and leave hand-in-hand—it all went blurry. Robert, my Robert—engaged, and he had referred to me as his *old* friend.

I plopped into my chair across from Henry. Any thoughts of a pleasant evening had walked out the door with Robert George. My head spun. *This can't be happening.*

Spiraling, I heard Henry's kind voice through the haze in my ears. "Are you all right, Samantha?"

Looking up, I met his eyes. "No, Henry. I'm not. I feel *empty.*" I blinked, my tears falling. I stared at the base of the vase holding the rose bud—not caring that my voice wasn't a whisper, "I have no direction. I'm not moving forward. My life is standing still." Hot tears rolled down my cheeks. "I don't know what I'm doing. Empty,

I'm just *empty*. And I have no one who can fill that void." Laying my head against the wooden table, I drenched it with my sobs.

"I thought..." Sitting up, my sob squeaky and loud, I continued. "I thought that Robert..." Sniffing, I wiped my nose with my linen napkin. "That Robert might be the one." Covering my face with my hands, I bawled in Henry's restaurant.

I had officially lost it.

The elegant, quiet atmosphere grew silent, except for my sobs. I didn't care about the staring eyes or embarrassing scene. Robert George would soon be a married man, leaving me more alone than ever.

"What will I do now, Henry? I'm going to die, old and single, and empty!"

Sitting straighter in his chair, I waited for Henry to hush me or even make me leave — my scene ridiculous. But he didn't. "You certainly will if you continue on this way." His soft and sweet voice took on a stern tone that made me jerk upright.

Henry's pep talk skills needed a little help. Did he want me to stop crying or not?

"You are a wonderful person, Samantha, but you are in a rut." He pounded his fist against the table, shaking our vase — and not caring that we attracted every eye in his quiet restaurant. "And not having a husband has nothing to do with it. You're empty? Well, you can't fill that void with a husband. It will never work. You need to *live* your life, young lady, full and well. You are not taking advantage of what you *do* have, of the opportunities right before you." Crossing his arms, he sat back and stared at me, his eyes narrowing into almonds. "If you are empty, my dear, it's your own damn fault. So, you don't have a husband. You've got a family who loves you, good friends who look out for you, and a good job. You are *young* and free to do anything. That goes away fast, and you are losing it to fantasies, daydreams — and whining. You thought Robert was the one? You said yourself you hadn't seen him in years. That, miss, is an impractical illusion. And your reality is pretty fortunate, so start living it."

For a minute I thought Henry had slapped me. My opened jaw wouldn't close. But — he was right. We sat in silence for a moment. He had said enough, and I couldn't say a thing.

Dad. Eve. Amanda. Liza. Nana. My nieces. My nephews… "Henry," I whispered, ignoring the lingering eyes. Henry hadn't bothered to lower his voice, they must not have bothered him either. "You're right."

"Of course I am."

"I am losing my life to nonsense." Henry had turned on a light bulb inside of me. One I didn't even know existed. I had talents. I had hopes and desires—that were mine—that I had forgotten. And I was losing them. I was losing myself. "I can't do this anymore. I have a great life with family and friends and work and—the problem is…" I gulped, not wanting to say the truth, but having to. "I am ungrateful for it all." Truth, almost revelatory, like someone had just explained physics and for the first time, I understood!

Smiling at me, Henry clasped his hands together. "So, start living!"

# *Chapter 6*

"Eve, I need to live my life," I yelled above the machines in the wood shop.

"No one else can but you." She held out her hand, and I handed her another long piece of wood, steadying the opposite end as she ran it through the router.

"Henry says I need to find my own direction." The machine died to a quiet hum, and I pulled my protective eyewear on top of my head. "Henry says it isn't about age, but readiness and experience. Henry says I can't wait for a man to make me feel better. If I feel empty inside, I have to fill that myself. Henry—"

"Did Henry charge you by the hour?"

"Ha. Ha." I shoved another line of wood into her palms. "You are hilarious."

"Just asking. I mean, this is kind of a one-eighty from where you were last week."

"I know." I shook my head. "I've been ridiculous."

"Well—"

"And ungrateful!"

"Maybe a little—"

"And stagnant!" I yelled. "I haven't been living, not really."

Eve started up the machine again. "Ah—"

"But I'm done with that now. I'm done with men."

Eve's eyes went wide—she didn't believe me.

"I am," I said. "at least for a little while. Henry's right. I have to find my happy. I need to live my life!"

Running the next strip through the router, Eve yelled above the noise. "I wish I could have been on that date!"

Laughing, I kept the back end of the ten foot board steady. "I could always set you two up."

*Live your life. Make your joy. Find yourself.* It was easier said than done in the Valley, at least for me, right now. My sisters were here. Dad wouldn't be alone. I needed a change. I needed to get out—not permanently—just for a while. I needed a *vacation.*

Searching the internet for vacation packages, I knew where I wanted to go. Vitiali's had inspired me. Henry had inspired me, and I had some money saved. I would pack my bags, get my passport, board a plane for the second time in my life and go to... *Italy.*

Killing my printer's ink cartridge, I printed every traveler's page on Venice I could find. Hotels, tours, historical sites—a dream I didn't even know I had, until I met Henry, came to life, page-after-page, through my computer screen.

Sunday, I invited Eve over to Dad's for dinner. My new found goal had brought on my inspiration for dinner: eggplant parmesan, homemade bread-sticks, and fried ravioli.

"Mmm, oh, my gosh, Samantha! What smells so great?" Amanda walked into the kitchen.

"Eggplant Parmesan," I said, a smile painted to my face.

"You look happy." Her hands went to her hips. "You must have had a good time on your date. Let's hear it."

Laughing, I continued to bread my eggplant slices. "There's nothing to tell." At least not in the way she meant.

Pointing at me, she said, "You just laughed!"

I held up my egg and floured hands, unsure of what she accused me of. "So?"

"You don't laugh after dates, you cringe." Crossing her arms, she walked over to the counter where I worked. Staring at me in silence, I could hear her tapping her toe on the tiled floor—waiting.

"Well, it was nice."

"So, you're going to see him again?"

"No, not on a date anyway." I would love to see Henry again, but as a friend. I could see the lecture coming, and I didn't want to hear it. "He's older, Amanda. Like, much older. He's in his sixties."

"Ew." Amanda's face scrunched in horror.

"No, he was sweet. It was by far my best date yet."

"Double ew."

"Amanda." I flicked flour at her. "He was nice. And he helped me."

"Really? Does he have son or something?"

"He has vision." I bounced my eyebrows. Washing my hands, I dried them off and pulled a stack of plates from the cupboard.

Trotting behind me like a puppy, she followed me into the dining room. "What does that mean?"

I let her stew. She'd see soon enough.

After Eve arrived, we sat at the table and I made my announcement. "Family," I said, including Eve in my endearment. "I am going to Italy."

"What for?" Nana asked, "Are there more men in Italy than Wyoming?"

"Nana!" Liza yelled, making my father jump in his seat.

Eve covered her mouth, no doubt holding in her laughter.

"It isn't always about men, Ellen." Dad smiled, and I nodded at his approval. "I think it's about time Samantha did something like this, something for herself."

"She deserves to have what her sisters have." Nana snapped, unafraid of Dad. He may not be her biological child, but he'd been her son by marriage for a long time.

"Stop." Their bickering sped my pulse and ruined my new found attitude and direction. I should have invited Henry to our dinner. He'd know what to say. "It's a trip, Nana. It isn't forever. I need to do this."

Twitching her lips, my little grandmother kept quiet. I could only imagine the argument flaring in her head. To her, I was wasting valuable time—I was, after all, almost thirty.

I brought in the meal and we ate—the Italy talk null and void, which didn't bother me. I didn't want to hear any more of Nana's disproving thoughts.

Volunteering Eve and I for dish duty, I pulled my friend up from the table. Once we'd cleaned the kitchen, I laid out my travel information all across the counter. With Eve, Liza, and Amanda standing around me, we fingered through everything.

41

"Oh my gosh," Amanda said, handing me a page I'd printed. "Look at this bridge."

"It's a water taxi tour." I pointed out the information. "And look at this one, Doge's Palace. Isn't it amazing? There are places like this all over Venice."

"How much is this going to cost?" Liza asked. Did she always have to be so sensible? Couldn't she be, I don't know, giddy for once?

"Well, a lot." I set the flyers in my hand back down. "But Liza, I'm getting out here. Doing something for myself."

"I know, and I'm proud of you. But Venice? This won't be cheap."

Biting my lip, I handed over the figures I'd gathered.

"Are you sure you can afford this?" Her eyes scanned over the list, not hiding their shock.

"I don't care what it costs—you need to do this." Amanda said. She might sneak into my suitcase if I wasn't careful.

"I know it's expensive." I turned to Liza, my big sister. I *needed* her support. "I think it will be worth it though."

Eve fingered through my flyers. "So, when are you leaving? How long will you be gone?"

"I have never taken a vacation or personal day from the mill." Stopping Amanda before she gasped in horror, I added, "I know. Pathetic. But that means I have plenty of time. More time than I can use. I'll be gone a week."

"A week?" Amanda's face fell, the bridge of her nose in a permanent, sad scrunch.

"Yes, one week. That's all I can afford. Liza is right, Venice isn't cheap." I slumped down, resting my head in my hands and my elbows on the counter.

"Are you depleting your savings for this?"

Clearing my throat, I stood up, defensive. They killed my happy. They stabbed, stomped on, and chewed up every ounce of happy I had attempted to gather. I crossed my arms over my chest. My jaw tight, I answered her. "Yes, Liza, I am."

"Wow, really?" Eve dropped the flyers in her hand.

No! Not Eve too!

"Well, yeah." My throat constricted as I squeaked out the words, attempting to bring back the joy to my voice. Holding my hands at my hips, I pinched my sides. If I cried, it would be for pain, not heartbreak. "There's plane tickets, food, hotel, tours, souvenirs, also I'd really like to go into a couple different cities."

"All of your savings for seven days? Are you sure about this?" Eve asked.

If it had been Liza, maybe I would have ignored it. Maybe I could have said, *she's just being my protective, worry-wart big sister.* But it was Eve.

The three of them stared at me, their faces wrinkled with concern. The air in the quiet room hung thick with their doubts. A knot swelled in my throat and tears sprang to my eyes. Shaking my head, I forced them back. I had to find my own direction. I had to fill my emptiness. But if not with help from Venice, how?

*I* called in sick to work the next day — I wasn't lying when I said I hadn't taken a day off in years. Still in my pajamas, I surfed the internet for some miracle-magic trip that wouldn't eat up all of my money. If I couldn't find anything — I would still go to Venice. Money had never made me happy, at least not while sitting in my bank doing nothing. Still, Liza and Eve had put doubt in my head, like a nagging ache, I couldn't get rid of it.

A knock at my door had me up. Eyeing my unkempt hair in a nearby mirror, I decided to leave the useless mess. The drawn blinds in my front room made it a dark safe haven, I could pretend to be gone. Tugging at the ends of my pajama shirt, I peeked through the peephole on my door. *Eve.* Whew. Just Eve.

Opening the door, I didn't bother to hide myself. "Hey," I said. "What are you doing here?" She shouldn't be off work yet.

"You called in sick today?"

"Um…" I looked down at my body — this should pass as sick apparel. "Yeah."

"You aren't sick." Shoving me to the side, she forced her way inside.

"Yeah? So?" Closing the door, I shuffled over to my couch and fell into the plush cushions.

43

"Well, I brought something to work for you today, and then you didn't even bother telling me you weren't going to show up." Plopping onto the couch, Eve sat next to me.

"Well, you didn't bother telling me you were going to bring me something." Rolling my eyes, my gaze dropped, noticing the shoebox in her hand. "Ooo." I sat up straight. "What is it?"

"You never call in sick." She moved the box just out of my reach.

Laying my head back against the couch, I closed my eyes. "I know. I just needed… a day. You know? After last night—ahh… I just needed a day."

"I know." She set the box on my coffee table and rubbed my arm. "You were so excited. You finally had a plan and then—"

"I should have just gone. Ya know? Instead of sharing and thinking about all the consequences, I should have left and sent you all a postcard."

"The thing is, Sam, I think you need more than a week. This rut you've gotten yourself into has been brewing for a while now, years. I just—I don't think a week would bring you out of it."

Great! She just added to my list of hole-filling problems. How could I fill this emptiness if I only found one problem after another?

"Now, I'm not Henry." Eve smiled. "But I think this all started when your mom died. You don't need to find a husband. You need to find yourself again."

I didn't like blaming my hole on Mom's death. I'd created this cavity myself. I had lost the real me, the cause didn't matter. "That, I've figured out. The *how* is what I'm having trouble with." My brain now understood, but I still couldn't flip a switch and feel okay. I still couldn't find my happy.

"I know," she said, an urgency in her tone, "and that's why I've brought you something." She handed me the cardboard box.

Sitting up, I grinned at my friend. I didn't deserve her. How long had she put up with me? I pulled the lid from the box and stared inside—not sure of what I should say. Nodding, I gazed from the box to her and back again. "Ah—woodchips. You bought me woodchips. From the mill?" I bit my lower lip. "How sweet?"

Laughing, she hit my arm. "They're *redwood* chips."

Setting the box of woodchips onto the table again, I stared at her, still lost.

"My aunt owns an Inn. It's kind of an amazing little place in San Francisco. It's called *The Redwood*. She rarely has openings; it's booked for years out." Standing up, she paced in front of me. "But I just had a feeling—so I called Aunt Grace. I asked her when her earliest opening was. She told me two years from July—*except* that she just had a three month cancellation. A client who works in San Francisco months at a time canceled at the last minute."

Her arms flared about and she spoke at a speed I'd never heard from Eve before. My body tingled from head to toe. Sitting up tall, I took her hand to stop the waving. "What are you saying, Eve?"

"I'm saying, I booked you a room at The Redwood, starting Friday. For the next *three* months."

I gasped, bringing my hands up to my face. Standing, I paced in front of the coffee table. "Can I afford this?"

"Well, that's the other part of your gift. I talked to my aunt—I get a family discount and—well, I've taken care of it."

"What? No."

"Yes." She pumped her fists in the air.

"Work—"

"Taken care of. I spoke to Mr. Bell this morning—you weren't kidding when you said you've never taken a day off." Taking my hand, she squeezed my fingers. "I know it's not Venice, but—"

"No." My heart raced inside my chest, and I smiled at Eve. "But it's *something*."

## Chapter 7

*F*our days after Eve presented her gift, I packed my car to the rim. At the crack of dawn, I poured myself into the driver's seat. My phone jingled. I opened it to find a text from Amanda.

> Amanda: Have a fantastic time in the sunny city.
> Get a tan for me!

I'd made an agreement with my sisters. Talking to them every day would keep me mentally home, in my quiet miserable comfort zone. So, texting only. I'd never been more ready. In fact, I couldn't wait to be out on my own in a foreign land—well, foreign to me anyway.

Driving, hours in, I couldn't stop Nana's words from echoing in my subconscious. *You're giving up. You are running off to California and giving up on your dreams.*

"No, Nana," I said to her, "I am running off to California to try and fulfill a few dreams." AKA filling my emptiness. She kissed me goodbye and wished out loud for a man to be waiting for me in California.

After playing every song on my iPod, including a selection of Christmas tunes, I saw San Francisco glimmering in the distance. The pounding in my heart thudded in my ears and the butterflies in my stomach came to life . *There she is.* A vacation shouldn't cause this much anxiety. Still, I hadn't been on a trip since high school, with Mom, Dad and all of us sisters. And I'd never been out on my own, but it was more than all that. California in my mind meant *Sam finds her happy.*

Stopping only for gas and food had helped me make make good time. Twelve hours in my Honda and I had made it; the sights of San Francisco danced before my eyes. Cars, and trolleys, and buildings taller than I'd ever seen before added to the glorious busyness and beautiful newness of it all — the adventure I needed. Using my cell's GPS, I followed the directions right up to *The Redwood.*

Pulling beside the vintage home  painted a pretty shade of canary blue, I stare up at the  old, unique architecture trimming the peaks. An ancient rock edge ran up the bottom quarter of the house, with stones aged and missing, it had probably been there a lifetime. The wide stairway out front led to the door and face of the building. To the left and right of the stairs ran a wraparound deck. The arched doorway had lattice beside it and flowered vines threading between the wooden slats. *The Redwood.* I looked at it, and it seemed as though it looked back. Waiting for me. Grabbing my purse, I walked up the porch steps, my hand running along the wooden banister. Breathing in, I turned the brass knob and walked inside.

"You must be Samantha," said an older woman rounding the corner. With long graying hair pulled back at her neck, she stood just my height. I peered into her happy blue eyes with ease.

"Yes, hello," I said, shaking her hand.

"I'm Grace. Eve is my favorite niece. It's nice to meet her best friend."

Smiling, I clasped my hands together. "It's very nice to meet you, too. Thank you again for accommodating me last minute."

"Oh, I'm happy to have you, but don't say that too loudly, I'd hate for my other guests to hear." She laughed, and the lines around her eyes and mouth scrunched together.

"This house is fantastic. I've never been in another like it." I turned a full circle to gaze around the entryway.

"Let me give you a tour." Grace started down the hall. "If you have any questions just let me know."

Walking past the parlor, across the large red area rug, I peered into a sitting room with two plush buttercup colored couches and an oversized chair. Large windows ran along the room, letting the light shine in through the sheer curtains.

My pulse quickened when Grace pointed in the direction of the kitchen just down the hall, a few more steps and she pushed open the entrance. Black and white tiles ran along the floor, as well as the countertops. A large island sat in the middle, sporting the same checkered tiles. The oversized stainless steel refrigerator sat next to two professional gas range ovens. I bit my lip. I would beg Grace to let me cook in here one night. I'd pay her to let me at this kitchen.

Walking across the room to a second swinging door, we entered the large dining room. Ten seats surrounded the long, dark wooden table. My heart skipped with a nervous twitch. I would be eating with strangers—part of *The Redwood's* breakfast and dinner services.

Backtracking, Grace pointed at a third door from the kitchen that led to her personal quarters. Following Grace to the back of the house, she held the door for me to the back porch. The enclosed room had a small table and chairs and a view of the yard, jungled with flowers, plants and trees.

Back in the sitting room where I'd entered the house, we climbed the stairs to the upper floor. At the top, a hallway veered to the left and one to the right. Each hall had two doors facing each other.

Pointing to the left side of the hall, Grace said, "This is The Sunflower room, and this one The Gardena." Turning to the right, she walked to the two doors, mid-hall. "Here we have The Sweet Pea room and your room, The Wild Rose."

"Just the four rooms?" The dim hallway with no windows made the space feel as if night had already come.

"Yes, only four rooms. That's all I can keep up with. I am the housekeeper, cook, front desk and bookkeeper. And my clients usually stay long periods of time, a couple weeks or longer. I want them to feel at home while they're here. So, I don't treat this place like a hotel with dozens of people around. Still, it's enough to keep me busy." She winked and I wondered if she was like this with all her customers—or if being Eve's best friend made her more open with me.

Nodding, I could only imagine how busy she must be.

"I want this to be your home while you're here. Wander around, come down in the middle of the night and get a snack from the kitchen, whatever, just make yourself comfortable."

"Thank you." Did everyone get to wander the house at all hours of the day? Or just me? My insides warmed. This had to be the perfect place to find my happy. I would have to search out one heck of a thank you present for Eve!

"Well, I'm happy to have you." Smiling, she reached out and squeezed my hand. With her other she held out an old metal key. *The Rose Room.* "I'll let you get settled." She spun on her heel and trotted down the stairs.

I waited for her to go and then turned to the oak door engraved with the large rose. Running my finger through the grooved markings, I saw that the circle around the rose was actually script. The words read again and again, *roses don't have to be red.*

Unlocking the door, I walked inside—ready to *find myself* in The Rose Room. A king-sized bed, centered along the back wall, sat made up in a pink, rose-patterned quilt. The same design papered one wall. The room could've been a magazine layout from *Pottery Barn.* The antique white bedroom set the focal point of the room. I gazed about, taking in the details and décor. Walking past a large wall clock and vase of pink roses, I stopped at the door inside my room. Bathroom, I thought as I opened the door. Yep, bathroom, but nothing like I'd ever seen—in real life anyway. The pinkish walls in the bathroom matched the real roses sitting on my dresser. Portraits of rose gardens hung on each wall and above the large porcelain bath tub. The space larger than my bedroom back home. "Beautiful," I whispered to myself. Skipping out of the bathroom, I threw myself onto the king-sized bed and laughed. *I'm here—I'm doing it!*

A text jingle from my phone brought me back from the heaven of my home away from home. I could get used to this place, no mill and that tub...

Sitting up, I searched through my tote for my cell.

Amanda: How's it going? Are you there yet?

Me:  It's, oh, just a bit… AMAZING! The ride
was long, but it's over and I'm getting
ready to take a bath in my HUGE tub.

I hadn't taken a bath since I lived with Dad. My little place had a tub that could fit my childhood border collie, Lewie, or maybe my niece, Jillian, but me? I'd have to fold myself in half to bathe in that thing. Ready to unpack and try out the tub, I threw my phone onto the bed. But my phone sang out again.

Amanda: Have you met any hotties yet?

Laughing, my fingers went to work, setting my baby sister straight.

Me: Of course not! #1 I've been here a whole
20 minutes. #2 No dating in California.
This is about me, not the opposite sex. I'm a
men-free zone right now, remember?
Amanda: I'm just saying, keep your eyes open.
Me: I'm shutting off my phone now. Love you,
sis. Bye.

Jogging down the stairs and out the door, I retrieved two bags from my car and headed back inside. I trudged up the wooden staircase, a suitcase in each hand. I opened the door to my room, threw the bags inside, and headed back down for a second trip of luggage. I had never packed so much in my life. With only a few days notice and such a long stay, I worried I'd forget something. So, Amanda helped me, and we packed it all!

With a duffle strapped around my chest to free up my hands for my last two bags, I started upward—again. Out of breath, I panted up each stair. With my head down, I focused on breathing. I had brought way too many bags—and who packed the rocks? I don't remember them being this heavy when I left Wyoming. I trudged forward, my bathtub cheering me on.  Turning down the hall, I lifted my gaze to the rose door. Almost there...then— smack! A knock to the side of my head had me on the ground. I had run into someone!—or they had run into me. A nearby rug beckoned me to crawl under it. Instead, I lay on my back, on top of the duffle strapped around my middle. Closing my eyes, I prayed whomever I had hit would leave before I opened them.

"Hello. Are you all right?" a man with an accent said.

What was that? Italian?"Oh, hello." I opened my eyes. Crap, a *good-looking* man with an accent. His dark hair fell to the side as he bent over to look at me.

"Can I help you up?"

*French!* "No. I can make it." Who cared if a French hottie with a lopsided smile stared at me sprawled about—*this is my manless trip.*

Without warning he swooped his large hands under my arms and swung me up into a standing position—like a two-year-old child. I wobbled as the duffel bounced into place at my back.

Looking up to see his face, I bit my lip. "You are a large man."

"Thank you." He smiled, thankfully, taking my loose tongue as a compliment.

"I meant to say—thank you for helping me." Thank goodness I hadn't come for the men; my lousy filter didn't exactly attract the opposite sex. "You're not really large—well—you certainly aren't small—I mean—you look very much in shape." I held out a hand and touched his hard bicep.

I work out," he said, smiling, and I drew my hand back as quick as I could.

"I... I am so sorry." Stumbling, I tried to pick up my two bags lying on the ground, but my balance wasn't quite back. I dropped them again. "I wasn't watching where I was going. I was thinking about my bathtub."

"Your bathtub? Oh. Okay. Are you in 'The Rose Room'?" He pointed toward my wooden door.

"Yes, I am. And you're—"

He pointed across from my room. "The Sweet Pea. I was coming out not necessarily watching where I was going either." He smiled at me and I examined him. He stood at least 6'3. His fancy suit coat lay along his wide shoulders as if it were painted on. His square jaw was clean shaven. With his dark eyes and hair, he encompassed the saying, *tall, dark and handsome.* "How long are you staying?"

"Umm, a while." Normal people didn't vacation for three months at a time. I didn't feel like further embarrassing myself with a quick rendition of I'm trying to fill my self-induced emptiness. "And you?"

"Six weeks."

Okay, maybe normal people did vacation for weeks at a time—who knew? "When did you get here?"

"Today." He grinned again. "Like you." His eyes went to the luggage I couldn't seem to pick up.

"Well, I guess we'll be seeing each other around then." I needed my tub more than ever now.

"Here, let me help," he said, picking up my bags like they didn't hold a ton of bricks.

Opening my door, I moved so he could set the bags inside. "Thank you."

"My pleasure, Mademoiselle, ah, what was your name?" He shoved his hands into his pants pockets and rocked on his heels.

"I'm Samantha, Samantha Blake."

"Victor Andrews," he said, pointing at himself. I reached out my hand to shake his, and he took it like we were in some French movie, bending and kissing the back of my hand. Standing, he said, "I'm here for work. I am originally from Eastern Canada, Montreal, but I've lived in Sacramento for the past ten years."

Was I supposed to give him my background information now? "Ah—"

"I'll let you get to your bathtub then."

"Oh, yes. Well, see you."

"Plan on it," Victor Andrews said, winking at me.

Shutting the door behind me, I leaned back against it and let out a breath I seemed to be holding. "Wow. I picked a *great time* to give up men."

# Chapter 8

A handwritten note from Grace told me dinner at The Redwood always served at seven and breakfast at nine. Lunch was on our own or upon request.

After my tour and my run-in with Mr. Andrews, I didn't have much time before dinner—either I'd go hungry or my tub would have to wait.

Looking in the mirror, I was even more horrified at running into Victor Andrews. With only an hour until dinner I didn't want to look like… *this*. Twelve hours of driving had not been kind to my clothes or hair. Lucky for me, I had an over-obsessed sister who'd packed me a bag of makeup and hair gadgets. I threw on some fresh, non-wrinkled clothes—nothing fancy. Grace had told me to make myself at home, and I didn't feel like dressing up, but I did comb through my hair and brush on a little mascara.

Stepping back, I studied the mirror. *Wow. Amanda wasn't kidding about this mascara stuff. It really works some magic. It just might—Whoa. Rewind. One pretty face and I had given up the quest? What am I doing? I am not here for the men. I am not here to find a date! I am here for me. For—*ugh!! Running one of Grace's rose-colored wash clothes under the tap, I rung out the water and scrubbed at my eyes, leaving black smeared across my face.

"Ow! Oh, ow!" I rubbed more frantic now with the wash-cloth. "Stupid magical eye gunk." Amanda never mentioned that beauty felt like shampoo when it seeped into the eye!

Officially late for dinner, I examined my bright red eyes.

All the rubbing it took to get Amanda's makeup off had left me looking like the Iggster's co-host. Already late and now looking like someone in a bar fight, I decided to yell at my sister. Blinking, I picked up my phone.

Me: Thank you, Amanda, for your bag of makeup. I look
 bruised!
Amanda: What did you do?
Me: Getting mascara off is much harder than putting it on.
Amanda: Sam, it's waterproof. You need to use the
    makeup remover I sent.

A few more jingles from my phone, and I had written instructions from Amanda on using the concealer and base. Attempting both, I did look a little less like a boxer.

Trotting down the stairs and into the dining room, I saw Victor and four other people already sitting at the table. Everyone but Victor dressed casual. He still wore his suit coat. Winking at me, he tapped the chair next to him. Scooching past a couple, I made my way to the seat.

"Samantha, have you met the other guests?" Victor asked.

Clearing my throat, I peeked up from the china plate at my place setting. "No, I haven't."

"Everyone, this is Samantha Blake." He spoke as if this dinner party and house belonged to him, Victor the host, introducing old friends. "Samantha, this is Jared and Jenny Little." He pointed to the couple I had snuck behind, and then, like Vanna White, he motioned to the left. "And this is Forest and Minnie Case."

"It's nice to meet you," I said, stretching out to shake their hands. I knocked the table as I reached and china clunked together, making an awful about-to-break sound.

The kitchen doors opened, and I crossed my arms in my seat — innocent. Grace came through with a platter of salads. Setting the food in front of us, I gave her a smile. "Thank you, Grace."

She grinned at me, but kept working.

"So, what are you doing here?" Victor poured dressing onto his salad and peeked over at me.

Laying a napkin in my lap, I met his gaze. "I'm just visiting—"

"Yes, I know you're visiting from Wyoming, but what are you here for?"

"How did you—"

"Your license plate." He set his elbow on the table, his chin resting on his hand and stared at me. Was he a model? That looked like something I'd seen in a magazine. "So? Why are you here, Samantha Blake?"

After years of no direction and months of my grandmother setting me up on not-so-great blind dates, I decided that happiness wasn't going to come from finding a husband, but from finding myself. So, I'm here to live, to learn, to experience.

Since that didn't roll off the tongue, I said, "Vacation."

"That's it? You're vacationing, alone?"

"Yep." Afraid of my candid tongue, I popped a carrot into my mouth.

Staring at me, Victor sat up and shook his finger at me. "Hmm, I can't quite figure you out. What do you do for a living?"

Coughing on the lettuce I'd just stuck in my mouth, I thought about lying. Not because I was ashamed of my job—but Victor with his posh suit and beautiful face, might look at me like I was a cave man. "Why?"

"Why?" he said in his fancy accent. "Is this such an odd question?" Ignoring the other chattering couples, he leaned in, inches from my face. "Are you a secret spy or something?"

Whoo—he smelled good. I hadn't noticed before—when we collided. "No. I, well, I work in a lumber mill."

Acting almost as if he hadn't heard my answer, he went on. "Are you single?"

I cleared my throat, his musky scent filling my senses. "Yes," I said, quiet, as if it were a secret. I didn't realize dinner at The Redwood meant baring your soul to strangers.

With Victor's nose only an inch from mine, he squinted, examining my face. "How old are you?" In thirty seconds Victor covered everything I tried to escape.

Sitting straight, I set my back against the chair, giving a good two feet of space between us. "Why? What does it matter?" I forced a laugh. "And what's with the twenty questions?" Did he know my Nana?

He smiled. Nah, Victor was too much of a catch for Nana to set me up with.

"Just trying to figure you out," he said, swishing the water in his goblet around and around.

"Maybe you should give it more time," I said, unable to hide my smile. Even with the twenty questions, I liked Victor—he was interesting. "Like maybe an hour."

He nodded and toasted his glass in the air. "Yes, you are right. It's just, you see…" He leaned in close again. "I can usually figure people out. Take these people, the Little's. They are forty-something, been married about ten, twelve years, and are here for a second honeymoon. The Case's, they have rings on, but they are young, very young. They are probably honeymooning, and her father is paying for it all."

I shook my head at him, trying to repress my grin. "You need a new hobby."

Bellowing a laugh, Victor smacked the table with his hand. The couples stopped their chatter and stared at us.

My eyes widened. "So! You're here for work?" I asked, changing the subject and ignoring the lingering eyes.

"Yes." Victor said, changing his demeanor. "I'm trying to expand my personal company. There is a conference here that should help me to do so."

I took a bite of my salad, listening to Victor talk about his business. Every word paired with an animation—Victor loved his work. And I envied him. I liked my job. I loved working with Eve, but I couldn't say molding brought me any joy, or passion. Grace refilled our drinks and Victor never stopped. His own boss, his own man, he ran a successful business consulting company—so successful he'd come to San Francisco to learn how to expand it.

"You find satisfaction at the mill?"

"I like my job." I swirled what was left of my salad. "I like working with my hands and seeing the finished product."

"But you aren't paid well."

"I'm paid enough."

"I suppose some financial benefits are more satisfying than others." His lips twitched, his fingers intertwining—and watching me, always watching. I felt like the main act at a circus show.

Leaning back in my chair, I crossed my arms. Okay, my turn for invading questions. "So, are you married?"

He smiled, and it reminded me of my nephews after they'd played a trick on Nana. "I am thirty-seven years old, and I've never even been close to marriage."

What would Nana do with him? "And you live in Sacramento?" I nodded at Grace who set a plate of lasagna in front of me.

"Ah, yes. I live in a big, beautiful ranch house. I can keep-up my hobby there."

"What's that?"

"Raising horses. Do you ride?"

"Horses? No."

"Of course horses." He laughed, his white teeth gleaming. "What else would you ride?"

"A bicycle. I love my bike."

He roared with laughter. "Really, you should try a horse some time."

"Maybe I will," I said. After all, I was trying a lot of new things these days.

I licked my fork clean. If this is how we ate every night someone would have to roll me home. I hadn't forgotten my tub, and I couldn't imagine Victor having anything left to ask me. Exhaustion and a fully belly made it easy to excuse myself. "Good night, everyone," I said, leaving the room.

At the bottom of the stairs, I yawned and tugged at the barrette holding my hair back. A sturdy hand on my elbow stopped me from walking any further. I turned to face Victor, and he let go of me.

"Would you like to get a drink?"

"Oh." Nope. No men, sorry. I bit my lip, listening to Victor's charming accent all night had me swooning—even with the game of twenty questions, but I couldn't. "Thank you, but I'm exhausted from the trip."

He nodded. "All right then, *bonne nuit.*"

High school French had done me very little good, but at least I knew he'd bid me goodnight. I could get used to a French goodnight—and it looked as if for the next six weeks I'd have it. "Night, Victor."

# Chapter 9

*I* woke early the next morning, dreaming about drowning in my giant rose room tub. The funny thing—it wasn't a bad dream, but peaceful and sort of heavenly. I loved that tub.

I didn't have time to lay in bed all day dreaming of my tub though. I had a city to explore. I showered and dressed, and left my hair down, using the straightening iron Amanda packed for me.

Everything I needed fit in my little cross-body purse: keys, cash and phone—my GPS and camera all contained in my smartphone.

"You're up early," Victor said, as I stepped out my door.

Crap, I didn't think I would see him this morning—otherwise I wouldn't have tried out the mascara again. It really did do something wonderful to my *blah* brown eyes. "Victor, hi. You're up early, too." I looked up to meet his eyes, very aware of mine frosted in the magical mascara, but then how egotistical of me to think a little mascara would have Victor Andrews swooning over me. Nope, the mascara wasn't for him—that happy discovery I wore for me. *Yes! Filling my emptiness already!*

"I have meetings."

"Right. Well, I am out to explore the city."

"Do you have a map or a plan?" he asked, hands on his tailored hips.

"No plan, that's the beauty of it." Fidgeting with my purse strap, I inched toward the stairs.

Raising his eyebrows, he shook a finger at me. "Maybe I better cancel my morning meeting and go with you."

Stopping my snail-like movement, I rolled my eyes at his joke.

I walked past him. "Go to your meeting."

Reaching the bottom of the stairs, I saw Grace. Her long hair pulled back and her jeans old and worn. "How did you sleep, Samantha?"

"Wonderful. Hey Grace, I won't be here for breakfast. I want to go out, any suggestions?"

"I've got the perfect place." She clapped her hands together and led me to the front parlor. "It's called Jack's. I used to take my son there every Saturday morning. Here's a map. It's not far from here."

Victor wasn't far behind us. "Glad to see you're taking my advice with the map."

"Oh hush, Vic, she'll be fine," Grace said, putting a reassuring arm around me.

"I have GPS." I held up my phone. "Besides, I am almost thirty years old. I think I can handle breakfast." Opening the front door to go, I paused and turned back to Grace. "It's Saturday. Do you want to join me?"

"Oh, no." She waved off my invitation. "My son is long grown, and I have work to do. But thank you, Sam."

Typing the address into my phone, I set out for Jack's. The small diner wasn't far from the inn though. I tapped the seat-yourself sign and took my pick of the booths. I may be a very single twenty-eight-year-old, but I had only eaten in a restaurant alone once. Being alone meant not having to approve my booth choice with anyone—second booth at the right. Only a couple other customers were in the place—not exactly a sign of deliciousness, but I trusted Grace. Three booths away from me a young man sat reading the paper. The waitress brought him out full plate of French toast. I thumbed through the menu, but nothing sounded as good as his smelled and looked.

The older woman, in her blue uniform and white lace trimmed apron, sat and talked with the man for a moment. Giggling, she walked toward me. "Can I help you, miss?" Her name tag read Maureen.

"Yes," I said, peeking past her. "I want what he's having."

Jack's reminded me of places I would find back home. Maybe

Grace thought she would ease me into San Francisco. Except for the occasional visit from Maureen, the diner had a hushed-library feel to it. A small hum came from a couple in the corner. The door's bell rang when another couple entered.

My food didn't take long to come. With the couples talking and the man busy reading his paper, no one around noticed me, and I seriously thought about licking my plate clean. Grace had good taste. I'd be back.

The quiet broke with the man's urgent tone. "Maureen! Is that the right time?" Gathering his things, he hurried to the door. "Thanks, Jack!" He waved to the cook behind the counter before pushing the glass door open. Soon the place would be empty — what a shame when so much goodness sat inside.

Leaving my cash, I headed outside. My phone jingled as I started my car.

> Liza: Are you having fun yet?
> Me: Hey sis. Yes, I'm out exploring.

With my car in reverse, I checked my mirrors and backed out into the parking lot when Liza rang again. I picked up my phone to read her reply.

> Liza: Good! Love ya!

*Crunch!* I wouldn't be texting her back — the sound of metal meeting metal made sure of that. The man from the restaurant stepped out of the blue Buick behind me. *Yes! My goal is to run into every man in this city.* I rolled my eyes at the thought. I was off to a fabulous start so far.

Exiting my Honda, I could see him already assessing the damage. His hands ran through his three-inch-long sandy hair — again and again. The sides had been buzzed short, but the long top looked as though he would pull it out strand by strand.

"I am so sorry," I said, my hands flailing about. "I swear I just looked." I bent to look at his car, the spot where he'd been staring.

"It appears that you didn't," he said without looking at me.

"Excuse me?" I stood straight, my arms crossed over my chest.

"Look, if you had been watching, you would have seen a guy in this big blue box right behind you."

Rude. Was he serious? *Big blue box*—I mean, what a jerk. "Ah—I *did*. I *just* looked. You must have been pretty fa—"

"Listen," he said shaking his head, again, his hands in his hair. "I don't have time for this. Everything *seems* to be okay, just in case though, why don't you give me your name and number."

I let the frustrated sigh I'd been holding in rush out. "Sure, okay," I said, my jaw tight with annoyance. I mean, I guess I did hit him. I suppose I should give him my information. "I *did* look."

He nodded, his eyebrows raised high on his head and handed me a pen and paper.

This guy might be tall—but he was nowhere near Victor's 6'3 or 6'4. Sure, he may have a few biceps discernible through his dress shirt, but I knew Victor could take him. I so wanted to sic the flirtatious Canadian I hardly knew on this callous man.

Scribbling my name down, I handed him the paper. I had said sorry—he showed zero concern for me and my vehicle. "Are you sure you were paying attention? Maybe I need your information. Maybe it was you."

He shoved the paper into his pocket. Sighing, he looked me in the face. "It was you."

My mouth opened. *What a—ooh!* Jogging around to his driver's side door, he backed away from our kissing cars, and sped around me onto the street.

"Rude. My first full day in San Francisco and I start off with… rude!" One thing was for certain, I wasn't in the Valley, anymore.

Shopping and lunch… success! Much better than breakfast, anyway. I bought a book at a shop I found downtown, then discovered a yummy bagel place for lunch—and nobody yelled at me. My book and my tub sounded like the perfect way to spend my evening until dinner.

"Samantha." Victor sat on a plush, buttercup couch in the sitting room.

I stopped on the first stair and turned back to him. "Oh, hi, Victor." I hadn't seen him there—my mystery book already in my hand.

"I returned just a bit ago. How was your outing? Did you drive over the Golden Gate Bridge?" He smiled as if he could read me like a book.

Grateful shopping had distracted me and postponed my plans to cross the bridge, I said, "No, I went shopping." I held up my book and the minuscule bag that held my new earrings.

"Looks like you didn't have much luck," he said, disapproving of my bag.

"On the contrary." I shook my head. Why did I feel the need to impress the handsome man—or maybe the accent made me feel the need to be more. "I had a wonderful day." Grr—*breakfast*. "Well, except for—nah." I took a breath. "Nevermind. I had a great day." I had handled it. I hadn't needed Victor's muscles— even if I wanted them at one point. My day had turned out well despite the grouch from the diner.

"No, what were you going to say?" Standing up, he leaned against the wall beside me.

"Nothing." I shook my head, rolling my eyes in the process— two very *unimpressive* actions. "Argh. I just—I bumped into a man's car today, barely a skiff. And he had a fit over it."

"Is this a habit of yours? You've been here twenty-four hours and you have two victims already." He smirked, teasing me.

"Hey, you weren't there. It could've happened to anyone." I started up the stairs again, stopping when he took hold of my wrist.

"Of course, I was teasing," he said, rubbing his thumb over the inside of my wrist. "I'm just sorry that your first encounter was unpleasant. We Californians really aren't all that bad."

"You're Canadian." I stared at him, eye-to-eye, with me two steps higher than him.

Raising his brows, he still held onto me. "Ah, I am, but I've lived here long enough to claim both."

Nodding, I pulled my hand from his light grasp and started up the stairs.

"Samantha," he said right behind me. "Let me make it up to you. Why don't I take you to dinner so you can see how charming we Californians can be?"

"Thank you, Victor, but I'm staying in tonight." Would I really be able to stick with my no men rule with Victor next door for the next six weeks? "Besides you've been a gentleman. In fact, I'm sure I think more of Canadians than of Californians at the moment."

Sitting on the edge of my tub, I ran the hot water into the basin. I set my novel on the ledge and went back to my bed where I'd laid out a bunch of brochures. I thumbed through them reading about ferry rides, the Golden Gate Bridge, Bay Bridge, Lombard Street and Alcatraz. I made mental notes for future plans.

By four o'clock my tub was full. I lay, soaking and reading until my water was close to cool. After dressing and adding a little mascara to my lashes, I trotted downstairs to the backyard porch. Grace's garden reminded me of a song—tall and short flowering vegetation all mixed in together, yet it worked. All colors spread across the grounds in what seemed like organized chaos. I breathed in the fragrant scent and scanned, letting myself take it all in. Beautiful.

"Hello, Samantha."

Turning, Victor stood feet from me on the stone path I walked along. "You know, it's funny. You told me you were here for work, yet twice I've seen you here, in the middle of day—when most people are working." Squinting in the sun, I smiled up at him.

"Well then, there is another thing I find rewarding in my career choice, being my own boss." Laughing, he stepped to the side to block the sun from blinding me.

"Would you like to walk around the garden?" I heard myself say. Where was that no men rule now?

"I would." Walking once around the large yard, we started again on a second trip. "Would you like to meet for lunch tomorrow? I'd love to show you around a little," Victor said, swaying closer to me with each word.

"You want to show me around?" I stopped, my hands on my

hips. "May I remind you that you arrived the same day that I did?"

"Yes, but I visit The Redwood every year. This time I happen to be working while I'm here." He tugged on my elbow and we started walking once more.

"Uhh—"

"Are you afraid of me?" His eyes creased, sad, but playful like.

"Of course not. It's just—"

"Then come now, it's not a date—no commitment, Samantha Blake. Just two friends, touring together."

"Oh." No men. No men. No men. "Well, I guess—"

"Great!" Victor clapped his hands.

Crap. Already. One day and I'd broken my own rule. But then Victor had a point. Lunch didn't have to mean a date. "Thank you for the walk, Victor," I said, stopping. "I'm going to see if I can help Grace in the kitchen."

"Why?" His brows knit together, confused.

I couldn't explain what she'd done for me, giving me this room above anyone else—giving Eve what must be the deal of a lifetime. Besides, the truth was—"I want to."

Walking into the house, I pulled my phone from my pocket to text my sisters and Eve.

> Me: One day. One lousy day, and I think I've already
>     broken my no men rule.
> Amanda: Oh, goody! It was a stupid rule.
> Liza: Twenty-four hours in the sunny state and you've
>     already met a man?! Nana will be thrilled.
> Eve: You made a no men rule? Sam, it's your rule,
>     you're allowed to change it. Or break it.
>     Whatever. Have fun.

"Arghhh!" I shoved my phone back into my pocket. My rule could have rules—lunch could be keeping within the no men rule... right? I would figure this out. The girls were no help, but then wasn't that why we made the no calling rule? Wow, how many rules could one vacation have? Still, I needed to live my own life. I couldn't have my sisters or Eve guiding me throughout every turn. If I wanted to spend the day with an attractive man, a new friend, I could. Experiencing life didn't mean I'd be an idiot. It meant I would go, I would live, I would try. I shut my eyes, blocking out everyone else's words and thought—Okay, the non-date outing with Victor is a go.

# Chapter 10

**B**y the time I peeked through the hall's swinging kitchen door I had a headache—too much thinking. "Grace, I thought I'd come help out." The kitchen would release my tension.

"Oh, dear, you are a guest here," she said, looking up frome the dough she kneaded.

"Well, see, I love to cook," I said, stepping into the room. "Really, you'd be helping me. This kitchen has been calling my name since I got here."

She stopped kneading and brushed a hair from her eyes with the back of her hand. "All right then. Have you ever made homemade noodles?"

I smiled. "As a matter of fact, I have."

Pulling my hair back into my standard ponytail, I washed my hands and dug into the dough. Cleaning off her sticky hands, Grace pulled ripe tomatoes and parsley from the fridge.

"How's my niece these days?" Grace asked, without looking up from her work.

"Eve? She's the best. Really, she is kind of amazing. I'm not sure how she found her way to Wyoming, but I'm glad she did."

"I know she likes it there. I wish I could make it out to visit, but this place keeps me busy—all day, every day."

"I can imagine, but it's wonderful. I could stay here—forever."

The kitchen door swung open and our conversation stopped. My working ceased and I stare at the door, waiting for the mystery person to appear. A man carrying a large crate up on his shoulder came through. I couldn't see his face. I didn't think

69

Grace had any employees though.

"Where do you want the apples, Mom?"

Grace's son—I wasn't even sure he lived around here. I went back to my work, rolling out the dough in front of me and glancing curious at the back of him.

"Hi, honey." Grace motioned to a section of empty countertop. "Thanks for picking up the fruit for me."

The old denim jacket he wore looked long before his time with its faded color and frayed edges. He towered over his petite mother. Setting the box of produce down, he kissed Grace's cheek.

Bowing my head toward the counter, I couldn't help but feel like I was intruding. My eyes darted between the dough in front of me and the couple across the room. He turned, and I wasn't sure I wanted him to see me, standing there—invading. I also didn't want to be rude and ignore him. Glancing his way again, I dropped the rolling pin. I spun around, facing the opposite direction. *No! No. No. No. Not him.*

With my back to the both of them, I tripped my way to the exit. "Uh, Grace, I need to clean up before dinner." I barreled out of the room, the flour covered apron still strapped to my body. I pulled it off and stuck my hand through the swinging doors, dropping it blindly onto what I hoped was a counter.

Running to my room, I unlocked the door and shut it closed behind me. Falling back against it, I closed my eyes, trying to control my breathing. "No, no, no—the *jerk* from the diner is Grace's son?" I knocked the back of my head on the door. "Aahh, please don't recognize me."

When the door thumped back, I jumped farther into the room, my breathing heavy and uneven.

"Samantha," Grace said, knocking again. "Are you okay, honey?"

Praying she hadn't heard me call her son a jerk, I opened the door. Beads of sweat slid down my forehead. "Oh! I'm fine."

Looking over my face, I could see she didn't believe me. "You left so suddenly."

"I know. I'm sorry, Grace." I wiped at the perspiration on my

head. "I didn't realize the time, and I need to change. That's all."
So much for cooking in my dream kitchen.

"Oh, sure. Well, come back into the kitchen before you sit down. I want you to meet my son."

"Your son?"

"Yes, the young man who brought in the box of apples. That's my Cole." Grace beamed—she must not realize her son was a cynical bum.

"That's lovely." I sucked in a breath. "I'd be happy to meet your son."

Fine. I had to meet *Cole*. Fine. I could do that. I could be the mature one—I couldn't say the same for him. Would he behave in front of his mother?

Closing the door behind Grace, my mind ran a mile. Yes, I could stop by the kitchen before dinner, and I would look like the most fabulous driver ever. *What would a fabulous driver wear?* I pulled out my security blanket—a.k.a. my cell phone.

> Me: Liza, what would a good driver wear?
> Liza: Sweats and a University of Wyoming T-shirt.
> Me: What?? Why?
> Liza: I'm a great driver. That's what I have on. LOL.
>
> Me: You're hilarious.

No help. These girls were no help!

Pulling every strand of my hair high up onto my head, I rolled the ponytail into a tight-no-nonsense bun. I pulled on slacks—also Amanda's addition—and a pink, button up blouse Dad had bought me years ago. It still had the tags on.

Standing in front of the elongated mirror, I examined myself. Yes—I looked like someone very sensible—someone smart—someone who would never drive carelessly.

"Are you practicing to be a librarian? Or maybe a very strict teacher?" Victor leaned against the wall in our hallway. One ankle crossed over the other, he looked as though he'd been waiting there for me.

*Was* he waiting for me? Maybe I should tell Victor about the no men rule. "Am I what?"

71

"I asked if you're instructing small children today or intimidating a juvenile. You very much resemble my sixth-grade math teacher with your hair pulled up like that."

"Oh." I patted the top of my bun, making sure no strays had fallen out of place. "Ah, well, sorry to bring back any bad memories."

"I didn't say I disliked it. I had a crush on my sixth-grade math teacher." Grinning, he leaned toward me.

Shaking my head, I put one finger on his chest and pushed him back against the wall. "I have something to do before dinner. I'll see you in there."

Smoothing my shirt, I cleared my throat before entering the kitchen. Cole wore a flowered apron, much too small for him. He stood at the sink, washing dishes. If clothes meant anything, I had the upper hand. His unshaven face and broad build didn't look right in the kitchen—and yet, it did. Ugh, and with that thought, all the confidence my bun and slacks had given me went out the window.

With Grace nowhere in sight, I considered sneaking back out the door behind me. But I was being mature—and adult—and living life—not running away, so hands on my hips, I cleared my throat.

Turning, he faced me and my hands fell to my sides. "I'm looking for Grace."

"She's in the pantry," he said, pointing to a small room within the kitchen.

Facing him didn't feel brave—more like standing in the middle of a busy street. Needing to escape him, I nodded and walked right into the storage room.

"Samantha." Grace laughed at my presence. "What are you doing in here?"

"Hiding." The word came out without thinking.

Cocking her head, her brows furrowed.

"Helping!" I said. "I wanted to see if I could help you."

"Sure, grab that sauce," she said, pointing to a large can of tomato sauce.

Walking out of the pantry with our arms full, I followed

close behind Grace. Cole smiled, a menacing grin, so menacing I thought he might laugh. *He's enjoying this. He is loving my misery.*

Grace set her armful on the counter and I did the same. "Cole," she said, and he turned around to face us. "This is Samantha Blake, Eve's friend from Wyoming."

Stretching out his hand, he said, "It's nice to meet you." Well, at least he hadn't talked bad about me to Grace—or if he had, she hadn't put two-and-two together. *Yes, Grace the reckless git from the diner is ME!*

Taking his hand, I shook it. "You too." I pulled my hand from his, and wiped the dampness on a nearby cloth. "I'm going to go sit down." I looked at Grace, ignoring her rude son.

"Yes, you go, dear." Grace patted my hand. Grabbing the pantry items and turning to Cole, she said, "How did your interview go today?"

Glancing back before going through the dining room door, I watched him take a jar from her hands and open it.

"I was late," he said, handing her back the bottle. "Not a great first impression."

Scooping the last bite of Grace's chicken noodle soup into my mouth, I wondered if there would be seconds. Grace had said I could come down in the night and search the fridge—I just might have to.

"I'm not kidding," Victor said. "That's how a goat became locked in my vehicle."

Forest smacked the table with his fist and threw his head back with laughter. Minnie and I laughed too. We'd been rolling at Victor's stories all night.

Grace gave me a smile and without a word cleared the plate in front of me. I hated not helping her. My grand plan to help make dinner didn't work out so well and now I sat while she cleared away my dishes.

"Divine," Victor said when Grace took his plate and bowl. "As always, Grace."

"Charming," Grace said, flashing Victor a big grin. "As always, Victor."

Standing from the table, Minnie looked at Victor and me, side-by-side. "We're going out for drinks. Do you guys want to come?"

Victor clapped his hands. "Yes, very good."

"Ah—no, thank you though."

Victor and I turned to the other, having spoken at the same time. I gave his arm a light punch. "You guys have fun." I wasn't opposed to making friends or going out—but she asked us like we were a couple. Even the idea violated my rules.

Minnie giggled. "You coming, Vic?"

He shrugged. "No, Samantha is right, we would only be interrupting your honeymoon," Victor said to the newlyweds—he'd been right about them.

"Thanks for the invitation." Walking to the entry way together, I waved goodbye to the couple.

"So," Victor's arm stretched out to the stair railing, putting himself right in front of me, "now that those pesky honeymooners are gone, let's you and me get a drink, eh?"

"Yeah, I don't think so." Oh, great, did he think I was trying to get rid of them? Victor Andrews would make this a long six weeks.

"All right my friend, but one of these days. . ." He shook a finger at me, his words trailing off. "Goodnight, Chéri." Bending down, he took my hand in his and kissed it before trotting up the stairs.

Was he for real? Victor did not feel like a real person to me—rather someone from one of Nana's romance novels. Still, the pressure he left on my hand made me laugh. I'd never had someone kiss my hand before, and in two days, Victor had done so twice.

Heading back into the dining room, I gathered the remaining dishes on the table. Taking them to the kitchen, I saw Cole instead of Grace cleaning up the room.

He didn't turn around from his work, but said, "You don't have to do that."

"Wow, you've got like super Spidey senses."

A quiet, breathy laugh escaped his throat. Maybe he *didn't* remember me.

"I don't mind helping."  I needed to help. I needed to be useful. You can't work in a lumber mill and take care of your dad for a decade and then suddenly spend all your time playing and lounging. Plus, Grace's kitchen could be a playground to me.

Turning around, he wiped his wet hands on his girly apron.

"Where's Grace?" I asked, my heart quickening with him peering at me. Maybe he *did* remember me.

"She was tired. I told her to lay down."

"That's kind of you?" It came out like a question — because it surprised me. He didn't strike me as a *kind* person.

"Can I help you with something?" he asked, crossing his arms over his broad chest. Huffing out a breath, he acted as if I were a child in the way of grown-up work.

"*I* was helping." I set the dishes on the countertop. Couldn't he see that I happened to be a nice person — a responsible person? I wasn't a run-into-someone-else's-car kind of a person. But then — yep, he could see that. *He knows exactly who I am, what I am trying to do, and he is still being a jerk.* Turning to leave, I stopped, swiveling back to face him again. "Actually," I stepped closer to him with my hands on my hips — through letting him intimidate me, "I wanted to ask you about this morning."

"Okay." He stepped in closer — playing the game. His arms were still crossed like a protective body guard.

"I, well," I said, hating the twinge of pressure in my stomach. "Is your car all right?"

"It's fine." He stared down at me and I wished I'd brought the high heels Amanda tried to sneak into my bag. They'd at least get me closer to eye level with him.

"Good." I narrowed my eyes. "*Mine* is all right, too, in case you were wondering."

Giving that breathy-almost-a-laugh again, he walked back to the sink and shoved his hands into the sudsy water. "Truthfully, I wasn't."

Picking up the stack of dessert plates I'd brought in, I walked over to the sink and dropped them in, suds splashed up onto Cole's stomach and chest.

"Shocker!" I stomped away and smacked the swinging door open. My heart racing, I continued my scuttle up the stairway to my room. I shut the door behind me—careful not to slam it with all the energy racing through my veins. I pulled out the pins keeping my hair in place. How could *he* come from Grace?

# Chapter 11

A shrill ring that didn't belong to my cell filled my room. Hopping out of the tub, I wrapped myself in a towel before peeking out into my room. The old fashioned phone on my end table buzzed.

Tip-toeing over, I picked up the corded receiver. "Uh-hello?"

"Hi, Sam, it's Grace."

"Grace. Hi." Had her son told on me? Was I getting kicked out all because his cynical-self couldn't get over a little accident? "Um—"

"Sunday's coming," she said, her tone too cheery to be evicting me.

"Yeah—"

"Sunday, I only offer dinner at The Redwood. I spend the day at the homeless shelter, helping with their meals. I thought maybe you'd like to come with me."

An invitation—not an eviction.

"Of course you don't have to—"

"No, Grace, I'd like that." I sat on the bed, the flowered spread wrinkling with my weight. I'd like that very much. "When do we leave?"

Cole. I had seen him three times—three times in just two days. He didn't glare at me, but he wasn't welcoming either. Why did he have to come over so often? Why couldn't I get over his crassness and just ignore him? His very presence ruined my self-finding-loving vacation!

Staring at the butter colored ceiling above me, I kicked at

77

the sheets wound around my legs. I was hot and annoyed, and the result—I couldn't sleep. How could someone so pretentious come from Grace? I wanted to call Liza. I needed to ask her why I allowed this to get to me. Or maybe I should call Eve, and ask her how her cousin became so pompous and smug.

Things happen! Bumps happen! It wasn't the end of the world. For heaven sake, in the sixth grade, Jamie Henderson's big brother backed into my bike with his truck. I couldn't ride it the rest of the summer. Even as an adolescent—a child, who grieved for the loss and walked everywhere, I forgave him when he apologized. I wasn't short, or rude, or ill-mannered— in fact, I think I told him I enjoyed walking. This man was an adult who behaved like a child, and then had the audacity to say it was my entire fault!

Kicking at the blankets around my feet, I defended myself—to myself, again and again. Between my tub and looking forward to spending the day with Grace tomorrow, I should be settled. I should be over this, but Cole's smugness circled in my brain.

My stomach growled. *Great! And now I'm hungry.* Grace had told me to make myself at home. I hadn't yet dared to be *so very* at home, but if I ate I would feel better. The food would take my mind off the man and I'd be able to sleep—I hoped.

I eyed my clock, 1:42 a.m. "Oh man, I have the shelter in seven hours."

Again, my stomach rumbled. "All right!" Grabbing my fuzzy blue robe, I threw it on over my knee length pajama shirt and snuck down the stairs to the kitchen.

Once inside the door, I patted around for the light. My fingers roamed over the knob of the switch, and I flipped it on. Covering my eyes from the new-found glow, I tip-toed to the counter. "She told me to do this," I said, feeling like a thief in the night as I opened one of Grace's cupboards. I pulled out a jar of peanut butter. Then I made my way over to the fridge and found a bottle of raspberry jam.

"She told you to do what?" A voice emerged from the pantry.

"Bwahh!" Dropping the jars on the ground, I balled my hands

into fists, protruding them outward like a boxer. "Bwahh!"

"Whoa." Cole held up a hand. "You might want to think of staying out of the kitchen. Do you always drop things?"

Cole. Of course it was *him*. He was destined to annoy me. I scowled at his stupid face. Looking down, I saw the jam bottle shattered, spattering red goo across Grace's spotless black and white tile.

"I do not often drop things. Only when people jump out of nowhere, frightening me—thoughtless,....Don't you think?" Snatching the garbage can, I crouched to a less-than intimidating pose to pick up my mess.

"I seem to bring out your jumpy side," he said, setting the contents in his own hands onto the counter.

"*You*... and pretty much only you, bring out my super annoyed side," I said, my face still to the floor. That wasn't true. Angela Bell had a knack at getting under my skin too—in fact, if Angela weren't happily married, I'd play Nana and fix the two up!

"Oh really?"

"Really." I scowled up at him again. "I'm normally a pretty together person." Was that true? When I said it, I meant it—but really when under a microscope—*I'm a mess.*

He raised his eyebrows in disbelief.

"You know," I said, standing and placing my hands on my furry blue hips. "There are no laws that say you *have* to be a jerk. What, is that a California thing? Or just a Cole thing?"

"Aren't you sweet?" he said, pointing a not-so-nice finger at me. "Besides, it's not as if you know me."

Sighing, I crossed my arms. "You're right, I don't. I guess you could blame it on first impressions—and second—and third—and let's face it, thus far all of my impressions have been just as *wonderful* as the first."

Nodding, he didn't argue. "Right," he said, his manner softening. "I suppose our encounters haven't been exactly pleasant, have they? Samantha, it sounds like my weakness is similar to your own."

"What does that mean?" His tone may have changed, but my defense still stood guard.

"I jump to conclusions too quickly at times." His feet didn't move, but his body seemed to inch nearer to me. "Often, I am *too* honest." He said it like a secret just the two of us knew.

Crossing my arms again, I glared at him, I wasn't buying his apologetic tone—besides he *hadn't* apologized. "Uh-huh." He thought he could claim to *know* me? Rolling my eyes, I bent again, to finish cleaning up.

Cole followed after me, a roll of paper towels in his hands. "Really," he said, holding the towels, but not using them. "I'm not *normally* rude. At least, I don't think I am."

"You're unsure, huh?" I threw more glass into the waste basket, not caring that sarcasm rang in my voice.

"The jury's still out."

"You're telling me." I shook my head.

He shut his eyes, squeezing them tight, like the moment pained him. "Hey, could you cut me a little slack? I'm trying really hard to believe that you aren't always... this *amiable*—at least, that's what my mom says."

My head shot up. "You told your mom—"

"No," he said, blowing out a puff of air. "I couldn't without mentioning what a *jerk* I had been. She's talked about you."

"Oh. Well..." I grabbed the paper towels from his hand and pulled off a strip, "...I can be *amiable*, you know."

"I'm sure." He rested his elbows on his knees, his head in his hands and I really examined him then. Sitting there, he looked...tired—not just one a.m. tired, but it's-been-a-long-life tired. "It's been a very long week," he said, confirming my suspicion.

The quiet lingered. I kept my eyes upon him. I could be outspoken and my emotions often provoked my bluntness—and I knew *tired*. I suppose I should give him a break. Maybe.

Sighing, he lifted his head to meet my stare.

Cowering, I wiped at the red mess still spattered about the floor. "Gosh, your mom gives me a great opportunity to be here, and I repay her by wasting food and making a mess."

"That's true. I know a twenty-four hour market. You should probably go buy her another jar of jam."

Looking up from the floor, I met him almost nose to nose. He cracked a grin, his blue eyes creasing as he did so.

"She's got a few dozen in the cellar, I think it'll be okay," he said, leaning his back against the bottom cupboards. He laughed and sighed again, like he needed to go to bed. "I am sorry about this week, Samantha. Although, I can't promise it won't happen again."

"That's not much of an apology," I said, but I wasn't angry anymore. Something in his exhaustion filled me with more compassion than anger.

Without looking, he reached up and slid open a drawer. Twisting his hand around, he pulled a couple spoons from the drawer and handed one to me. Leaning over, he picked up the jar of peanut butter that had slid beneath the island. He dipped into the crunchy goodness and then handed the jar to me. I leaned against the island cupboard opposite of Cole, scooped out a tablespoon of peanut butter and set the jar on the ground between us.

"So, what's the definition of: bwhaa?"

"Ahh…" I managed through a sticky mouth.

"You know—*bwahh*!" Cole flared his hands and mimicked my scream. "Probably some bohemian word for jerk, right?"

Sputtering out half my mouthful, I laughed and choke all at the same time. Jumping up from his seat on the floor, he filled a glass with water and handed it to me.

Gulping down the water, I caught my breath. "Exactly," I said through a wheeze. With my hand on my chest, I stretched out my bare legs and leaned my head back against the cupboards behind me. "So, what's with the rough week?"

"You don't want to hear about my troubles, Samantha."

I shrugged my shoulders. Maybe I didn't. I hadn't made up my mind about liking him just yet. If I heard his problems, I'd feel sorry for him. Then, I might forget my anger altogether. Still, I said, "You want to know why I can't sleep?" I pointed at him and then balled my hands into fists.

"I must have really upset you," he said, smiling.

"I was just so infuriated by you. You. Mr. it-was-you-not-me

81

belonged to sweet Grace. I couldn't see how that was possible. You, with your glares and snarky remarks and—"

"I get it," he said, his forehead scrunched and his hand held up to stop me.

"Right." I nodded—that's right, we were trying to avoid the insults, now. "Okay. So, you know why I'm up. Maybe if you spill your guts, we'll both be able to sleep."

"Ahh." He ran a hand through his thick ash hair. "I've been interviewing for jobs the past couple weeks. I was late to my last interview. It didn't bode well." Raising his eyebrows, he rested his arms on his knees bent to his chest.

Biting my lip, I said, "Hmm... car trouble that morning?"

Cole nodded and let out a light laugh.

"Sorry," I said, feeling a twinge of guilt for all the times I'd used the word *jerk*.

"Don't apologize again." He laid his head against the cupboard with a *thump*. "The real problem is, I don't want any of the jobs I'm applying for."

I put my spoon down. "Then why apply?"

"I need a job. Bills. Rent. Food. You know, the basics."

"Grace charges you rent?"

He laughed again and stretched out his long legs out. "I don't live here, Samantha. I stay from time to time, but I have my own place."

"Oh—" Really? He's *always* around!

"Tomorrow is my mom and dad's anniversary. With Dad gone, I like to keep her company, kind of celebrate with her."

Pressing my lips together, I let out a full breath. Hmm... not a jerk type move.

"How many years would it have been?" I said, thinking of Dad. We didn't celebrate, but it never surprised him when I made Mom's favorite dish on those special occasions when we missed her—if possible even more than usual.

"Thirty-two." He smiled, sad.

I knew his pain. I knew the heartache of having your parent gone too soon, but I couldn't say as much. My mind—my heart—something kept all that inside, kept it all mine. Instead, I handed

Cole my spoon. "I better be off to bed. Thanks for the talk."

Standing, he offered a hand and pulled me to my feet. "Yeah, me too."

Pins pricked at my fingers. Letting go of Cole's hand, I rubbed mine against my robe. I'd sworn off men and now they surrounded me — none of them clowns or cousins.

## Chapter 12

Nine o'clock came all too soon. My four-minute shower lasted just long enough to wash my hair. I twisted the long-wet mess into a tight bun once again. Slipping into my skinny jeans, I threw on an old Aerosmith T-shirt that I had packed. The one Amanda begged me to leave behind.

Seconds later I met Grace downstairs. Her graying hair pulled back in a ponytail. The worn ripped up jeans she wore made her look too youthful for her years.

"Good morning, Sam." She smiled and adjusted a backpack before slipping it over her shoulders. "Ready to go?"

Nodding, I followed her outside where Cole waited in the driver's seat of his old blue Buick. "Does Cole always go with you?"

"Nah," she said. "He's a bit of a worrier. He doesn't like me to be alone, but I'm fine. I have plenty of wonderful memories to fill my not so spare time." Opening the passenger door, she turned back to wink at me.

"Happy anniversary, Grace."

She smiled, seeming unsurprised that I knew.

Slipping into the back seat of the small car left me claustrophobic and out of my comfort zone. Going to an unknown place, to do what, I wasn't sure, with someone I hadn't decided I liked yet. Sure, we'd had a visit, shared some peanut butter, but I wasn't ready to call Cole Casey my friend.

"Good morning," Cole said, peaking at me through the rear view mirror.

Clearing my throat, I didn't stare back at him. Instead I

focused on my seat belt buckle. "Good morning."

The half hour ride loosened my discomfort and calmed me. I enjoyed sitting quiet, examining the different homes, buildings and greenery pass by.

Brown brick tiled the side of an old corner lot building. The brick had aged from what must have been a bright red. Walking around to the rear side Grace pulled a key from her backpack and unlocked a back door. Stepping inside, we walked into the tight galley kitchen of the shelter.

I'm not sure what I pictured—loads of people serving, and mending, and helping those less fortunate, and then the line of the needy waiting for our help—maybe. But in the end it was Grace, Cole, me and a young couple, Ashley and Dawson. Grace gave instructions and then we worked. I washed dishes while Grace and Cole prepped and packaged food that would be eaten days from now. The portions all looked child-size to me. The plastic containers were lined up inside two oversized refrigerators.

"This is a small shelter," Ashley said, drying the dishes I handed her. Most of the chatter in the room came from her. She was young and sweet, and liked telling me all of the things a country girl from Wyoming just wouldn't know. "We don't have the facility or the means that some shelters in the city have to serve a lot of people here, but Grace and a few local vendors keep this place afloat."

I nodded and continued to wash. The pile of dirty dishes never seemed to get any smaller. "So, how'd you and Dawson meet?"

"Oh." She giggled. "I can't even tell you."

"You can't tell me?" I stopped mid scrub to look over at her.

Walking over, his hands full, Cole set down another pile of dirty dishes for me. Leaning past me, he rinsed off his dough covered hands in the wash tub. Ashley ignored him, but then, he wasn't in her way.

"No, really, I can't remember. We grew up together. We've always known each other. It felt like a life time before we could be together. My parents made me wait until I graduated high school," she said, still irritated about the *long* wait.

Maybe it was the inflection in her voice, or the way her eyes had widened as if in shock when she told me—maybe both. With my insides all shook up and Cole almost standing on me, I couldn't stop the chortle that burst from my lips.

Ashley cleared her throat and dried her hands. Without looking at either of us, she said, "I'm going to help Dawson."

I hadn't meant to offend her. My never-ending home town story interrupted my vacation and… well, it was too ironic and humorous not to laugh.

With his hands now clean, Cole took Ashley's spot beside me to dry. "Do you often laugh in homeless shelters? You find something funny?"

He's right. *I am a horrible person*—this wasn't the time or the place.

"I'm sorry." I washed with renewed vigor now. "I didn't mean any disrespect. It's just, Ashley, she reminds me of someone back home. It's stupid. And not at all an interesting story."

"I bet it's not." He smiled, making fun of me for defending myself. "People are actually allowed to laugh, *even* here. It's okay." He stressed his exaggerated tone.

Ignoring him, I looked behind me, at Ashley. She seemed okay.

"Are you going to tell me?"

"What?" I handed him another dish and looked up at him.

"You're story. I'm waiting. We've got time." He cocked his head toward my ever-growing pile of dishes.

"Ahh—" Why not? He had to be close to thirty *and* single too. Maybe he'd shed some light—or at least laugh at someone other than me. So, I started in on Miss Angela Bell—err Mrs. Cash.

"You have to be exaggerating." He ran his cloth over the pot I just handed him.

"I'm not. Remember I have that honesty disease just like you. Her weekly work message ended with the theme of, 'find yourself a husband.'"

He flicked suds from my own sink into my face. "Well, sometimes the honesty disease is accompanied with the *lay it on thick* illness."

Wiping the droplets from my face, I shoved my hands back into the sink only to bring out two palmfuls of bubbles. Patting him on the shoulder, I soaked the top of his sleeve. "Oops, sorry about that." I held my hand in front of my face, feigning shock.

"No, you're not." He rubbed away the remaining suds from his shoulder. "That's the *lay it on thick* disease talking."

Hours past. We didn't stop for breaks. We didn't stop to eat. Grace cooked and boxed. Ashley, Dawson, and Cole took turns helping her along with other jobs — things, it would seem, they'd been doing for years. All while I washed dishes — dish after dish, after dish, something that didn't need instructing. I think I washed the same pot eight different times. By two o'clock we had lunches for forty for the entire next week.

Maybe vacation had weakened me. I had worked ten-hour days before coming here. But after five hours in that kitchen with non-stop work, I stood drenched in sweat and ready to collapse. Why I'd taken the time to shower, because I'd need to again the minute we got back.

Back at The Redwood I spent the next few hours in my room reading in my tub and resting. Lying on my bed, I sat up to look at the clock. "Two hours," I yawned, "until dinner."

In front of the mirror in my bathroom, I let my hair out of its bun and brushed through it. It was still a little damp from being tucked up all day. I applied some of Amanda's mascara — I'd gotten good at it. There wasn't much to it. Besides, as a girl, shouldn't it be part of my DNA to understand how to put on makeup? Twenty-eight years of not caring had killed that part of my DNA, but little-by-little I'd get it back, because now I wanted it.

Trotting down the stairs and into the kitchen, I tapped on the door belonging to Grace's private quarters. Cole answered.

"You're still here?" I said, my eyebrows rising. I thought he would have gone home by now.

"Nice to see you, too." He smirked. "I'm spending the day with my mom, remember?"

"Oh, yeah." I bit down on my thumbnail.

Smiling, he waited — shooting for *patience.*

"Uh, is Grace around?" I looked past him into Grace's room.

"Come on in." He stepped aside, making room for me to enter.

Unsure, I stepped over the threshold. Following Cole, I realized Grace's "room" could have fit my little home within it, and there would still be space to live. We passed a bedroom, a small kitchen, and entered a little living area where Grace sat on a blue ribbed couch. Her home appeared so different than the rest of The Redwood, her personal style mixed with photos and knick knacks.

"Samantha," she said, standing up. "Did you need something?"

I held up a protesting hand. I didn't want her fussing over me, feeling less like a customer and more like an old friend when it came to Grace. "Please sit. I didn't mean to disturb you."

"Mom, Samantha just asked to speak to you. I didn't think you'd mind—"

"It's fine." She brushed her hand along Cole's upper arm and offered him a smile. *I'm not an old friend though, maybe I have crossed a line.*

Breathing in, the air entered my lungs more like humid smog with everyone waiting on me. Guests didn't normally saunter back into Grace's private space. Biting my lip, my eyes bounced from Grace to Cole. "Ah, I was just hoping to help you with dinner."

"Honey, I told you, that's nonsense. You are my guest."

Shoving his hands into his pockets, Cole cleared his throat, his brows knit together. "Mom, I think it's a great idea. Sam and I can take care of dinner tonight. You deserve a break."

*Sam and I.* Not how I imagined this playing out. But I didn't cringe inside. It wasn't like the first time I saw him in the kitchen— after our run in. Then, I had wanted to run and hide or punch his stupid face. Total cringe. But now, I don't know, it's...better. Grace, the shelter, dishes, talking, peanut butter—something had made it better. "Cole is right." Grace needed a break. "Besides, it's your anniversary."

She smiled, but despite what she had said to me earlier about feeling content, I could see the sadness in it. Either our offer would help her or we'd be taking away her distraction. I didn't know which, so whichever choice she made, I wouldn't argue.

"Okay, then," Grace said, rubbing her palms along her pant legs. She did look sleepy.

Grace sat back down and Cole walked me to the door.

"Maybe you should stay with her," I said, peeking past him into her home, though I couldn't see her from the door. "I think she could use your company."

Shuffling his feet, he rested his hand on the door jam. "You're sweet, Sam, but you'll need my help and she'll want a of couple hours alone."

He should know better than me. "All right then. When do we start?"

Lifting at his hand, he peeked at his watch. "Five minutes okay?"

Nodding, I rubbed my hands together—being this excited to cook may have been irrational. "I'll meet you in the kitchen."

I washed up while Cole went back to speak with Grace about dinner. Five minutes later he met me in the kitchen with a list. Holding it up, he said, "Here's what Mom has planned for tonight. It's just you and Victor. The others are going out."

Checking out the list, I busied myself rinsing and chopping vegetables. I couldn't help but notice how Grace had spoken to Victor so casually and even Cole seemed to know him. "Victor said he's been coming here a while. Do you know him very well?"

"A bit, I guess." He didn't look up from his work.

"So, you like him? You'd call him a friend?"

He snorted. "I talk to the guy a little every time he's here. That doesn't make me an expert on him. So, friend is not the word I'd use." Meeting my eyes, he squinted. "Why? Do you like him?"

"Yes, he's interesting."

Nodding, he looked back down, his lips twitching.

"What?" I stopped my work, staring at his twitching mouth. He appeared to have more to say on the subject.

"Nothing." Cole didn't meet my eyes, he just kept working.

Blowing out the breath I'd been holding, I went back to my chopping.

"It's just—"

90

"What Cole?" I slapped my knife onto the countertop. "It's just what? It was a simple question. I was just curious." He could win an award for annoying me.

"I guess I'm curious why *you're* so curious." He stood at the stove, browning the ground turkey in his pan. "Has he asked you out? —is that why?"

"No." Okay—sort of, but as new acquaintances and that isn't what Cole meant. For some reason, he read a lot into a simple question. "Besides, I am *not* here for men!" I said, killing the carrot left on my cutting board.

Cole laughed. "Wow, you're pretty adamant about that. Why? I thought you were single."

Embarrassed, my face burned, sweat droplets trickled down my neck. Grateful I didn't face him, I said, "I am. Should unmarried women always be on the lookout for single men? We have other interests you know."

"So, you aren't asking about Vic because you're interested in him?"

Did he know no boundaries? Still, I'd started this. I suppose I would have to finish it. "No. Just. Curious."

"Little defensive, aren't you?" He didn't wait for me to answer, but walked over to the counter where I stood and looked me in the eye. "You aren't in this kitchen, cooking on your vacation, because you want *me* to ask you out?"

"What?" I jutted backward. Was he serious? I'd asked to cook with Grace, not Cole! "*No!* Are you always this cocky?"

Standing inches away, he smiled. "Just. Curious."

"Are you kidding?" Stumbling from behind the counter, I met him without the boundary to block me, in case I needed to punch him. My face on fire, I poked him. "Fine. You want the story. You can have it. Believe me Cole when I say, I DO NOT want to date you. I did not come here for men. I came here for *me* and to get away from men—"

"Uh, Sam." He interrupted my ugly tale by flashing me a crooked smile.

"Oh." I covered my mouth, more heat rising into my cheeks and looked away from him. "You're kidding around."

"I don't *mean* to give you such a hard time. It's just so easy to do."

"You're lucky I already ran into your car. If I didn't owe you — ooo!" I glared at him, trying to find some dignity, but I wanted to hide my face in a paper bag.

Cole took a plate into Grace and I brought two dishes out into the dining room. And there he sat, waiting for me.

"I thought you might be in there," Victor said, his toothy grin shining at me.

"Oh, really, why is that?" I held up his quiche.

"You seem to like the kitchen." He laughed as if he'd made a joke.

"You might want to be careful. You don't want to make me laugh or insult me." I waved his dinner plate from side to side. "I am carrying your dinner."

"And you will drop it in my lap, eh?"

I pursed my lips. "It could happen."

"We're still on for dinner tomorrow?"

Our non-date outing… "Oh, yeah, sure." I sat in a pool of my own guilt. I'm not sure why it mattered. Sure, I'd told Cole, Victor hadn't asked me out, that I wasn't interested — and really I wasn't. But why should Cole care? Really — why should I care if he cared? Oh, confusing. In the end, I didn't see tomorrow as a date. Just two friends going dutch and that's what mattered — right? But now Cole had me wondering, how did Victor see it?

# Chapter 13

"What do you think of dessert?" Victor's dark suit went perfect with his tall, dark and handsome persona.

Still working on my Spoupe à L'oignon, I looked up at him about to lick the bowl, but I didn't have room for dessert. Not to mention Victor and I were on hour three of our non-date outing and it had begun to feel—well, like one great date. We walked across Bay Bridge just as the sun set below the horizon and then Victor had taken me to his favorite French restaurant. I'd never eaten French food before, but the cheesy oniony dish I ordered sent me into a full-fledged love fest. "Ah, I don't think I'll have room."

"Nonsense." Victor smiled, watching me eat the last drops of my dish. "The girl who has never eaten French, has never eaten! We can share, I'll order."

"Well—ah—"

"Well what? You think you can resist Brioche Perdu?" He spoke so beautifully—I could have eaten his words and called it dessert.

"But how will we split the check if we share?" I tried once again to spell out how casual I saw this.

Laughing at me, he wiped at the tears pooling in his eyes and then motioned to the waiter to come. Speaking so fast and so… French, I didn't understand a word he said.

"*Oui magnifique!*" The waiter kissed his fingers.

"*Oui.*" Victor picked up my hand from across the table. He kissed my fingers and shooed the waiter away.

Pulling my hand from his lips, I rubbed it on my skirt beneath the table. "Uh, Vic, I think you have this wrong. I'm not interested in dating—or seeing anyone as more than a friend."

"No?" he said, smiling as if he didn't believe me.

"No." I kept my voice stern—I liked my interesting French Rosewood neighbor, but he hadn't made me lose my focus. "I am not." I had to say more. I had to—he wouldn't believe me, he wouldn't understand if I didn't. "I'd been searching for *someone*... to share my life with for months, when my epiphany came."

"*Oui?*"

"I need to find myself." I tried with every fiber of my being to exude confidence.

"And have you?"

I sounded silly... and sharing this with Victor of all people... He was too sophisticated for my nonsense. I couldn't imagine what he thought of me—but that's the thing about finding yourself, you don't really care what others think of you. It's what you think of you that matters. "I'm getting there," I said. "Besides, as long as I'm being honest, when I do look for someone again—I want it all, Vic. I want marriage and kids and—well, everything you don't."

"So, friends?" He grinned at me.

"Yeah." I nodded, a slow breath leaving my chest. "Friends."

The couple of weeks that followed went by fast. I couldn't believe I hadn't run out of things to do. This vacation might have ruined me for the real world. I toured the city more—once again with Victor. I ate at Jack's a few more times. No one made French toast like Jack. Cole doubled as Grace's handyman it seemed—so I ran into him a few times, too. But even with the strides we'd made, I would forever be known to him as the easy-to-irritate-spinster who hit his car.

Wearing my cut-off shorts, the ones Amanda had wanted to burn, and a plain gray T-shirt, I pushed open Grace's front door. I had my hair in its usual pulled back ponytail—which was almost a treat. I granted myself the easy comfort since I hadn't sported one since my first day in California. And I'd become attached to Amanda's mascara. I'd probably wear it to the mill.

A booming noise filled Grace's manor, the minute I entered. Cole must be fixing something again. Grace was in the parlor with a new guest, placing a pamphlet in her hand, she sent her out the door I still held open.

"Hi there," Grace said, smiling. "How was your outing?"

"It was great. It's so beautiful here. I have to say Lombard Street was a better view than a drive though."

"That was Cole's favorite when he was boy. When he'd start talking about Disneyland, I'd take him for a drive on Lombard Street and he'd be content for a couple more weeks."

Laughing, I shook my head. "Really? It's so slow. It's not exactly a roller coaster."

"It's not," Grace said as the pounding above us stopped. "But it worked—well, at five and six years it worked."

"That's sweet—and funny!"

Walking inside, his blue T-shirt filthy, Cole ran his hand through his hair, damp from sweat. "What's funny?"

"You've been working too hard." Grace looked him up and down, her face scrunched in disgust.

He ignored her comment and stared at me, waiting for an answer. Sweat ran from his forehead to his chin. His blonde hair seemed lighter, bleached from spending all day on the roof in the sun.

"Ahh—your deep passionate love for Lombard Street."

"Oh, did you go there today?" He lifted the tail of his shirt and wiped his wet forehead. My eyes darted to Grace, avoiding his bare chest.

"You are just grimy." Grace waved her hand in front of her nose.

"I did," I said, glancing back at him—now that he'd covered himself. I cleared my throat. "It was better than *Disneyland*."

Rolling his eyes, he walked between us. "*Mother*. Why do you like that story so much?"

"It's a good one. I liked it." I bit my lip, stopping the laugh fighting to escape at his squirm.

"It's funny? You think being a deprived child is funny?" Narrowing his eyes at me, he pursed his lips.

95

Squinting, Grace abandoned her one-sided conversation and joined us. "You were not deprived." She slapped his shoulder and then gasped at the residue it left on her hand. "Daniel and I were always working on this house and we didn't have the time to go to Disneyland. We planned to later, but then Daniel passed away and I couldn't afford to take Cole."

My mischievous smile faded.

Cole kissed Grace's cheek. "You're right, Mom," he said, the humor gone from his voice. "I am filthy. I'm going to go clean up. See you later, Samantha."

"Oh, Sam," Grace said, "you might want to go out for dinner tonight. Cole isn't done on the roof, it's going to be a noisy evening I'm afraid."

"Oh, that's fine. Victor wanted me to try out his favorite Japanese place tonight anyway," My peripheral vision found Cole staring at me. I knew he misunderstood. He didn't know I had explained things to Victor. He didn't know we were only friends. For some dumb reason I found myself wanting to explain it all to him.

$V$ictor snatched up the check. "A friend can buy another friend dinner every now and again."

I liked the restaurant and the conversation wasn't bad, but I was off, distracted all night. I would have enjoyed the evening more if I'd explained myself to Cole—*which is stupid*. I didn't owe him an explanation, but I didn't like him out there thinking I'd lied. I'm sure to him I was a walking contradiction. He just didn't have all the facts. Victor knew what this was, he—*whoa*!

"Hey, but—" I managed before Victor took a wad of cash from his wallet.

"Besides, remember the rewards to my job are very different than yours. Let me get this one." In our short time together I'd learned Victor enjoyed his money—and he knew my funds were limited. "How about a trip to China Town?"

This "non-date" my head defended so strongly would appear to any outsider as a…well, a date—again! "Nah. Thanks, Vic, it's been fun, but I want to get back."

*D*rifting off, I soaked in my tub when my phone jingled. Blinking awake, I reached for my cell on the hamper.

Liza: I've been fighting with two little boys to go to bed
    and nursing a sick baby all night. What have you
  been up to in your dream land?

My laugh echoed with the acoustics of the bathroom.

Me:  Went to dinner with Vic tonight. . . Didn't know I
    lived in a dream land.
Liza:  You don't live there. Remember you're only visiting.
Me:  That's right. Thanks for reminding me.
Liza:  Miss you. Love you. Be good. Don't let Vic woo you
too much.
Me:  My FRIEND Vic isn't wooing me at all. Give my boys
and my niece a kiss for me. Good night.

*Grr.* Why would Liza say that? Lying in bed, I listened to my stomach. Once again, I had a mind full of thoughts and a stomach that believed it needed attention, despite my filling it at dinner. It had to be psychological. I ate more Yakisoba chicken than anyone ever should, but it seemed when my head filled with thoughts, my stomach emptied.

*I'm not dating Victor.* He knew that, I knew that, but no else seemed to. I was figuring my life out, and I liked that. I'm not worried about marriage or dating or my age. So, why am I worried about this? Who cares what Cole or Liza think? My stomach cared.

*S*neaking down to the kitchen, I opened the fridge, searching for leftovers from the night before.

"What are you doing up?"

Like a reoccurring dream, I jumped at the sound of Cole's voice, hitting my head on the roof of the refrigerator. "Ouch. Hi." Standing up, I rubbed the back of my head. "I couldn't sleep so I thought I'd look for pasta leftovers."

"Sounds good. Is there enough for two?"

Pulling a container from the fridge, I held it up. "Looks like it." I turned around, the tiles cold on my bare feet. "Wait—what are you still doing here?" I didn't mean to sound rude, but if we were going to keep meeting like this, then I wanted to come prepared with witty comebacks and a longer pajama shirt.

"I've been working on the house all day." Cole took the pasta from my hands and pulled two bowls from the cupboard. He dumped the contents into the dishes and placed them in the microwave. "It got late. And even though I'm thirty-years old, Mom wouldn't let me drive home."

"Ah, I see." I watched his arm, his hand resting on the door of the microwave. His sleeveless shirt left his bicep, defined from all the house climbing and roof pounding, just hanging out.

The microwave dinged and the spell broke. My eyes darted from his face to the floor and back again. Cole removed the steaming pasta. I pulled two cups from the cupboard and filled them with water. We bustled around the kitchen in silence.

Setting the bowls on the island counter, Cole pulled over two stools. I followed after him, setting a water glass in front of each bowl. Sitting on the stools, we lifted our forks in silence.

Taking a swig of water, I cleared my throat. "Can I ask you a question?"

"I guess." He scooped up another spoonful of ziti.

"So, you're thirty, right?" My insides tingled with the question. I hated when people focused on my age. A number couldn't define me—and yet here I sat bringing up his as if it did.

Cole only smiled. "Right." He shoveled a bite into his mouth.

I pressed my lips together hating myself, but I had to ask. "And you aren't married?" I knew the answer. Why did I need to ask? Had an alien possessed my body? Or at least my voice?

Looking down at his left hand, Cole gasped. "Look at that. Nope, I'm not."

"Ahh…" I rolled my eyes—at myself—not him or even his annoying response. "I'm sorry. I don't know why I'm doing this." I shook my head, whispering to myself. "Stupid! And I was doing so well." I stood, picking up my bowl of half eaten pasta. *Stupid. Stupid. Stupid.*

"Hey," he said, putting a hand on my shoulder. "What are you mumbling about?"

And then it happened. My ramblings burst free, like an overturned cup of milk, everything spilled out. "It's just, you're thirty, you're not married. Why? You're a good-looking guy, you're intelligent. I've seen you be kind. Sure, at times you're infuriating, but still overall a seemingly good person. So, why isn't a guy like you married?" It was a question for myself—not him—not really. I had been happier in California than I had been in years. Living my life the way I always should have, but the question still remained unanswered. As much and as far as I shoved it away, it wouldn't leave my mind—no matter how many baths I took or desserts I ate.

He took another bite of his ziti and I sat back in my chair, waiting while he chewed for a long twenty seconds. "Well, uh, thanks for the praise—I think. But the honest answer is, I don't know."

"That's not true." I pressed—which on some level I knew wasn't fair. I couldn't understand why, but I wanted an answer. I needed an answer. "I think you do know."

His full lips turned up into a smile, making me gawk. Biting the inside of my cheek, I waited, staring at his mouth, willing it to speak. "You're right, Sam, I do know." He crossed his arms, resigned. "I'm not supposed to get married."

"That sounds like a copout." I didn't buy it.

Laughing, he let his arms fall to his sides. He rubbed his five o'clock shadow again and again. I liked the way his side burns ran down his face, and the whiskers on his chin—*whoa*, side tracked. I crossed my own arms, still waiting for a real answer, and forced myself to make eye contact.

"All right, but you asked for it." His cynical tone returned. "Seven years ago, I met a girl, Nadia."

I nodded and kept my eyes locked with his, ignoring his grouchy disposition.

"A blind date." He raised his eyebrows as if just the words were toxic, and in a way, I agreed with him. "We hit it off right away."

99

Well, I'd never had that experience.

"We spent every minute together—it seemed."

Pinching a sliver of my lip between my teeth, I tasted blood—nope I'd never had anything close to that experience. His tone told me how this would end. I almost regretted asking. Like a thriller movie with its intense, spine-chilling music just before the killing starts, I listened. I watched. Just waiting for someone to die.

"I just knew." His words came out like knives pulled from a wound. "I had found the girl for me." He shook his head. "I proposed a year later."

"You were *engaged*?" I blurted the words, surprised he'd been devoted to something so official, something to celebrate, and yet he spoke as if a crime had been committed.

"I was." He leaned in, his eyes locked on me without blinking.

Sitting up straighter, I moved back on my stool. "For how long?"

His eyes met mine. "Ten months. She had to have time to plan! To prepare! What was the rush?" Spitting the words like poison, the fold in his arms tightened, more and more until I thought he'd lose all circulation. "She sure *rushed* when she left town."

How terrible. Did I just force that out of him? Ugh. "I'm sorry." My voice shook. I laid a hand on his crossed arms—attempting comfort. "That's... that's awful." I pulled back, entertwining my fingers together and hiding them between my legs.

Blowing out a sigh, he waved his hand in the air. "Yeah, well, it is what it is. It's in the past. And now I know—I'm not supposed to get married." Forcing out a laugh, he ran his fingers through his sandy hair. He no longer sounded cynical, but sad.

"I don't believe that." I don't know why it could be fine for Victor, but I couldn't accept it of Cole. Maybe because the thought of Grace not being a grandmother seemed perverse. Maybe it was because Victor had chosen that path and Cole had it ripped away from him. Maybe the pathetic look on Cole's face or the sad tone in his voice, but I couldn't believe what he said. One lousy girl—one awful failure didn't mean he couldn't have that life one day.

100

"Believe it." Resting his elbows on the table, he stared at me again. "So, what about you? Do you get to ask all the questions? You're what? Twenty-six? You're vacationing alone? Not even looking — so you say."

I couldn't help my blushing cheeks or the passing thought of kissing him with the compliment he didn't even realize he had paid me. *Twenty-six? So, there, Nana!* "Ah — I'm twenty-eight."

"Okay, so you're twenty-eight and..."

"And I haven't found him yet." I faced away from him. We'd reached dangerous teritory, the hazardous truth I happened to be vacationing from. But I had pried, and he had answered. I owed him that much, I guess.

"It's hard to *find* him, Sam, when you say you aren't looking. With your hiatus from guys — or whatever it is you're doing."

"It's complicated." To say the least. I turned back at him, but the word *complicated* hadn't scared him away. He waited, and watched.

"So... you're seeing someone back home? Back in Wyoming?"

Maybe the late hour had gotten to me. Maybe it had just all built up over time, but I laughed at his serious question, and I couldn't stop. I held my stomach, my eyes pouring with delirious tears. Was there a single someone in the Valley I hadn't seen yet?

"I didn't realize I'd made a joke." He smiled crooked, watching me in my ridiculous state.

"Oh, I've been dating a lot — lately." My voice squeaked higher than normal with the confession, sending me into a laughing fit once more. Cole handed me a tissue and I wiped at the tears streaming from my eye sockets. "Whoo." I took a deep breath, calming myself and held my aching stomach.

Shaking a finger at me, he said, "Vic doesn't count."

In seconds my laughter died and my smile faded. I knew he had the wrong impression. "I have never dated Victor."

"No? So, how was dinner tonight?" he asked, his eyebrows practically on top of his head.

"Victor is my friend. Friends are allowed to eat together." Wasn't our late-night meal proof of that? Then again, maybe he didn't consider me a friend. *Since when did I think we were?*

"Did he pick you up? Did he pay the bill?"

Pointing at him, I tried to form a sentence. "That's—you—he—"

"That's a date." He crossed his arms.

"You've got it wrong." I slammed my fist on the countertop. "Think what you like, but Victor knows it, and so do I."

"Well, you can think whatever you like, but he's a guy."

Pressing my lips together, I thought before speaking. He made it so difficult to be nice! Rude comments flying from my tongue would only leave me with regret. I wanted to say—*True, are you all a bunch of idiots?* Thinking… and breathing…and thinking, I opted for, "Why do you care?"

# *Chapter 14*

He couldn't answer my question. He just shrugged, but at least he stopped talking. I liked the silence, and either I'd flustered Cole to muteness or he didn't mind. Picking up both our empty bowls, Cole rinsed them off and placed them inside the dishwasher. I wiped down the counter where we'd eaten and set the wash rag at the edge of the sink. "Goodnight."

"Hey, Sam." He held out his hand, his fingertips brushing my arm, stopping me from leaving.

"Yes?" I peered up to meet his blue eyes.

He grinned, crooked. "Why did my question about you dating someone back home make you laugh like that?"

"Ah…" I stepped back, ready to escape rather than bare my soul to him. Trying to laugh it off, I said, "Talk about long stories—"

"I told you mine."

"Yeah, well," looking down, I scratched behind my ear, "yours didn't exactly make you sound like a pathetic loser. Mine on the other hand—yeah, well, 'night." Turning, I placed my hand on the swinging door, hoping he would let me get away. *Show a little mercy, Cole – once!*

"It can't be that bad." He followed me over to the door, leaning his hip against the counter next to me.

Peeking back around, he waited for me. Sighing, I frowned and rubbed the back of my neck. I would have a tension ache in the morning, I knew it. Staring at the ceiling, I shut my eyes. "It is."

Walking back to the counter, Cole sat and pulled a stool out for me.

103

The late hour grew even later. I told Cole every horrid detail of my past year. He listened. He didn't interrupt. And he didn't laugh until I did. Maybe we *could* be friends.

"*Nana*, huh?"

I rubbed my temples and nodded. "Yep," I said, popping the "p" sound. "You should only be so lucky."

"Yeah," he said, his eyebrows rising. "She'd have a hay day with me."

"She absolutely would. You're despicable. A disgrace. Don't you realize you can ask a girl out? A dozen girls! Show some initiative man!" I punched his shoulder. "I was speaking for Nana — not me."

"Ah." He rubbed his arm and gave me a small grimace. "So, if you're not here for 'the men', then what brought you here?"

"You know the last man I told you about?"

"Yeah, the old guy, Henry."

"That was by far the best of all my blind dates. It was Henry who helped me see that all this searching for a husband, not love, or fun, or experience, but a husband, had made me forget one very important person. Myself. I can't find someone who will be happy with me, until I am happy with myself. And I wasn't."

"Wasn't?" Cole slouched, his elbows on the island counter, meeting me eye level.

"Yeah." I smiled. "Wasn't. I am now. Thanks to your cousin." I looked around Grace's kitchen. "And this beautiful place, a little California fun, and my giant tub."

Sitting up, he spun in his stool, using the counter as a back rest. "So when you go home to your little house and stall shower, will you go back to being miserable?"

"No," I said, resolutely, more sure of that answer than I ever had been. "It's not the tub that makes me happy. It's me using it. Making the most of the life I've been given, rather than sulking for what I don't have." I crossed my arms, hiding what I could of myself — this was all so baring. Like he could see inside of me, spaces no one else had ever witnessed. I scratched my head, looked away from him, and folded my arms in again. Counting the black and white tiles on the ground, I said, "So, when I go back home to my family, my job, and my teeny tiny tub, I will appreciate it. I will love myself, my life—what I have and who I am."

He smiled at me, and mimicked my crossed arms. "I didn't know Mom was running a healing home."

"Well, she is." I stood, moving over to the door again. I bore my soul—the naked, ugly truth and I didn't regret it. No more regrets. Still, I needed the space between us. "And now I'm going to bed." I pushed open the door, but twisted back to him. "Thank you, Cole." He hadn't laughed at me or even looked at me like an alien. I bit my lip and peered at him—I needed his kindness. "I love it here. My heart is here. I am grateful to be in California, but I miss home. I miss Eve. I miss my sisters. I need a friend. Thank you for listening."

His mouth pressed closed, but he smiled. "Goodnight, Samantha."

My heart ached—in a way I didn't understand. Like a child who couldn't express what they want, or maybe they just didn't know. I offered a small smile. "Goodnight, Cole."

## *Chapter 15*

Trotting down the stairs, Cole's whining came into earshot. "Mom, I've got to go. I've got ten minutes to get there." He wore that suit again, the one he wore at the diner. It didn't look bad on him at all—but it didn't work for him, either. Not like a suit looked on Victor. Now that I knew him better, it just wasn't *Cole*. A sweaty old T-shirt and tool-belt seemed more appropriate.

Shoving a blueberry muffin into his hand, Grace said, "Eat it in the car then."

"You should always listen to your mother." I teased him as I passed on my way to the dining room.

"Thank you, Samantha," Grace said, her glare never leaving Cole.

"Okay, okay." I heard him say. "Thank you, I'll see you soon."

I sat at the empty grand table I peered around the colonial room. I ran my hand along the grain in the wooden table, but stopped when Grace came in. "It's just you this morning, Sam."

"Oh, well, don't make breakfast for just me. I'm off for a ferry ride this morning anyway." I had time to grab something from Jack's beforehand.

"Don't be silly. I'll fix you something."

"Really, I'll just take one of your muffins," I said, trying to appease her.

Following Grace into the kitchen, she said, "Nonsense, you came down here for breakfast and that's what you're going to get."

"Grace." I tilted my head, narrowing my eyes at her. "Why

don't I make you breakfast?"

Laughing, she covered her mouth. "I haven't had someone make *me* breakfast in years."

"Then you're greatly overdue. Sit." Walking over to the fridge, I opened the steel doors "Crepes okay?"

Giggling again, she nodded.

Finding it comfortable, I took my place as chef in Grace's kitchen. I searched through cupboards and drawers until I found all I needed. Cracking eggs into my flour concoction, I whisked the batter together. "So, Grace, do you have any more children?"

"No." She leaned back in her chair. "We felt pretty lucky to get our Cole. We'd been married almost ten years when we found out I was expecting. I think we were both in shock. We had about given up."

"My sister Amanda tried for—well, not that long, but she and her husband can't have children. A couple years ago they adopted a little girl."

"What a blessing." Grace made everything sound like a blessing.

Finding the perfect pan for my crepes, I scraped a tab of butter onto the side of the pan, heating it over the stove top. "My oldest sister has three kids, two boys and a baby girl."

"My brother and two sisters all have large families," Grace said. "I loved being an aunt. Still do."

"Me too." I flipped my first crepe. Perfect.

"Just wait till you have your own." She rested her elbow on the counter.

I could see in her face what I'd seen in my sister's. It was the mother look. I wasn't sure I'd ever wear it—or understand it. But in the meantime, and maybe for the rest of time—I would perfect the art of being the best aunt ever.

"Grace, how did you meet your husband?" I had another crepe cooking in my perfect crepe pan, so I grabbed a knife and cut up the strawberries I'd found in the fridge.

Smiling at her own thoughts, she said, "I met Daniel my senior year of college. He was an aide for a professor in a class I took. Gosh, I don't even remember what class that was now, but he offered to tutor me. When I told him I had an A and didn't need his help, he offered to buy me dinner."

"Cute." I grinned at her.

"Yeah, I thought so too."

"My mom studied chemistry in college." I couldn't brag of any accomplishment of my own, but my mother had enough brilliance for both of us.

"Your mother is a chemist? That is wonderful. College wasn't like it is today—back then there were just a handful of women who went to college."

"I know. She's amazing," I said. I knew how it sounded, like she waited at home for me. But I didn't stop there. "She's done more than I ever thought about doing. I wish I were more like her."

"You have a lot to be pleased with, young lady. I'm sure your mom is very proud of you."

I couldn't help the tears that welled in my eyes. For someone suffering from the 'honesty disease' it was sure hard to get out that my mother had died. I turned in toward the counter, away from Grace at the island, and wiped at the one tear refusing to stay in my eye socket. Filling our crepes with fruit and cream, I folded them neatly and dusted them with confectioners' sugar. I set a plate in front of Grace, pleased with how pretty they'd turned out. Sitting next to her with my own breakfast, I smiled, silent, hoping my face didn't give away my emotions.

Before either of us could take a bite, Cole bounded into the room. Throwing his briefcase onto the counter, he kissed his mom and grinned—reminding me somewhat of Clark Kent with his disheveled hair.

"Well, that didn't take long" Grace sat up straight, fork in hand, waiting to hear whatever he had to say.

"No, no it didn't. I think it went really well." He was out of breath, like he'd run all the way home.

Grace clapped her hands together and stood up. "Wonderful!" Her hands held his face and she stretched on her toes to kiss him. "Sit down," she said, pushing him into her seat. "Samantha has made us breakfast." She handed him her fork and went to the counter to cook another crepe for herself.

"Hey," Cole said, still out of breath and still blaring his grin. "Oh, hey," his brows furrowed, "you okay?"

"Me?" I blew off the concern on his face. "Psh—a, yeah." Shaking my head, I shrugged—like he was crazy to ask. "Congratulations."

Cocking his head to the side, he examined me better. "You don't look all right."

"Weird-o." I pushed his shoulder. It worked too. He faltered backwards and broke his stare-down. Standing, I walked over to Grace. "Grace, sit! I'm serving you this morning, remember?"

Laughing, still giddy with Cole's news, she patted my hand before taking my seat next to him. It only took a minute to cook up Grace's crepe and assemble it. I placed it on a new plate and set it in front of her.

Thirty seconds later Cole's food had disappeared. Leaping out of his chair, he threw his suit coat off. "Thank you, ladies, that was delicious." With his coat over his arm, he rubbed his hands together. "I am gonna get that roof finished before lunch. See you two later."

"Oh, wait," Grace said. "No, no, no. Cole, sweetheart, you deserve a break! You've been at that roof all week..." Her eyes creased with compassion. "Oh, I know! Why don't you go with Samantha on her ferry ride this morning? Celebrate!"

"Ma, I need to get the roof finished." He glanced my way and then back to Grace. "And you were the one who taught me not to invite myself to other's festivities."

"Every day Samantha heads out alone." Grace threw her arms out, exasperated. "Every day you work your tail off—without pay. She might enjoy the company, and you could use a day off." She shook her finger at him, before resting her hands on her hips.

His eyes went wide. "Ma—"

"You're welcome to come." Why not? It might not be terrible having someone to talk to, and at least he should believe me about Vic now. Cole and I could spend a couple non-dating hours together. It might be fun—and it would prove my point!

His face softened, and I noticed he'd shaved away all his whiskers. Nodding, he agreed to come. "I'll change. Meet you back here in five?"

"Yeah," I said, my stomach fluttering.

*P*ulling a backpack over his shoulders, he opened the front door. "I hope we don't run into any clowns on this trip." He stared straight out the door into space. "I'd really hate for you to embarrass me in my own city."

I pushed passed him, trotting down The Redwood's steps and breathing in the floral scent of the gardenias. "I'm going to regret telling you my stories, aren't I?"

"Probably," he said, opening the car door for me.

Getting into the vehicle, I threw my head back. "You better behave."

"My mother taught me to be polite—I think I can manage." Shutting the door, he ran around to the driver's side.

I wondered how long it had been since Cole had gone out. He had that little boy excited grin on his face—all his cynicism left behind.

"Where to?" he asked, his hands on the steering wheel.

"The Bay Cruise. We'll see Alcatraz, Angel Island, the Golden Gate and Bay Bridges all from the bay." I held up my flyer.

"Wow." He turned the key, starting the car. "You sound like a walking advertisement. Anyway, you don't want to go on that ferry."

"I don't?" Turning to him, I tapped my chin. "Because I'm pretty sure I do."

"Believe me," he said, still reminding me of that happy little boy. "You want to go on the ferry cruise to Sausalito."

"Why? What's the difference?"

"Trust me." He put the car in drive and we flew out onto the main road. "You'll get to see all of those attractions and so much more! We'll go to a small seaside village just north of the Golden Gate Bridge, Sausalito. We'll get to walk through the village, about two and a half miles, and explore their one-of-a-kind art and craft boutiques."

"Now who's the advertisement?"

He smirked, keeping his eyes on the road.

"All right. Okay. I'll trust you." He's the local—I suppose I should. "Besides, how can I resist that sales pitch? Do you work on commission?"

Cole drove entirely too fast. Sightseeing couldn't happen at that speed. I held onto the dash with every turn and waited for sirens to roar. *Sure*—that accident was my entire fault. Crazy driver... he hadn't driven like this with his mother in the car. Without a doubt, he knew where to go.

Instinct—conviction—rules—something should have kicked in when the teller asked me "how many". It's one—it was always one. It certainly wasn't a date. *But* I said, "Two," and paid for Cole's ferry ride.

"What are you doing?" he asked, when I held his ticket out toward him.

"Ah—come on. You *don't* have that job just yet. So... my treat." At least the lie held some truth. My head swam with confusion—I couldn't explain, I didn't have the answer. My hand with his ticket, tremored.

Silent, he took the ticket from my hand.

The beautiful view floated along—blue sky, green trees, the bridges arching in the background. A cool breeze blew in my face, and I breathed it all in—lulling along, my stomach waving with the water. It wasn't a sick feeling, but relaxing, almost slumbering. Very little small talk exchanged between Cole and I, but I didn't mind. Grace had been right. I'd become used to solace. I didn't feel uncomfortable with Cole— just normal.

Floating closer and closer to the little island, sail boats seemed to come out of nowhere, growing full-size the nearer we got. A hundred different colors mixed in with the blue from the water and sky. Buildings ran up the green mountainside, covering the island—that didn't seem so little now up close. Some establishments stretched out right over the water. I had never been anywhere like it before. Following Cole's advice had proved right. This was where I wanted to go.

Reaching for my hand, Cole helped me off the edge of the boat. "Ready?"

"For what?" Keeping my hand in his, tingles shot from my hand, to my elbow, to my shoulder.

"Come on. This way." He pulled me along behind him.

Climbing up the mountainside on a wooden dock, we reached the streets and buildings. Walking through the crowd, we passed people and shops. Pulling me along, Cole guided me through the mob. A little boy, no older than my nephews, ran out in front of us. His tan pants were too short for his long legs and his brown chest bare.

Holding up the bucket in his hand he said, "Hello, sir. Would you like to buy a flower for your pretty lady?"

Taking my hand from Cole's, my cheeks burned. "Oh, I'm not *his* lady."

The boy smiled, his front teeth missing.

Bending to meet his eye, Cole asked, "Can I see what you've got there?"

Holding up the bucket, the boy's grin grew wide.

"Purple pansies," Cole said. "Very nice. Did you grow them?"

"No, *Madre*." He held his hand out to Cole for payment.

"Oh, sure." Cole dug in his wallet, while the boy held the bucket up to me. I picked out a couple of the little flowers floating in the water at the bottom of the bucket. Holding out a five-dollar bill, the boy snatched it up and skipped away through the crowd.

Spinning the flowers by their skinny stems, I pressed my lips together. Flowers. Tickets. Hands. Non-date. Friends. I let a shaky breath fall from my chest. Trying to sound normal, I said, "You're the man with the plan, where are we off to?"

Searching through the crowd, he said, "Last time I was here there was this little — ah-ha! There it is." Grabbing my hand again, he pulled me along. "There's this great little herb boutique. I didn't have much use for it, but with your gift for cooking... I think you'll love it."

Biting the inside of my lip, I repressed a smile. "I enjoy cooking, Cole. I wouldn't say I have a gift for it."

Stopping, his hand still holding mine, he looked back at me.

"Where's your honesty when it counts?"

Rolling my eyes, I shook my head. "I am being honest." To him, yes. To myself, I wasn't sure—the pressure of his palm, hard, yet soft, against mine made it hard for me to believe myself. *This isn't a date.*

"Sam, I've cooked beside you. I've seen how you go all gushy in my mother's kitchen."

"Gushy?" I couldn't help my dumb smile. "I don't go gushy."

"You're going gushy right now just thinking about it. Now, come on."

Pulling me along again, I followed him across the pebble road, passing vendors and shops without taking a second to be a tourist. He dropped my hand when we stopped at an outdoor booth. Fresh plants and herbs surrounded the petite stand. My arm hung at my side, my hand a heavy weight without his to hold it up. The earthy smell filled my nose and breath. *What a beautiful little place.* The smell of the dark soil alone had me deliriously distracted. Picking up a small wooden shopping basket and holding it from the braided handle, I inspected each seasoning.

"I would love to grow my own herbs," I said. "Our growing season is so short. I've grown them indoors and then transplanted outside once I'm certain the frost is gone for the season… but this, mine looked nothing like this." I held up a large bunch of parsley.

Cole followed behind me.

"Do you think your mom would let me plan and prepare dinner one night? If I bought a few of these, I would have to use them while they're fresh." I picked up the next herb in line, bringing the boxthorn leaves to my nose. "I mean, you can dry them—keep them forever. But this!" Turning, I shoved the boxthorn in his face. "Look at this. This should be used now, today. You know?"

Smirking, he shoved his hands into his pockets. "Yeah, I don't think that would be a problem," he said. "It's not like Mom has chefs knocking down her door to give her a break…for free."

Touching everything, smelling everything, I took my time and breathed it all in. I wouldn't find a place like this back home. I held up a bowl of lemon balm for him. He bounced his eyebrows, nodding approval. I acted nonsensical, like a kid in toy store, but I didn't care.

Picking up a long pottery bowl filled with rosemary, I held it out to him. "Smell this." Then circling the bowl under my own nose, I inhaled the aromatic pine scent.

"You are a funny girl."

Shoving the bowl under his nose again, I said, "This is fresh rosemary, it's magnificent. Smell it."

"I did! It's great." He scrunched his nose. "What will you make with that?"

"Hmm, I don't know, but we're getting some. I'll figure out what later."

"Is there an herb here that would help you bake a delicious chocolate cake?"

Laughing, I shoved his shoulder. "Yeah, sure. I'll get some thyme for that."

Picking up a twig of leaves from the bowl marked thyme, he placed them in my basket. "Perfect."

Once I'd gone through all the herbs—twice, I stepped back, searching through my basket. I wished I could take more home, but I wasn't as confident as Cole that Grace would let me just take over her kitchen.

Taking it from me, he looked in the basket too. "Is this all you want then?"

As I dug through my bag for cash, Cole handed my basket to the older woman sitting in a chair next to the stand. She had skin kissed with sunshine, with hair as white as the Wyoming snow.

Her expert, wrinkled fingers placed my things in a small brown paper bag. She handed it to Cole and he thanked her, offering her his own money. Passing the bag onto me, he smiled. "Here you go."

"Thanks," I said. "What do I owe you?"

"How about one chocolate cake?"

Looking up from my wallet, I pressed my lips together, holding in my grin. "You got it. One thyme and chocolate cake, just as soon as we get home." I didn't correct my mistake—The

Redwood was my home for the next couple months, anyway.

His face softened, and I wasn't sure if it were his expression or that he'd shaved for his interview that morning. Smiling at him, I could feel the strangeness of it, but couldn't wipe the silly thing from my face either.

"What?" he asked.

And without thought I answered him. "You shaved."

Letting out a quiet, confused chuckle, he said, "Yeah, I did."

And then someone who had confidence with men — someone trying — invaded my body and reached up to feel Cole's smooth cheek. "I like your whiskers."

His smiled faded, but a soft expression still warmed his face. He leaned in toward me. "I'll try and remember that."

With great thought now — thoughts that seemed to sting every part of my body, I withdrew my hand. What was I doing standing there, in the middle of a crowd, in the middle of Sausalito, caressing Cole's cheek? Did I not remember what brought me here? His breath warmed my lips, lips he could have kissed for how close his were to mine. One whiskered chin, one thoughtless action, and I'd almost ruined everything.

I hadn't come for this.

Afraid to look at him, I searched the ground, keeping my lips a fair distance from his. He didn't move. He didn't talk. I peeked up, he smiled at my nonsense. "Come on," he said. "Let's eat."

Following him out of the herb hut, we crossed the road to a small tarnished building with Japanese writing on the outside.

"Do you like sushi?" His hands tucked inside his pockets, he motioned to the building with his head.

"Yeah." I examined the building rather than meet his eyes, my face still burning with my careless actions. Working at the mill, I had quite a few male friends… I had *never* caressed one of their cheeks and told them I liked their scruff! Even in my dating life — as fleeting as it may be, I'd never felt the urge to say or do anything so insane.

Staring at me, I realized Cole had asked another question while I'd been drowning in my reflections. "Ahhh— "

"If it doesn't sound good, we can—"

"Sushi?" My brows knit together — were we still talking food? "Yes, sushi."

"Oh, no, or yes, I mean, it sounds great." I bit down on my thumb nail, playing catch up in my own conversation.

The line into the restaurant ran all the way outside. Standing together, side by side, my phone jingled. I dug into my bag to find it.

> Amanda: Nana wants to know how many kids Victor's
>    willing to have.

I peeked up to see Cole staring at me. I shoved the phone back into my purse. "Sorry," I said, knowing my eyes were opened much too wide. "It's a just text from my sister."

"Aren't you going to write her back?" He ran a hand through the long part of his sandy hair.

Peering back into my bag, I could still see the words she'd written — "Uh, no. That's okay. If I text her back, you'll be watching me reply to her all afternoon." I laughed, short and hysterical. "That Amanda, she's a gabber."

"But if you don't reply, will she —"

"Oh, she won't call." I pressed my lips together. "I came on this trip — as selfishly as it sounds, for self-discovery. So that's one of our rules. No phone calls. My sisters didn't want me driving more than a dozen hours from home just to be on the phone with them all day. Ya know, and not finding myself."

"I get that." He nodded, again showing kindness when I needed it most. "It helps you to step out of your comfort zone."

"Exactly," I said pointing at him. "For example," I kept my tone teasing, "that night you startled me in the kitchen, the same day we met, I normally would have called one of my sisters and told them about the *jerk* I ran into."

Teasing, he pointed to himself, as if to confirm that I'd meant him.

I laughed, but kept talking. "Instead," I said, more relaxed by the minute — my inappropriate behavior almost forgotten. "I went to the kitchen for a snack, saw you and we talked things out. So, you see, out of the comfort zone — it's a good thing."

"Come on." He grinned and moved up in line. "So you're pretty close to your sisters?"

"Yes, very close."

"How many are there in your family?" Cole leaned against the wall of the building.

"Three girls, I'm right in the middle." Pointing at him, I said, "And you are an only child."

"I forgot, you live with my mother." He let out a moan.

Laughing, I crossed my arms. "You say that like it's a bad thing."

"No, not at all. Mom's the best. She just doesn't have any secrets."

"That you know of." I poked him in the bicep. Why did I keep touching him? "Well, in her defense, everything I know, I asked about."

"I see." His eyebrows rose, ready to rib me. "So, you say you aren't here for men, but then I find out you've been digging up info on me."

"Ha! Yeah, for blackmail! How else will I sue you for hitting my car!" Joking, I poked him again. Something had to be wrong with me. "Actually." I had to save myself and my obnoxious poking finger. "It was Grace I was asking about. It's not my fault she likes you so much."

"Sure." He smiled and winked, like a reflex. "So what else did she tell you?"

Stepping forward, we moved inside the building. "She told me how she met your dad and that you're a *miracle*."

"Well, that part is true." Blowing on his nails, he pretended to shine them across his chest.

"What a *miracle* it was they were able to have you," I said, shoving him—again! I crossed my arms, forcing my fingers into my armpits. "I wouldn't want your head to get any bigger than it already is."

"Hey! It's my lucky day." He rocked on his feet. "Besides, I'm joking."

Moving up, close enough to smell the rice and ginger, our conversation lulled. "So," I said. "Since your mom isn't around…

tell me more about your family."

"What do you want to know?" He shrugged as if there couldn't be anything more to tell.

"What about your dad? Were you two close?"

Shuffling his feet, his eyes darted to the ground and I didn't know if he'd answer me. "Yeah, I guess."

He guessed? Wouldn't he know? Unless… "How old were you when he died?"

Clearing his throat, he crossed his arms, guarded. "I was ten."

So young, no wonder he *supposed* they were close. "What happened?"

Ignoring his caution and resistance, I just kept going—kept asking. I'd become the polar opposite of myself. All the things I tried so hard to avoid I did my best to drag out of Cole.

His folded arms tightened and he studied me. His narrowing eyes looked as if he were deciding whether or not to tell me. And then at once he opened his mouth. "He was in a car accident on his way to my grandparent's house. Mom and I would have gone with him, but I caught a cold. My fever peaked pretty high, and at the last minute Mom told him we couldn't go with him. Dad's brother was visiting from Vermont, so he went without us. His car was totaled. There wasn't much left. If Mom and I had gone, I wouldn't be here with you."

"*Miracle*," I said. His flu had saved them. "I'm sorry." I thought of my own situation. How many times had I pitied myself? It didn't make Mom not being around okay, but it did make me grateful that I had her as long as I did. I had a whole six years more with my mom than Cole had with his dad. So many memories, so many holidays and talks—so many things in those six years that Cole would never have. And I knew the future we faced. I said goodbye. I made as much peace as I could. Poor Cole, he hadn't had a clue.

His eyes lost their sad wrinkles and glistened their pretty blue as his mouth turned up in a closed lip grin. "It's okay," he said, shaking his head—but we both knew it wasn't. "My grandparents, well mainly my dad's father, really stepped up for me. He and Grandma lived in San Diego before they passed. Even though

119

they had to travel, they came to everything I ever did—school awards, sports, scouts—it didn't matter what, they were there. My grandpa tried really hard to play the role of 'dad' for me."

Smiling, my eyes teared up, thinking of Nana. I blinked back the moisture easily. Nana had done the same thing—like Cole's grandfather. As pestering as she could be, she'd been there, teaching, loving, caring, for all three of us girls. "My grandmother's like that," I said, still in my own thoughts.

"Your match maker?" He couldn't say it without the small chuckle.

Laughing with him, I nodded. "Yep, my Nana."

Adjusting in his seat, he said, "Sorry, but why?" His tone light, but his arms tight in their fold again.

"Ahh—" He didn't know me. He didn't know my loss.

Letting his arms fall, he shoved his hands into his pockets. "Before my dad died I remember my grandparents came every now and again for special events, but they didn't come for *everything*. I don't know if you *can* understand." His face softened—he wasn't trying to be rude. "And that's okay. But it's different. My grandfather's role in my life has been huge, unlike a regular grandpa." His eyebrows pushed together, and he stared at me, sad, as if I were a child he had to explain hard things to. "I don't quite understand why your Nana would behave like a mother." With kindness, he pressed his point. One I understood, more than he knew.

So, I didn't argue. "You're right. It is different." I don't know why I couldn't say it, I just couldn't. He may have been guarded at times, but at least he spoke truth. Everyone back home knew about Mom. I didn't have to say the words, they knew. It had been a loss for the entire Valley. Everyone mourned. I'd never had to explain myself before. No one here knew my sad truth. And I didn't feel like telling them.

# Chapter 16

Sitting at the Sushi counter, we faced each other in our swivel chairs.

"You're not saying something." He looked at me, too perceptive.

"What?" I twisted my chair to face forward. "I don't have anything to say."

"Sam, I've heard you be too honest, I've heard you justify your dates with Victor, but I've never heard you lie." He said it as though we'd had dozens of conversations.

Whirling back to face him, my dark hair spun out, the ends smacking me in the face. I kept my voice strong. "I have never dated Victor."

"That's what you keep saying, and I'm sure you believe it."

"Are you trying to get me mad at you?" I wanted to poke him again—hard. "I thought we were trying to have a nice day. I may not have my car with me now, but I will soon. We both know how good I am at backing into you."

"No, hey, come on." He ran a hand through his hair. "I am not trying to get you mad at me. I know where you stand with Vic, but I'm pretty sure it's not in the same place Vic is standing—not even the same state."

Tucking my long bangs behind my right ear, I stared at him. "And you would know this, how?"

"I know Victor. And you're avoiding the real question here—you talk—whether or not you should—you do—"

"Hey!"

"It's true. And it's seems you're not telling me the whole

121

story…"

I shrugged. "What else would I have to tell?" He saw too much, like back at the house — Grace didn't notice my about-to-lose-it face. I thought I'd held myself together well, but Cole saw right through me.

"Something," he said, his eyes boring into mine.

Crossing my arms, I studied his hands held together on the counter. "I'm glad you can speak about your dad so easily."

Swiveling forward and then back to me, he tilted his head. "I can't usually. Normally, I only talk about him with Mom."

In that moment, I wondered if people who have suffered traumatic losses could share an unexplainable connection. Why would Cole feel like baring his soul to me? Maybe because I had asked, but really, I knew he wouldn't have said anything if he didn't want to. People, even strangers, can be connected for different reasons. Maybe fate connected us in this way, maybe our sad link is how Cole and I had formed a friendship — despite our horrid beginning. We shared one of those unseen links — even if I was too chicken to explain why.

Cole ordered for both of us and the chef spun up our California Maki. We didn't talk about Cole's dad again — or Victor. We just talked. My sides hurt from laughing and my cheeks ached from smiling. The awkwardness left and we could just be friends once more.

Glancing at the clock on the back wall, I stood from my bar stool. "Cole, we have to go!"

He followed my glance. "Oh, yep." But he didn't get up. He stuffed another rolled Maki into his mouth.

"What are you doing?" I snatched up my purse and bundle of herbs, "We need to go. We'll miss the ferry."

"We've missed the ferry," he said, his mouth still half full.

"They wouldn't leave without us," I said, still on the balls of my feet, ready to run.

"Uh, yes, they would." He licked his fingers. "We are stuck here, for eternity. We may have to live in a hut and form a plan to repopulate California."

I shoved his shoulder. He joked. We'd missed our ride home

and he still shoved food in his face, kidding around.

"Sam, sit." He wiped his fingers on a paper napkin and motioned to my stool. "There will be another ferry."

"When?"

"Do you have date or something? What's the hurry?"

"No... I just..." I plopped back into my seat. "I just thought..."

"You thought we'd have to swim back to The Redwood?"

"Maybe!" I picked up my last bite of Maki and popped it into my mouth.

With our stomachs filled and my nerves on edge, we walked out the door. "So, when is the next ferry?"

Taking out his ticket, Cole read to himself, and then said, "Three hours. There's actually a lot we haven't seen yet. Are you up for a walk?"

I followed him along the hard-concrete ground, past the different boutiques, to the soft sand of the beach. With the green mountainside next to us and the wooden boardwalk just behind, we strolled along the shoreline. The village sat nearby, but separate from this part of the island. The sound of the water seemed to quiet the sound of habitation. The town, the tourists, the cars all died away with the whir of the waves.

"Let's stop here."

The sandy spot had large rocks speckled throughout, some within the water and some outside of it. The breeze on my cheeks was cool, but welcome. I breathed in the air, smelling the salt from the ocean. Chirps from birds mingled with the sound of rolling waves.

"Okay." I sat, the sand compacting beneath my weight. "This really is a lovely place. I would never have found it on my own."

"It's my favorite." He took a seat next to me.

"You haven't told me about your job."

"Well, it's not *my* job yet. The interview did go well. Here's to hoping."

Pulling my knees up to my chest, I wrapped my arms around them. "So, what is it?"

"It's a supervising managerial position. I'd be over all of the managers for their plumbing company in this region." And as excited as he'd been when he bounded into the kitchen this morning, you would have thought now it was a prison sentence the way he spoke.

"Ahh, okay." I stare out at the waves instead of at Cole, forcing my fingers into the soft sand beneath me.

"What?" He peered over at me. "Don't go quiet on me now, Sam."

I chuckled. "It just... it doesn't sound like something you *want* to do. I'm just surprised at your excitement this morning."

Standing, he brushed the sand off his pants, his face turned back to the sea. "It's a job. I'm not looking forward to telling people who have been doing their jobs for years how to do them better, but I need to work."

"I understand that." I did—sort of, but his rejoicing earlier when he spoke with Grace this morning, I did not. Shouldn't you actually want the job you're excited about? "Don't you feel like you're settling though?"

"No, Sam, I don't." He spat the words at me, his jaw twitching. "Settling? Who cares what it is? This job would relieve my stress—my mom's stress. She shouldn't be worrying about how her thirty-year-old son is going to pay his bills."

"Hey." I stood. "I was just being honest. You asked me to be honest, remember?" Throwing a stone into the ocean, I crossed my arms, keeping him out of my view. For someone who'd hit the ripe ol' age of thirty, he sure knew how to act childish.

"I didn't mean—ahh." He stopped talking and pressed his lips together. "I mean," he said each word slow—careful-like. "I'm sorry." I could see him facing me, but I didn't return the gesture. "I hate her worrying over me, ya know? It's bad enough I can't figure life out, but it causes her grief and pain—and that isn't fair." Stepping closer to me, he nudged my shoulder with his own. "You're right. I did ask you to be honest. It's just—"

Sitting, I made space between us. "What do you *really* want to do, Cole?" Over his tongue lashing, I wanted to know. His frustration had to have an outlet. What did he want?

He stared out, quiet. I waited for his answer. Instead of giving one, he plopped down to the ground and began untying his shoelaces. "Right now, I want to see your face when I get you wet."

I scooted away from him.

"Come on," he said, getting up again, his anger forgotten. "If you don't walk in, I'll have to throw you in."

"You wouldn't!" The water didn't scare me, or even his threats. But wondering how it would feel to have Cole wrap his arms around, even to throw me into the ocean, that had me on edge.

"No, maybe not," he said, ending my insane delusional daydream. He walked out into the water. "But I would splash you." Leaning down, he cupped a handful of water.

Standing, I backed up again, hitting the mountainside. "Oh, all right." I threw my sandals to the side. I'd been in San Francisco a while now, without getting in the water — besides in my tub.

Walking out until the cool water drenched up to my ankles, I made my way across the bank alongside him. Cole shoved his hands into his pockets. "So, do you want kids? Big family, small family?"

"Where did that come from?" I chuckled, staring at our reflections in the water below.

"I don't know, just something we haven't talked about yet." He walked out ahead of me.

Following behind him, the rocky sand in the shallow water bit at my bare feet. "I don't know."

"What do you mean you don't know?" He glanced back at me, stopping and waiting for me to catch up. "I thought every girl had her life planned out by the time she was thirteen."

"You watch too much TV."

"No, really, every girl I've ever been around knew exactly what she wanted, down to her husband's eye color." I didn't like the high mocking voice he used — making fun of all those girls.

"Okay, now who has the *lay-it-on-thick* disease?" I cocked my head his way. "I. Don't. Know. Okay?"

He raised his eyebrows, not buying my non-answer.

"Okay." He wanted an answer. I'd give him an answer. "If you'd asked me that question ten years ago I would have given you my thirteen-year-old answer. Which was yes, definitely a great big happy family — four kids at least."

125

His eyes widened, feigning shock.

"And his eyes would have been green." I kicked the water beneath me, sending a spray of cold droplets his way. "If you had asked five years ago I would have said, yeah, a big family would be wonderful. Who cares what color his eyes are? But now, I don't know, is my honest answer. I am almost twenty-nine years old, with my Nana reminding me every day that I'm not getting any younger. My prospects are a boy scout and my cousin. Being alone isn't ideal, but it's better than settling for something I don't want."

"You say that like twenty-nine is ancient. Most people don't start their families until twenty-nine — or later." He shook his head at me.

Wriggling my feet until they sunk into the sand under the water, I didn't speak. Maybe the rest of the world started the most important part of their lives at thirty — but we didn't. My whole life and everything important to me consisted of my *family* — and they all moved on without me. Mom in death. My sisters' in life.

"And those aren't your prospects, Sam." He stood a few feet in front of me, his body facing the mountain his head turned to me.

"Well, that's what I've been dating." I tried to laugh — the late night comedy act we called *Sam's dating life*.

"That doesn't mean those are your prospects." His hands were shoved into the pockets of his khaki shorts, but I could see them form into fists through the cloth. "Roses don't have to be red."

Tilting my head up at him, I grinned. "That's what it says on my door. My Rose door, that's exactly what it says."

"Yeah, I know." He grinned back — happy that I'd noticed, I think. "My dad used to say that. He engraved that on your door."

Closing my eyes, I bit my lip and pointed my face in the direction of the setting sun. Sure, I'd been standing still, but part of that, I'd learned, had been my choice. And the wisdom in Cole's words touched me. *Roses don't have to be red*. I'm not my sisters. I don't need to be. At least now I lived, I experienced. I think Mom would be proud of that.

Like a mirror the water reflected our images. I stare at him and him at me in the watery glass.

"My point being," he said, his eyes on the water. "Everyone is different. Every situation is unique. Besides, Sam, look at you..."

Dropping my eyes, I saw my calves buried in water, the ends of the white Capri's I wore soaked. Wading toward me, he stood just inches away. Wriggling my toes into the sand, I anchored myself, so not to fall backward. Lifting my chin with the tips of his fingers, my gaze went from our reflection to his eyes, bluer than the water beneath us. "You're *it*. You have everything any sane man would want."

My stomach flipped inside my body and I held it still with my hands. I could see the flecks of green beneath the blue in his eyes. I smelled the mint of his gum and the aftershave he must have put on this morning. I felt the callouses of his fingers that worked so hard making The Redwood beautiful. Breaking away from his stare, I tried to joke. "Well, that explains why I'm still single."

"You're still single," he said, his hand still holding my face, "for the same reason I still don't have a job."

Clearing my throat, I managed, "And that would be?"

"No one can tell you what you want, but you. Do you know what you want, Samantha?" Lifting my chin again, he forced me to look at him once more.

Pulling my face away from him, I stepped back and walked to the shoreline. He stood too close and I needed to remind myself why I'd come here. It wasn't for Cole — or any man.

Standing in the water, he watched me on the shore before following me out and sitting down beside me. "I didn't mean to offend you."

"You didn't." I forced a smile and kept my eyes focused in the distance. The space I had needed wasn't because he'd hurt my feelings. He stood so close if he tried to kiss me I didn't think I'd have the strength to stop him.

The irony I called my life! I knew why I'd come here and the remedy had been mending my broken so-called life. And now men seemed to be coming out of the woodwork! Well, let them come. I wouldn't mess up the friendship Cole and I had worked so hard to achieve. And I wouldn't lose myself now.

Waves rolled along the water as we sat in silence. I could feel him next to me. I didn't understand why I'd let him affect me so. Victor had charm and looks—he's every bit as handsome as Cole—yet I had no problem setting him straight. Maybe that unseen connection drew me to him—or this place. Maybe—

"So, you really like The Redwood?"

Taking a breath, I smiled. "I love it." I kept my gaze towards the water.

"I think Mom could expand her business, hire on help, and maybe even open up another inn somewhere else."

My head shot toward him, my brow scrunched together. "Yeah?"

"Yeah, I mean she'd just need—"

"You astonish me," I said, not worried about the confrontational tone in my voice—anger would stop me from breaking the rules and kissing.

"What? No, I'm serious, Sam. I have a mountain of paperwork at home." His hands stretched, showing me the mountain. "I have figured down to the last detail what she would need to do," he said, still thinking I didn't believe him.

"I don't doubt that, Cole. You astonish me because you *know* what you want, but you're too scared to realize it."

His eyes narrowed—his turn to be ticked—my no kissing guarantee. "Wha—"

Turning to face him with my whole body—unafraid to look at him now. My brain had left the kissing isle as it entered scolding mode. "I'm talking about your job, Cole Casey. Your heart is in The Redwood. Why are you afraid of that?"

"I have a few ideas, that doesn't mean I should be the one to execute them. Just because I haven't figured out what to do for work doesn't mean I should steal my mother's business from her."

"You wouldn't be stealing your mother's business, Cole. You'd be her partner—just like your dad. You're telling me you haven't found your passion yet, but you happen to have a million ideas for—not just any business, but for The Redwood. That's not your dream job?" I spat the words, not caring that I sounded cross. "That's anything but the truth."

He didn't respond to my scolding. We sat in silence until he got up and brushed the sand from his shorts. "Time to go."

The sun sat on the water, like a tea cup on a saucer, and I didn't want to leave. Even after our argument, the peace of the water, the smell of the sea, it comforted me. No words, no people, just peace. "We have to leave *now*?"

"Yeah, we do." Bending down, he took my hand and helped me up.

Leaving my hand in his, we walked the short journey back to the boat dock. A different boat than the one we'd arrived on waved on the water. The large ferry held more passengers than the one from the morning.

We boarded and took a seat along the edge of the ferry. Folding my arms along the ledge of the boat, I rested my head upon my arms and stared at the blue-green sea below us.

"You haven't told me much about your parents." Cole tilted his head my way.

Sitting up, I studied him.

"It's just, you've talked about your sisters, your nieces and nephews, even your brothers-in-law, but you haven't said anything about your parents."

"Well, they're wonderful. What do you want to know?" I folded my hands in my lap — no escape now.

"I don't know." He shrugged. "What does your dad do?"

"He's a counselor at the high school in the Valley. He'll probably retire soon."

"What about your mom? Does she work?"

The boat rocked and I thought my stomach would give out on me. Would I ever be okay stating the awful truth? Did I have to? Here? This was *vacation* — why did Cole need to know everything about me anyway? Sure, we were friends, but how much do *vacation* friends really need to tell to each other? "No, she doesn't," I said unable to keep my demeanor from changing.

"That's it?" He shrugged, one brow raised above the other.

Breathing out until all the air within me left my body with a final wheeze, I held my stomach, certain we'd be seeing the aftermath of California Maki. Sitting straighter, I took a deep, salty air breath. I could talk about Mom's life all day, but her death... Why did her story have to end that way? She didn't get to finish. It's a story with a forced ending and a lifetime stolen away. People who live in happy oblivion didn't need to know that story.

The inevitable truth would come out though, and Cole had talked to me. I couldn't straight-face lie to him, not about this. I didn't fear talking to him, but bonding over tragic experiences didn't sound like self-empowering vaca material. I had better things to do, like sit in the sun, spend too much money and forget about my age. But, I had to speak, and I had to tell the truth. "My mom got sick when I was sixteen. She had colon cancer." Turning away from him, back to the water, I kept going. The serenity of the waves helping me through. "She fought so hard, but it was too much. After suffering for months, she let herself go. She stopped fighting, stopped hurting, and she died." Turning back around, I faced him, my eyes boring into his. "My mother is dead."

His forehead wrinkled—confused. "Why didn't you say anything before?"

"When?" I asked, feeling cruel with the word. I knew what he meant. When he'd told me about the death of his father, he wanted to know why I hadn't told him then. But I didn't have an answer—not really. Saying *I didn't want to* just seemed like more cruelty. And I hadn't been shooting for mean—private maybe. Living for three months in a fantasy world left my problems, my heartaches, my age all behind, and I wanted to keep them there.

"Before," he said, sounding hurt. Gripping the ledge of the boat, he stared outward. "I bore my soul to you." The hurt in his tone left. His voice had more of a numb anger to it, now. "I told you all about my dad. I was trying to explain to you about my grandfather. You just let me go on and on." Twisting back to me, I could see the chagrin in his stare. "You didn't think that might be a good time to clue me in?"

Where was my remorse? I should have apologized. I should let guilt fill my insides. He had a point after all. But I couldn't. How dare he? "*My* heartbreak," I stabbed the ferry seat with my pointer finger, "*my* trial, *my* grief—they are *mine!* And I will tell who I want when I want." Getting up from my spot, I walked away. He didn't follow after me.

We drove home to The Redwood in silence. I didn't thank him, I didn't say goodbye. I got out of the car and without looking back went to my room. Like a robot, I walked to the tub in my rose room and turned on the hot water. Shutting the door, I let the steam and fresh rose buds on the counter fill my senses. We'd made it back just in time for dinner, but I didn't care. I didn't want to see anyone and, for once in my life, I couldn't have eaten even if I wanted to.

Soaking, I let my tears fall into the basin. The hot water hugged me like an old friend until I fell asleep. Waking up, a chill ran through my body. Four hours later my hot sauna had turned into one cold bath. Getting out, I dried my goose-pimpled body and twisted my hair up into a towel. Shaking, I threw on my blue furry robe, but the short length it did nothing for my cold legs. I slipped into a pair of sweatpants too.

Sitting on the edge of my bed, I rubbed my heavy eyes. I needed Tylenol and food—my California Maki just a nice memory.

Bending forward, I dropped my towel to the ground and threw my damp tangled hair behind me. Pulling a bottle of Tylenol from my purse, I walked gently down the stairs for a glass of water and hopefully leftovers.

I tip-toed through the quiet house, the only noise my rattling medicine bottle as I opened the swinging kitchen door. Already on, the light from the kitchen flooded the hall. I blinked in the glow, trying to get my eyes to adjust. Open and closed, open and closed, open and—Cole. He sat on a bar stool, facing the door as if he waited for me.

"Of course, you're here," I said, my tone grouchier than my actual feelings.

"If you knew, then why did you come?" His brows knit together like a sad little boy.

"I need food—and Tylenol." I shook the medicine bottle at him. "—and because I didn't actually know you'd be here."

Getting up from the stool, he walked closer to me. "Listen, don't be mad at me. I'm sorry. I was a jerk and—"

131

"Yeah, you were."

Running his hands through his hair, he closed his eyes. "I just don't understand—why would you withhold information—"

"Withhold information? Am I on trial, Cole?" I moved past him, careful not to touch him, and filled myself a glass of water.

"No," he said, his voice soft. "Of course not. I'm sorry, Samantha. I was taken aback. I told you all these—I was just... I was surprised. I don't like being surprised."

Glaring at him, I popped the little white pills into my mouth and gulped down my water.

"Sam, please." His shoulders drooped and his jaw clenched. I hadn't made this easy on him. "I am sorry. I know what it's like to lose a parent and I know it's not always easy to share." He rubbed his hand over his five o'clock shadow that had formed sometime in the night—distracting me. "The truth is, since we've been back, I've been thinking about your mom. I can't imagine watching someone I love go through so much agony. I can't imagine the last picture of them in my head being their saddest version. That has to be miserable. I don't blame you for not telling me."

My hot head left with his apology. And if I were to tell anyone of my heartbreak—it should be Cole. He, at least, understand on some level—the misery.

"I'm not a very good friend." He reached out to touch me, but stopped, his hand in midair and brought it back to his side. "I'm sorry I got angry."

"It's okay." I whispered the words, clenching my glass with both hands, my eyes blurring with tears.

He tucked my dark bangs behind my left ear and lifted my chin until my watering eyes met his. "It's not." He wrapped his arms around me, pulling me close to his chest. Tears gushed from my eyes, drenching the front of Cole's T-shirt. His body, so close, warmed me from my recent chill. Physical and mental— he soaked up all of my pain, allowing me a release I didn't even know I needed. Sobbing, he held me upright and, without worrying about my rules or reasoning's for once, I let him.

## Chapter 17

*I* woke the next morning with my head racing. What a long
night, with very little sleep—more tossing and turning than
anything. How could dreaming of work make you literally
tired the next day? I didn't know, but somehow it did. I didn't
dream of the mill though. I dreamt of Cole, Grace, and The
Redwood. We worked and bustled about The Redwood—all of
us smiling and happy. At times, an older version of Cole would
help us. This morning, I'd decided he had to be Daniel, Cole's
dad. What a happy dream—tiring, but happy. My poor friend
Grace had been working this business, this dream by herself for
far too long. Not exactly how she'd planned to do it.

Rolling out of bed, I opted for a shower instead of my tub. Still
in my dream-work mode—I needed a fast pace, get something
done day. I thought about Sausalito and the kitchen with Cole
too—my brain all over the place.

Amanda: You never got back to me last night. Were you
and Vic discussing tuxedo sizes?
Me: Ha. Ha. You're so funny. I was sightseeing with Cole.
Amanda: Another date? Another guy? Nana will be thrilled.
Options!
Me: It wasn't a date. Zero dates. Cole and I are friends.
Amanda: I'm glad you have a friend, sis, but it's okay to
date. You can say you went on a date with Cole.
It doesn't mean you've failed. I'm afraid Nana has
ruined dating for you.
Me: Nana didn't ruin anything for me. I'm just happy being
carefree and not worrying about things like that here.
It's working.

Amanda: Hmmm... But is it working for them? Are they
     happy?

I never wrote her back. She'd said "they", but with the thought I only pictured Cole working next to his parents — my dream. I needed to speak to him. Tossing my phone onto the bed, I opened my rose door, almost bumping into Victor.

"Oh, hello, Vic." I laughed, holding my thumping chest.

"Samantha, how are you?" Vic's smile brightened up his already handsome face.

I was on a mission though — no chit-chat. I needed to see Cole before I lost the courage or everything that seemed so right in my head became jumbled and confused. Hurrying down the hall, I turned my head to answer him. "I'm great. See you, Vic."

Running down to Grace's quarters, I knocked on the door. Tapping my feet, I checked my watch and waited for someone to answer.

"Sam," Grace said, beaming at me. How did she do that? She made me feel welcome as I intruded in her personal space just with her tone, just with her smile.

"Hello, Grace." I returned her smile, and then looked past her. "Is Cole still around?"

"No, the company he interviewed with called pretty early this morning and wanted to see him again. So, I woke him and off he went."

"Oh, I see." I bit down on my thumbnail.

"Did you guys have a good time yesterday? I barely saw Cole last night."

"Oh, yeah, we did." Nodding, I crossed my arms. *I am a terrible person — hoping Cole would get a rejection from the plumbing place today. But then you didn't have people come back in to reject them...*

"Cole said you found a little herb boutique you were quite fond of."

"Oh," I said, my rude thoughts interrupted. "Yes! That's right, I almost forgot. You decide which night you want off and I'll cook. I bought herbs just for that reason!"

"Well, all right." She giggled, slapping her leg. I laughed, thankful the idea appealed to her.

Still, I had a one-track mind at the moment—I needed to get this out before my brain exploded. "When Cole gets in will you tell him I was looking for him?"

Grace's eyes creased and her grin changed. She nodded. "I will," she said. Somehow that grin reminded me of Nana.

I went back to my room, still in my own thoughts and world. I lay on my bed with a book. After rereading the same page three times I threw the book onto my night stand. I closed my eyes in thought, but abruptly opened them at the knock upon my door.

Jumping up, I raced to my door. I had to get this out. I had to—and then, then I could sleep, read—move on. "Cole!" I said, before I had the door all the way opened.

"No, Victor." Vic pointed to himself.

"Oh, gosh, sorry Victor." I leaned against the door frame, my mind still somewhere else. "What do you need?"

"Aren't you friendly today?"

Standing straighter, I gave him a weak smile. "I'm sorry. I didn't mean to be rude. I just have a few things on my mind today."

"Would you like to go out for lunch and talk about it?"

"Rain check? I think I'll stay in." I couldn't take a chance missing Cole's return.

"I'm sure I could make you forget your troubles." He bounced his eyebrows, ribbing me.

Laughing, I shook my head. "No, thanks, Vic."

"Okay, then." Vic sighed. "I tried. I saw Grace in the kitchen. She asked me to see if you were here before I went to my room. She'd like a word with you when you aren't busy."

"Oh, okay." I stepped out next to him and closed my door.

Pursing his lips, his bottom lip protruded in a pout. "You will make time for a friend later?"

"Sure." I could do that. My friend may be extravagant, but I found him fun and exciting. Sure, at times a little exhausting, but I didn't want to push him away.

Grace crouched at the windows in the sitting room, a rag in hand, scrubbing away at the non-existent smears there.

"Hi, Grace." I trotted over to her. "Is he back?"

135

"No, he called, though. He got the job!" She clapped her hands, the rag muffling any noise she might have made. "They wanted him to start training right away." She grinned, the joy evident on her face.

I felt the punch of guilt for wishing he'd been rejected.

"I told him you wanted to speak to him and he said he'd meet you for breakfast tomorrow at Jack's."

Tomorrow? "Oh, all right." I tried to hide my disappointment. Tomorrow would I feel this conviction? Would I be brave enough to tell someone else how to live—when I just learned myself?

Giving the window one last shine, she set the rag on top of her bottle of glass cleaner. "I called a friend of mine. Our schedules just never seem to coincide. Anyway, I asked her if she'd like to go to a movie and dinner Friday night. Will that work for you?"

"To make dinner? Yeah, Friday will be great," I said, happy for the distraction. If I couldn't talk to Cole until tomorrow, I could occupy my brain by planning a feast.

"Wonderful, and Cole said he'd be happy to help you." She took both my hands in hers. "You're a doll, Samantha." Squeezing my fingers, she let them drop. "Well, I better get back to work."

His suit coat buttoned and his hair slicked back, Victor sauntered down the stairway. "Samantha, my friend. You cannot turn me down twice, no?" Standing next to me, he shoved his hands in the pockets of his suit pants. "Friday. What about Friday? I'm free that evening and I have reservations for two at one of my favorite restaurants, Parallel 37."

"Oh." My cheeks warmed up, and for some stupid reason I was grateful I had an excuse not to go. "I just promised Grace I'd make dinner for her that night, but thank you for inviting me, Victor."

His eye twitched and he took a couple of steps closer to me. "Samantha," he said, lowering his voice. "I was hoping to speak to you alone."

Glancing around the space, I shrugged, balling my hands together. "Vic, we are alone," I said, and his mouth pursed, aggravated. "Or we could go down to the garden."

Smiling, he nodded. He followed me through the house

until we made our way to the indoor porch and then out to the fragrant garden. He didn't say anything though. The only noises from the garden were the birds and our tapping feet along the stone walkway.

I waited for him to say something—anything. What could he possibly have to talk to me about? Bending down, he plucked a daisy from its spot in Grace's flower bed and handed it to me. I took it, but looked down at the bushel of flowers in the garden. The one bush must have had two hundred daisies—I couldn't tell where he'd taken it from, and yet, I wanted to return it to its rightful home in the ground.

"I only have a couple more weeks here, Samantha." Victor walked beside me, his dress shoes clicking against the stones.

"That's right. Then you'll be going home." I knew this, he'd told me before. I couldn't think of why he'd need to bring it up again. "I'm sure you miss your home. Your horses, your—"

"Yes." Again he sounded agitated. "I do. But. . ."

I waited for him to continue.

"Samantha, I like you. I wish that we would have spent more time together. We still have two weeks though—and then if you wanted me to, I could stay." One of his eyebrows rose, waiting.

My mouth dropped. What was he— Why would he— This made no sense. Victor and I weren't even from the same puzzle— how could he think we'd fit together? And hadn't I explained? Hadn't I told him— "Victor why would you do that? Don't you remember—I mean I told you—I—"

"I just told you," he said, brushing a finger across my cheek. "I like you. You're unusual, rustic, interesting."

I sputtered, I couldn't speak. I wasn't sure rustic was a compliment either.

"I—Victor, I told you—I said—I made it very clear that we could only be friends." Shock had taken over my language skills.

"You said it was *important* for us to be friends, *oui*, I remember."

Walking fast, I dropped the daisy to the ground. "No, Victor. I said it was important for us to *just* be friends. My whole—happy and single mission. Remember?"

His long legs didn't even have to try to keep up with my

scurry. Snatching my hand, he brought it up to his lips. "So, let's be single and friends."

Jerking my hand away, I stomped off. "You aren't listening to me. I'm going to my room." How could Cole be right? I'd never hear the end of it—but then I'd never tell him either!

The rest of the day I kept my eyes open for Victor, avoiding him at all costs. The man only heard what he wanted to. I couldn't communicate with that.

The next morning my inner alarm clock woke me early. I showered, dressed, applied a little mascara and threw my hair into a ponytail. Nana would completely disapprove. I beat Cole to Jack's and found us a booth.

"Can I get you a drink?" Maureen asked, her name tag skewed and a hand on her hip.

"Orange juice."

The front door jingled. Cole walked in wearing a suit with his face clean shaven and his hair combed back with gel. "Good morning." Smiling, he scooched in across from me. He had a new job, he'd walked in light as air—this is what he'd been waiting for, stability. And I wanted him to ditch it all because of dream, a hunch?

"You look all grown up." How could I do this? What gave me the right to screw up someone else's life—or even attempt to?

"So, curiosity is killing me—mom said you *needed* to see me? What's up?"

My face warmed with embarrassment. That meaning could go a whole other way. "Ahh…" I could see him—so vivid, in that dream, smiling, working—*happy.* Okay, forget pride and fear—and heck, why not mess with someone else's life? *I am Nana's granddaughter, after all.* "I think you should quit your job."

Laughing, he threw his head back. When I didn't laugh—or speak, he cocked one eyebrow. "You're serious?"

I nodded.

"And you've gone crazy since I saw you last?"

Before I could defend my sanity, Maureen sauntered back. "Cole, hey honey. I didn't know this little girl was with you."

"Maureen, this is my friend, Samantha. Sam, Maureen—she

and her husband own Jack's."

I shook the older woman's hand. I'd seen her half a dozen times for breakfast, but maybe she didn't remember me. "It's good to meet you."

"Well, I can't tell you how lovely it is to meet you," she said, grinning. Cole ordered a grape juice and Maureen left with the silly grin still plastered to her face.

"Now, back to why you want me to join the unemployed again." His hands flattened on the tabletop.

"Cole, you already have a job, you just don't realize it." I pressed my lips together — waiting to see if he understood.

His eyes widened, he didn't know — he only knew my insane state had been confirmed.

"Seriously," I said taking his empty hand across the table, "you told me a dozen different ideas you have for The Redwood in just an afternoon."

Bouncing back over to us, pressing her lips, it seemed as if she were trying hard not to grin. Maureen set Cole's drink in front of him. Pulling back my arm, I tightened my hand into a fist and we placed our orders.

With Maureen gone, I went on, keeping my hands in my lap. "Cole, you are the only person who can make that to-do list a reality. You love that place. Just like your dad did. Grace can't do all that alone. That was never the plan. She was supposed to have a partner." I cleared my throat, resting my elbows on the table. "Besides, I had this dream—"

"Wait, whoa," he said, trying not laugh. "You had a dream? I'm supposed to quit my job because Samantha Blake had a dream. You never mentioned these psychic powers of yours before—"

"Oh, shush. I know it's stupid. Forget the dream. Think about all of the other really intelligent things I just mentioned."

"I don't think I'll be able to do anything until I hear about this dream of yours." He sighed, blowing out his lips with a puff of air.

The two-minute version of my dream I gave him seemed more ridiculous by the second. I sighed. *This is right. I know it.* "Cole, you're pretty brilliant. You know what needs done and more importantly you have the plan to do it. If you offer more booking dates for The Redwood, if you have another establishment, there will be income enough for you and Grace — maybe just to survive at first, but eventually to thrive on. I know it. You don't need to settle. You need to talk to your mother. You love that place. And when you talk about The Redwood, I feel like I know Daniel."

His eyes, shiny with moisture, narrowed at my words. We sat quiet and when he spoke, his voice came out just above a whisper. I almost didn't hear him. "I *do* love that place."

"You do," I said, reaching for his hand.

"I don't know." Quiet and still, he intertwined his fingers with mine. "I have no idea how my mom will feel about this. I couldn't do anything she wasn't comfortable with. And Sam, she's never wanted to follow through with any of my ideas before. Why would she now?"

"Because you'll be there," I said, squeezing his fingers and feeling a buzz ride up my arm with the motion, "doing it with her. Before, you were presenting an idea for her to do on her own. Now, she'll have a partner, like she did before, with Daniel."

I still didn't have him. He needed another Nana nudge.

"You'll never know until you talk to her," I said. "Try."

Running a hand through his sandy hair, he shook his head. "Agh. I started this job yesterday!"

"So, don't quit today, talk to Grace today." Taking his other hand, I tried to transfer my assurance to him. "Try."

Sidling up next to us, her hands full, Maureen set our plates in front of us. She'd watched me  pull my hands back from Cole. My cheeks went warm at the thought of someone seeing us like that, and getting the wrong idea. I wasn't Cole's girlfriend — friends, just friends. I needed to tell my hands that... Still, the friendship we'd formed seemed important to me and I wanted to be a good friend to him. At least I tried to be.

We left the conversation alone and turned to our food.

"Can I ask you something?" he asked, once we'd finished our meal.

"Sure." Of course, I could allow him that. I had just intervened in his life — I could answer a question.

"Why would you tell me all this? You're on vacation? I'm pretty sure this isn't why you're here."

I knew it sounded silly, but I didn't know what else to say. "Because I think I'm right. And I think it'll make you happy."

His mouth broke into his crooked grin. "And because you've been dreaming about me?"

Rolling my eyes, I wanted to poke him, but attempting to keep my hands to myself, I didn't. "It wasn't like that."

"I know." He laughed at me. "Thank you for thinking about me."

"You're welcome." I bit my lip, examining the pattern in the ceramic tabletop.

I spent the rest of the day exploring Chinatown. After several hours, I came back to The Redwood, souvenirs in hand. Walking over to the kitchen, I swung the door opened. Grace stood in her green striped apron, cutting apart a whole chicken. Pots simmered on the stove with steam rising up from their openings. An empty cutting board lay next to the stove with a used knife lying on top. Savory aroma filled the room. It made me giddy. I loved walking into a working kitchen.

"Hi. Is Cole back yet?"

"I haven't seen him, but I can't say I expect to. I figured he'd go home after work." She stopped mid-cut and looked at me.

"Oh." Cole had been around so much, I almost forgot he had a different home. "Well, if you do, will you let me know?" I felt like a second grader sending notes through a mutual friend.

Heading up to my room, I needed to freshen up before dinner. I had my tub on full blast and sifted through my shopping bags when someone knocked on my door.

Peeking in the bathroom at my half-filled tub, I hurried to the door. Cole. "Hey!" Anxious to see him, I needed to feel out his emotional state with all I gave him to think about this morning.

"I can't do this," he said. His right arm stretched out against the inside of the door. His combed hair wasn't quite so perfect anymore and his eyes drooped tired.

Okay, so I wouldn't need to pry it out of him. "Why not?"

Standing straight, he crossed his arms, a tired sigh falling from his chest.

"Come inside." I pulled on his arm until he'd stepped inside and closed the door. "Oh! One second!" Hurrying to the bathroom I turned off the roaring water.

He'd set himself in the rose covered arm chair in my room. Climbing onto my bed, I crossed my legs, facing him.

"I'm not ready."

"What do you mean? You are ready. You have a plethora of ideas and —" I squeezed fistfuls of comforter beneath me. "You're afraid."

"No, Sam, I'm not afraid." He sat up, leaning forward, his elbows propped on his thighs. "My mother is a smart woman, a businesswoman. She's been doing this a long time. If I come to her with a hundred ideas and nothing to back them up, she won't listen to me. I've got my ideas and I've even done some homework, but not enough." He held his head in his hands.

"Okay." This we could do. Fear I couldn't fix, but this, this merely involved *preparation*. I rubbed my hands together. "So, what do we need to do?"

Giving me a half smile, he sat straight. "I like how you're including yourself in this."

Scooting to the edge of the bed, I let my legs fall to the floor. "Cole, you're going to need my help if you're going to make this happen anytime soon. You're working nine to five, five days a week. You won't quit your job until she agrees. I can help. You *need* my help. Tell me what to do."

142

# Chapter 18

"*D*o you have information on the real-estate in Sacramento and Oakland?" I stood in front of a short plump woman at Ocean View Real Estate. She scribbled in a notebook, but she stopped to answer me.

"That's a vast area—I have a website that should help you." Taking a post-it-note, she scrawled a website down and handed it to me.

"Thank you!" I'd never been so giddy about someone else's real-estate before. My heart sped as I took the square note from her hand. Just one little web-site scrawled in red ink , but that one address would lead to life changing opportunities for Cole.

I spent the rest of the afternoon in the library on their computer. I had Cole's list of "need to haves" and "hope to haves." So, I searched for the right square footage, number of rooms, location, and price. There were two homes in Sacramento and a handful in Oakland that looked like contenders. Printing off the info I'd gathered, I headed back to The Redwood.

Lying on my bed, I flipped through the pages of houses I'd found. Some had pictures, but they were black and white and too grainy to really get the feel for the places. I tried to picture another Redwood, a Redwood like this one, but different. It wasn't hard to picture Cole working bedside Grace at their unique bed and breakfast—but an entirely other place— that took some imagination. Yawning, I flipped to my back, holding the pages above my head, when someone tapped on my rose door.

"Ah, hi, Vic." I didn't open the door all the way, just enough

143

for him to see me. Our last conversation had been more than awkward.

"Hello, Samantha." His smile shone on his face—I guess that awkwardness was one-sided. "What are you doing this afternoon?"

"Just a little work."

"What are you working on?" He pushed my door open an inch more.

"I'm just helping Cole out a little. What are you up to today?" I held to the knob of the door and changed the subject.

Tilting his head, he grinned again. His dark hair and eyes—his sleek expensive clothing— like a piece of eye-candy, he stood there allowing me look on him. I could easily imagine Victor breaking a few hearts. "I can tell you what I am not doing." He sighed, like life had been a   struggle. "I am not taking you out for dinner. Why, again, am I not doing this, Samantha?" Victor picked up my empty hand and held it in his. Leaning down, he kissed the inside of my palm, sending a shiver down my back.

A small laugh escaped my mouth at the tickle from his touch. Pulling my hand from his, I rubbed it against my jeans. The better I knew Vic, the more I imagined Nana's endless battle attempting to straighten out the man's perfectly happy ideals to be single and ever playing the field. "I'm cooking for Grace tonight, remember?"

"Ah, yes." His head bent toward the ground and he shook it. Looking back up, his pretty brown eyes confused, he said, "I do remember, but I do not understand when I have reservations..."

"I already—we talked—" I sighed. "I'm sorry, but I really do have some work to do."

"Fine, fine, I will go, but I will be back." He winked. Bending toward me, his lips puckered near my earlobe.

"Victor, stop it. We're friends. In Wyoming friends don't go around kissing each other's hands and ears—err anything!"

Laughing, he winked—again. "See you." He backed up, into his open door and  closed it.

Nana would be so appalled that I just let him walk away—a handsome, single, interested man walking away from me. I shook my hands. The winks, the hand-kisses, the not catching a clue... *I must be crazy.* Had I met Victor in Wyoming, months ago, I would have been happy to drown in his affection. But even then, we were so different. And neither of us was willing to change for the other. He didn't want what I needed and I couldn't picture a life with Vic—a real life. An amazing night on the town, some steamy kisses—but a life... kids, Christmas, arguments, making dinner together—all that I really wanted—*that* I couldn't even picture a little bit.

I needed a drink, I needed air—something. Trudging my way down the stairs, my eyes on the ground, I grumbled to myself. "How could he be so dense? How could I—" My grumbling stopped when I rammed into someone. "Oh, I'm so—Cole! What are you doing here?"

"It's Friday. I work a half day on Fridays." He held me upright, giving me a funny smile. "What were you mumbling about?"

"Me? Ah—I wasn't mumbling." I forced a laugh. "I'm so happy to see you. I have ads to show you."

"Wow, already?" Cole set his bag in the entryway closet. "You don't waste time, do you, Samantha?"

Biting my lip to keep my grin minimal, my frustration with Vic melted away.

"Why don't we look them over after dinner?"

"Yeah. Okay." A flushed, fluttery sensation filled my insides, replacing my frustration. Staring at him, my mind wandered to the little purple bag Amanda gave me for my mascara. I needed to reapply and find the skinny jeans that Amanda bought me—she said my backside looked good in them.

"I'm going to see if Mom has anything she needs me to do." He shot his thumb toward the kitchen door.

"Okay." I shook off my foolish thoughts.

Picking up my hand, he squeezed. "Hey, thanks, Sam." He let me go, his shoulder brushing mine as he passed.

My cheeks burned pink and my hands tingled with the absence of his touch. Smiling, I watched him go.

"Now everyone will be attending dinner, except Victor — he's going out," Grace said, standing in the entryway next to me. "I can stay and help if you —"

"Don't be silly." I wrapped an arm around her shoulders. "We'll be fine. I've been cooking forever — and Cole will be there to help me."

"Right. Yes." She kissed my cheek and reached for the doorknob. "Thank you, dear."

I nodded — feeling like a kid ready to throw a secret party with Mom and Dad out of the house.

We had two hours until dinner. Rubbing my jittery hands together, I entered the swinging door, ready to cook a feast. Cole had beat me there, looking 1950s housewife-ish with his trusty apron already draped around his neck and tied about his waist. I couldn't help the chuckle that bubbled from my lips.

"Laugh all you want." He threw a matching printed apron at me. "You get one too."

Ducking into the purple apron strings, I reached behind me for the ties, but my fingers touched Cole's already there. He tied the strings at my waist. I brushed flat the wild flower pattern at my front and shoved my hands into the large pockets.

"Looks good on you."

Turning, I examined him. I pursed my lips and squinted. "But better on you."

He shrugged, taking the compliment. "So, what are we making?"

Taking out the list I'd made for the meal, I scanned over my own instructions. "The first course is going to be light, White Bean Fennel Soup. It's simple. I've written down instructions for you. The main course is pork roast with a raspberry sauce, an artichoke tossed salad and parmesan herb bread. After you finish with the soup, I want you to work on Nana's sour cream chocolate cake." I babbled on instructions and ingredients, all the while reading over my list. Glancing up from my handwritten note, I noticed Cole *staring* at me. "What?"

"You're loving this, aren't you?"

Taking a deep breath, I shut my eyes. "Immensely."

"You do look good in the apron, maybe I'll have to hire you." He shrugged again, as if he were still considering the idea.

Laughing, I pointed at him. "I already told you, you wear that apron better than I ever could. Hire yourself."

"I don't think you mean that. I think you're making fun of my smock." He ran his hand along a fabric purple lily, feigning offense. I laughed at his face and the fact that he'd just used the word "smock." Picking up a squeeze bottle of ranch dressing, Cole removed the cap and pointed the opened end at me. "So? Do you dare to make fun of my apron again?"

Pretending to ignore him, I wandered over to the fridge and opened it up. Whirling around, I held out a plastic container of chocolate. "It's a lovely apron. You wouldn't want to get it all mucked up—now would you?"

"Are you threatening the apron?" He motioned down and we circled the kitchen island in slow motion.

After a full circle, I held up my hands, the chocolate sauce still clutched in one. "Truce? We need to get to work."

"All right." He sighed, slamming the dressing bottle onto the island, just cock-eyed enough to point it toward me. The bottle sputtered and ranch dressing rained onto my face and apron front.

"Cole!" I wiped at a droplet on my face. "You did that on purpose!"

"Yes." He nodded. "You really can't mess with a man's apron."

I walked around the island, stopping next to him. He held out his bottle, ready to fire again—depending on my actions. Rolling my eyes at him, I grabbed the nearby rag and wiped my face clean. Laying it down, I glared at him, with an *I'm a grown up* persona.

With his bottle on the counter and his guard down, I swooped my chocolate sauce into the air, circling his head until brown goo ran through his hair and dripped down his face. Cole stood there, taking the punishment. Blinking back the thick liquid, he stared at my face—assuring me I was not all that adult, but I didn't care.

"I can't believe you just did that. So unprofessional." Chocolate dripped down his nose.

Laughing, I dabbed at the sauce between his eyes and licked my finger. "Mmm."

Squinting, he blinked through the chocolate on his eyelids and lashes.

"You know," I said, my tone lecturing, "you deserved—

Cole jolted forward, grabbing my left hand, and pinning it to the bottle I still held. Grabbing my waist with his free hand, he turned me around until my back lay flush to his chest and my right arm sat trapped between his hold and my body. He raised my left hand, still clutching the chocolate sauce until it hovered above my head.

Struggling in his hold, I tried to bring my arm down without any luck. I squirmed, circling my body until I faced him, my right arm pinned between our stomachs. "Give me the bottle, Cole." I glanced up at the sauce pointing down on me. A dribble fell from the un-squeezed bottle, landing in the center of my forehead.

Stronger than me, he squeezed my hand holding the bottle.

"Cole, no!" I squealed. The gloppy sauce trickled down my face and onto my apron.

Letting go of my hand, the bottle dropped to the ground. With his one hand free hand, he smeared the sauce on my forehead and cheeks, still clutching me tight against him. Then licking his fingers, he looked down at me. "You're right, this is good."

He loosened his grip, but wrapped his free arm around my back keeping me in place. Squeezing my arms in between us, I lay my hands against his chest. Peering up to him, he leaned down— my eyes found his lips. Breathing in, I waited for the inevitable to come. Pushing vacation rules from my head, I closed my eyes.

The kitchen door swung open, bumping the cupboards behind it. Jerking, I blinked. Grace zoomed in and out of focus. Pushing against Cole's chest, he stumbled away from me. We faced forward—in a line up, guilty as ever.

Coughing, Cole gaped down at his chocolate spattered apron. "Hey, Mom—I thought you left." One of his arms still draped around my shoulders in our hustle to separate. I circled my shoulder, making it fall from its spot. Chocolate and sweat ran down the sides of his face.

"What's happened in here?" Her face contorted in disgust and she looked around, examining the dirty floor around us. She didn't seem to notice that I had been wrapped in her son's arms two seconds previous.

"Ah—nothing." Cole shook his head like a not-so-innocent ten-year-old.

Standing in our police line-up, she studied us up and down. "You two are a disaster."

Feigning a laugh, Cole waved a hand. "Oh, you know, we were just fooling around."

Letting out an inaudible gasp, I shoved him with my elbow.

"What?" His eyes widened, peering at me.

"I just forgot my purse." She bit her lip. "You two are certain you can handle this?" She shook her head, still examining what we'd done to her kitchen.

"Yes, of course." I held my hands together. *Great, one little mess and Grace had lost her faith in me.*

"Go," Cole said, pushing her out the door.

"Okay, okay." She glanced back over her shoulder before he'd forced her over the threshold. "Call if you need anything. I've got my cell." She brushed at her shoulder, the spot Cole touched, afraid he'd soiled her.

"We'll be fine, Mom. You go, have a great time." He held the swinging door open and kissed her goodbye.

"Cole!" Leaning in she grabbed a napkin from the counter and wiped chocolate sauce from her face.

I waved—oh, if she had come in two seconds later... But she hadn't. She'd come. She'd stopped us. And the rules I'd so carefully made and then somehow so easily forgotten were still intact, still unbroken. Walking to the sink, I found a clean cloth and washed the goop from my face. Tossing the rag to Cole, I pinched my unkissed lips together. "Time to cook."

Even with his face covered with the rag, I still heard his sigh. "She's always had impeccable timing."

Handing him his dinner instructions and a mop, I said

nothing. I was grateful for Grace's interruption. As much as it embarrassed me and as much as I wanted that kiss—where would we have gone from there? I was here for a reason, we both knew that. All that kiss would have done is ruin our friendship.

We kept busy with our own recipes. My menu didn't allow for down time or another game of handsy chocolate sauce. Soon the kitchen filled with a rich and savory aroma. Opening the oven, I rattled the metal inside, placing my roast on its shelves. Onto the fridge, I filled my arms with ingredients for my sauce.

I poured and mixed—not bothering to measure, and then tasted the concoction I'd made. Grinding a bit of the fresh rosemary into the sauce, I tried it again.

"You should have been a chef." Cole looked up from his pot of soup

Smiling, I watched my own pot. "I thought about it."

"Yeah? What changed your mind?"

"I've always loved to cook. When I was little I spent hours in the kitchen helping my mom. But then… Mom died and I cooked for survival, not fun. Plus, I couldn't leave my dad. He needed me. And now, cooking—well, it's just a hobby." Looking up, I met his eyes for a second before returning to the pot. "In the end, I chose mill work." *Or it chose me.* "It's actually fun. I get to work with my hands and create things. I get to work with Eve. I'm in the Valley—with my family."

"But zero *options*," he said, and I knew what he meant. I talked about it entirely too much not to follow his thoughts.

I laughed at the way he said it—at how it sounded. "That's the truth." But I didn't care anymore.

"Do you regret it?"

Peeking over at him, I shook my head. "No."

Cole stared at me, he opened his mouth to speak, but the swinging door from the dining room opened again. Victor's dark hair and strong jaw poked their way inside. Scanning the kitchen, he stopped, finding me.

"Samantha," he smiled, baring his perfect teeth, "I just wanted to let you know that I'll be staying for dinner."

"What about your reservation?" I stopped my stirring. Thankful I'd made enough for everyone times two — too busy thinking about food to worry about Victor's misdirected ideas.

"And miss your big night, no way." Winking, he disappeared into the dining room.

Grunting, Cole stirred his chocolate cake batter as if it were a punching bag.

The roast needed twenty more minutes in the oven. Perfect timing. Dishing up seven bowls of soup, I placed each terracotta bowl on a matching plate.

"I'll take these out." Cole picked up a couple of bowls. "You're a guest here, you probably shouldn't be serving."

"Okay." I wiped the edge of one of the plates with my dish cloth before letting him take it. He started to move again, but I held his arm to stop him. Using the clean end of the rag, I held it to his face. "You've got a little chocolate." I wiped the brown sauce from his forehead. It still speckled his hair, his attempt to rinse it out in the sink earlier hadn't done much.

"Thanks." He peered down at me — so serious. I couldn't look away from him. His blue eyes stared into mine. I continued to wipe at his now sparkling clean head.

Blinking, I forced myself back to reality — to rules. "There you go." I moved away from him.

My stomach fluttered watching him leave. *I have got to get control of myself. I'm acting like a schoolgirl. He is just a man — a tall, handsome, sweet —* "Stop this!" *I've made so much progress. I'm happy, truly completely content and happy. I cannot do this. Not now.*

The door swung open and Cole walked back into the room. I jumped at the sight of him — so busy giving myself a pep talk, I almost forgot he'd be back.

"You okay?"

"Yeah, yeah, I'm fine," I said a little too high pitched. Moving to the other side of the kitchen, I peeked in the oven and opened a cupboard — hopefully appearing like I had something important to do.

"Do you want to go sit down and eat? I'm sure I can manage in here."

"No, no. I want to stay in here and finish things up. I'll eat with you."

Smiling, he nodded.

My stomach twisted at giving him the wrong idea. I found myself feeling dreamy and fanciful around Cole. Something I wasn't used to and something I wasn't prepared for. And at this moment in my life, this joy finding, self-loving moment—not the best idea.

"Is the cake ready?" Work was a safe subject.

He nodded. "It's ready to go into the oven, just as soon as the roast or bread is done." Grace had two ovens in her massive kitchen. It wasn't a wonder why. She might as well have run a restaurant—cooking for often a large group twice a day.

Arranging plates on the island top, I kept myself busy. Cole walked around, standing beside me. "So, after we're done here, we'll eat and go over the ads you found today?"

"Oh, the ads, I almost forgot about them." My body leaned his direction, my arm brushing his. Jerking upright, I smelled the soft scent of his cologne mingled with chocolate sauce.

"I haven't," Cole said, taking my hand. "I can't wait to see what you've found." He intertwined our fingers and shivers ran down the half of my body nearest to him.

Paralyzed, I stared up at him, holding onto the hand he'd given me. The *ding* from the oven saved me—bread. Capering back, I let go of his hand. Another *ding*—time to let the roast rest. My back to Cole, I busied myself with things that truly needed to get done. Things I couldn't feel guilty about leaving him for. Things that probably saved me from a lot of future guilt.

In work mode, I asked him, "Will you melt a couple tablespoons of butter for the bread?" Pulling the roast out of the oven, I reveled at the sight of it. The savory scent alone had me swooning. Setting it next to the bread, I grabbed the pan with the raspberry sauce and drizzled it back and forth over the meat. Placing more fresh rosemary on top, I stepped back to look at it better. "Perfect."

"Are you sure you're in the right profession? You look...

you look enchanted when you cook." I didn't realize he'd been watching me. Shouldn't he be melting butter?

Making light of his comment, I shrugged. "You should see me when I strip wood."

He laughed so loud I jumped and couldn't help but join him. "Go," I said through my giggles. "Clear the dishes. The main course is ready."

Swirling butter on top of the sliced bread, I pressed my lips together to keep from smiling. The dining room door swung open, Cole's arms were full of dishes and his mouth in a flat, straight line.

"Victor is requesting your presence. He would like you to meet the new guests." The dishes in his hands clanged into the sink. "Maybe inform him that I'm not his personal butler."

Biting my lip, I studied his face. I'd seen that expression before. He wore it whenever Victor's name came up or when anyone backed into his car.

"Well, they know I'm in here now. I guess I better go out and say hello." Removing my apron, I brushed off the puffs of flour sprinkled on my jeans. Taking my hair out of its ponytail—I shook it out, letting it fall to my shoulders. I hoped the dark brown would hide the chocolate sauce. I could see Cole in my peripheral, staring at me, again. Combing my fingers through my hair once more, I glanced over to him. "Do I have any chocolate on my face?"

His arms at his side, he looked defeated—or maybe just tired. He walked over, inches away, his eyes roved over my face. "Yeah, you do," he said, almost sounding sad.

I didn't know why he let Victor affect his moods so much.

Cupping my chin with one hand, he brought the end of his apron up, smoothing my face clean.

"Thank you." My eyes glued to his face. I wished I could force him to smile, to not let Vic's confidence, his superiority, bother him. I wished I could forget the rules—just for a minute—just long enough to—

Tearing my eyes from him, I sucked in a deep breath. Taking a step backward, I kept my eyes safely on the ground. Turning away from Cole, I walked into the dining room and smiled at the four strangers and Victor seated at the table. But no one noticed me.

"And then I asked him if Mr. Hoffman always wore leopard print," Victor said, making the group roar with laughter. He dumped the remains of a wine bottle neither Cole nor I had brought out into his glass and downed it before seeing me. "Samantha, dear, come, sit." Moving his chair closer to mine, Victor draped an arm around my shoulders. "Everyone," he said, "this is Samantha."

"So," the woman at my right said, "The two of you met here at The Redwood."

"Ah, yes." I glared at Victor, wondering what he'd told them.

Vic squeezed my shoulder. "She literally ran into me, the blow knocked her to the ground!"

"Talk about falling for someone!" The woman said, and the group laughed again.

What *had* Victor told everyone? Why would someone with so much going for him need to fabricate any relationship? Surely, Victor had women falling for him wherever he went—this, this made no sense.

The kitchen door opened its swing quiet and halfway. Cole squeezed through with his arms full. Setting a plate in front of the woman who'd last spoke to me, he peered over at me and then Victor. My nerves on edge, I offered a smile, but it didn't feel normal.

Standing, I needed to get back to the comfort of the kitchen. "I should get back to work. Cole and I have to finish up dessert."

"Oh, no you don't." Victor pulled me back down. "Sit for a while. I'm sure Cole can handle dessert." He threw a hand out toward Cole.

The woman next to me sighed, like Vic yanking me back into my seat and bossing me around was the sweetest thing she'd ever seen.

With his hands on either side of my face, Victor forced my stare to him, planting a hard, quick kiss on my lips.

Wrenching my head away, I sucked in a gasping breath. "Victor!" I yelled without any accusation attached. He's lucky I got out his name instead of what I wanted to call him.

Getting to my feet, I held my mouth — my kiss free lips until that minute. Victor was wealthy, handsome and charming — and so insolent, it made me sick. Nana, Amanda, they both might call me crazy for it, but it took all my self-control not to punch Victor right in his beautiful mouth.

Pushing my way into the kitchen, I rubbed my lips with my fist. "Pphh." I blew air out my buzzing lips and ran my hands through my hair. How humiliating. How stupid. How —

"Wow." Cole leaned against the counter, his arms crossed tight over his chest. "And here I believed you when you said you two weren't dating."

"Wha — No. It's not like that." My brows furrowed, how could he jump to that conclusion? Didn't Cole see my disgust? Didn't he see how wholly unwanted that kiss had been?

Shaking his head at me, he grimaced his face in revulsion. How dare he be repulsed by me?

"Are you calling me a liar?" My hands gripped my hips until I thought I'd have bruises. "I've told you again and again that I'm not involved with Victor. I've told you why I'm here. Why I — "

"I know. You've made it all very clear," he said, but his voice sounded wrong — so wrong — mocking and rude. His hand flung in the direction of the dining room door — where Victor waited saying who knows what.

"Are you really blaming me for this? You're that stupid, huh?"

Widening his eyes, he gave me one of his cynical laughs, but he didn't get a chance to speak. Victor's head popped into the kitchen. "Samantha, my dear, what's going on?" He stared at me, not acknowledging Cole's presence at all. "The others wanted to compliment your meal. Come back."

"What's going on?" I whispered, though I didn't care if anyone heard me. I overcompensated. It was either whisper or scream. "What is going on with you, Victor? What was *that*?"

"Can we speak in private?" He glanced at Cole for the first time.

Cole had turned away from me and he wasn't looking back.

Shaking my head, I pressed my lips together. "Yeah, I don't

think so. I don't feel like talking right now, or being alone with you, or even looking at you."

His brows knit together and he reached for my arm. "But I—"

I jerked away from him, my hands out, ready to slap any limb that came near me. "Don't grab me. And don't kiss me. Don't even talk to me, until I tell you it's allowed."

I started for the exit—the door to the hallway, not the dining room. I wouldn't walk through the ogling eyes of Victor's audience again.

Peering over at me, Cole raised his head. "Sam—"

"Don't!" I pointed to him and then Victor. "Either of you." I left them to deal with the crowd and the dessert and the mess all on their own.

# Chapter 19

How on earth was I to blame for what had happened? And why did Cole care? Better yet, why did I care that Cole cared? The chaos in my brain made my head hurt—another California night tossing and turning. Why couldn't I let go of this? I hadn't lost sleep over any man in Wyoming.

My stomach had been growling for hours. Because of Victor—because of Cole, I didn't get to have one bite of my roast, or my bread…or anything. But the thought of once again trucking down to Grace's kitchen just to see Cole sitting there waiting for me—*Ooo! No, I could not do that, not again.* I loved that kitchen. That kitchen could have been my second home—and those stupid boys ruined it for me.

My stomach refused to shut up—not used to being denied. So, concocting a plan, I grabbed my robe. Tip-toeing down the stairs, I listened next to the kitchen door…nothing. Peeking under the door, no light shone through the crack. Still, I paused before pushing the swinging door open. *I swear if Cole Casey is in this kitchen, I will pummel him.* Flipping on the light, I braced myself, ready to run or punch at the sight of him.

No Cole.

Sighing I glanced at the clock—almost one. Tomorrow would be a long day—no, actually vacation. Tomorrow I would sleep in. I would spend the day in my bed and my tub and order my meals in!

The kitchen was in pristine condition. I smiled, thinking of Cole cleaning up the huge mess we'd made by himself. My head in the fridge, I found the leftovers that had been singing to me half the night.

Fixing myself a plate, I stuck it in the stainless-steel microwave. Sitting on a bar stool, I yawned. I loved this kitchen. The black and white tiles, the long cupboards in a row, the pantry as big as my closet back home, the worth-more-than-I-make-in-a-year appliances, they always smelled good—either clean or with food. It's a happy place. Laying my head on the cold island counter, my eyes opened and closed, Grace's black and white tiles appearing and disappearing. I emptied my head of rash, stupid men and breathed in rosemary and pork, listening to the hum of the microwave like a lullaby. Moving my arms up to pillow my head, I closed my eyes—just for a minute.

Blinking, I stumbled off my bar stool.

Nana stood in front of me. "Samantha," she said her little hands on her hips.

"Nana?"

And then Victor appeared on her right.

"Samantha," she said again, glancing at Vic.

Bouncing my head from Nana to Victor and back again, I gasped. "Nana, what are you doing here?"

Cole walked up from behind her—standing at her left.

"Samantha," she said a third time. And behind them I could see my cousin, a clown, the salesman she'd sent to my door, and Henry… "Samantha, are you thirty yet? Are you thirty yet?" Walking over to the bar, leaving a sea of men behind her, she picked up my left hand, eyeing it for a wedding band. "Are you thirty yet?" Her voice echoed in Grace's kitchen. Her mouth had stopped moving, but her question remained, bouncing off the walls, asking me again and again and—

And then the room broke apart. Pieces of tile, chunks of countertop fell to some bottomless blackness, men falling with it. I held to the island counter, shaking while Nana still shouted at me.

Gasping in a breath, I sat up—opening my eyes from the nightmare. "Am I thirty yet?"

"I don't think so."

Standing beside me, Cole still had a hand on my shoulder. "Ohhh." I moaned, holding my head. "Nightmare."

158

"How long have you been here?"

Holding my head in my hands, I squinted toward the clock. "Couple of hours." Though I could have sworn it had been minutes. Too tired, too startled with the dream, I forgot to be angry.

Dishing himself a plate, Cole opened the microwave. My plate still sat inside. "Is this yours?"

Closing my eyes, I nodded. Turning the oven back on, he reheated my food and then his. Setting both of our dishes onto the bar, he sat next to me.

"Thank you," I said, not meeting his eyes.

"I'm glad to see you're talking to me."

"Yeah, well, don't get used to it." My anger hadn't dissipated, but my exhaustion made me unable to do anything about it.

"I'm sorry," he said, not eating. He wouldn't quit staring at me.

But I didn't want to see his face. I didn't want to forgive him. He had thought the worst of me. I didn't want to just forgive and forget.

"I shouldn't have jumped to conclusions. I shouldn't—will you look at me?"

He wanted me to look at him—fine. I turned, hoping my sleepiness wouldn't lessen the effect of my glare. "You called me a liar."

"No! I didn't—I mean I wouldn't."

"You did! Don't do it again." I stabbed the countertop, meaning here and now. I know what I heard. I know what he said. He thought I'd lied to him, or at least fabricated the truth.

"Okay, but it's really not what I meant." His hands fisted in his hair. "I just—it's Victor. *Victor.* He's so cocky. He just takes whatever he wants and—"

"And that's my fault?" I crossed my arms, defensive and staring him down now. I was right, why shouldn't I look him in the eye? "I'm the one who was assaulted. Maybe instead of holding me in contempt, you should have defended me. You could have yelled at him—made him feel like crap—slugged *him* in the face. He was the one—"

"You would have wanted me to hit Victor?" His voice rang with surprise—pleasure even.

"No." *Idiot.* "That's not what I meant. I just meant I didn't do anything. I was innocent, yet I'm the one who went to bed without dinner."

"I know." He pushed his eyebrows together. "I'm sorry. I am. I can still punch Victor if you want."

Shaking my head, I didn't want him to make me laugh—not yet. He didn't deserve it. I didn't say anything, just turned back to my food.

"I did love seeing you yell at Victor."

"That was as much for you, as him," I said, not giving him a glance. "You're both idiots. It must be that Y chromosome."

I saw it in his face, even though I only saw him through my peripheral. Cole hated being lumped in the same category as Vic. Good—as long as he suffered. His sad eyes stared at me. "I am sorry, Sam. I really, *really* am."

My fork hovered in front of my mouth. "You're getting good at saying that."

His laugh came out small—sad. "I guess I am. It's just..." He paused, running his hands over his face. "I feel crazy. Things have been crazy since you came. You drive me crazy. I don't normally act like this, it's just—"

"I know. I know," I said, if possible even more irritated. "I drive you crazy. Are you seriously blaming me for your reaction tonight?"

"I'm not blaming you." His cheeks turned pink. Standing, he ran his hands through his hair. "Ah," he groaned. "I... I was jealous."

My head whipped around to him, my eyebrows raised. He was jealous of Victor? Why? When he wasn't being an idiot, Cole happened to be kind of amazing—funny, smart, genuine.... just Cole. He didn't even like Victor.

He rubbed his hand across his chin—like I interrogated him rather than waiting for him to volunteer information. He cleared his throat. His hand drew my eyes to his whiskers... his chin, his mouth... "I was jealous," he said, reading my confused expression, "because I so badly wanted to kiss you tonight, and somehow, *Victor* beat me to it."

Swallowing hard, I stared at my friend. With all that had happened, with all the signals and signs—I'd only thought about my own feelings—my stupid, foolish, offended feelings. My head shouted warnings at me. Rules—there were rules, but I had wanted that kiss just as much, possibly more. And then something changed me, maybe the naked truth in the room, maybe the tension, maybe my exhaustion, maybe Cole's unshaven chin—I don't know. But standing, I walked to him, lifting my hand to his face—brushing the whiskers that occupied too much of my thoughts. Cole's hands came up to my hair, sweeping my long unkempt bangs from my eyes. My stare roved from his eyes to his lips, waiting...

Running his hands down my back, he pulled me closer, leaning down until our lips met. Wrapping my arms around his neck, I lifted up on my toes, crushing myself closer to him. Feeling his arms wrap tighter around me, I kissed him back.

# Chapter 20

There's nothing like a night of making-out to send you off to sleep. I hadn't kissed someone like that since…I'd never kissed anyone like that. Closing my eyes, I could almost imagine Cole's lips on mine, the pressure there, the zing in my insides—*oh no, no, no, what had I done?* I turned the best friend I had in California into my make-out buddy. Worse than a make-out buddy—I *liked* Cole. I had broken every no-men vacationing rule in the book!

Lying in bed, I kicked at the sheet around my feet. I didn't know what happened. I'd never had a make-out buddy before. I just got caught up in the emotion, in the moment. Sure, I enjoyed it… way too much did I enjoy it. *Crap.* I couldn't let it happen again. Cole was my friend, and I didn't want to lose that. I could tape my rules back together—right?

A friend from high school—Lacy, she had make-out-buddies… that's how she referred to them. But they never remained friends! Grabbing a little paper-sack from my nightstand, I tossed the chewing gum I'd bought from inside to the ground, and started breathing into the bag. Trying not to hyperventilate. I needed Cole—we needed to stay friends. I'd lost my focus. Stupid, but I wouldn't let that cost me my friend.

Staying in bed, I closed my eyes again—though sleep wouldn't come. Peeking through my lashes, the clock on my nightstand read noon. Closing my sleepless eyes, I hoped I could wake up from this nightmare. It wasn't working though. Grabbing my phone, I stood and stretched my tired muscles. Flopping into my oversized chair, I debated over whom to text. I could not text Eve!

How horrifying. *Hey, thanks for the amazing gift, oh and the bonus gift – cousin Cole is a great kisser.* Liza would reprimand me – all so sensible. I wasn't up for a lecture. I'd been lecturing myself all morning. Amanda – yes, Amanda would be full of advice.

> Me: Help. I kissed Cole last night. And Victor kissed me.
> Holy... things are screwed up.
> Amanda: Wow! Both? You kissed both of them?? And Nana
>      thought you couldn't have fun.
> Me: Pay attention Amanda. I said I kissed Cole. I didn't
>      kiss Victor, he forced himself on me.
>
> Amanda: Jerk. I can send Nana to beat him.

Her comment had me laughing, before I could write her back, I got another message.

> Amanda: But Cole... that's great, sis! I didn't see that
>      coming. How did it happen?

She wanted a story and I needed advice. I wanted to call her, at least then I could interrupt her when she got all mushy on me. I could get out what I needed to say, zipping her lips in the process. I considered... but I'd already broken one vacation rule.

> Me: I don't know, one minute we were fighting, the next
>      we were kissing.
> Amanda: Ah, romantic.
> Me: No, it's not romantic. It was a big fat mistake and
>      now I have to try and fix it.
> Amanda: You like him?
> Me: Of course I like him. He's my friend. Thus, my
>      predicament.

Maybe I should have texted sensible Liza...

> Amanda: Obviously, it's more than that. You don't make-out
>      with someone you don't feel more than friendship
>      for.

Bah!! She was no help at all!

Me: LACY WILLIAMS!!
Amanda: You aren't Lacy, Sam. YOU wouldn't kiss someone
      you didn't have feelings for.
Me: Who knows… maybe I would.
Amanda: You wouldn't.
Me: How do you know???

She was starting to annoy me. Tempted to throw my phone across the room, I opted for covering my face with a throw pillow and screaming into the cushion. I had been trying to convince myself that I didn't have *feelings* for Cole — other than friendship feelings, anyway. I needed help fixing this mess and Amanda, ugh, Amanda, couldn't get off of feeling feelings.

Amanda: I'm your sister, Sam. I know. But fine, if you
      need a hard fact, then: Victor. Victor is your
      friend too. You didn't feel the need to make-out
      with him, did you? You're not a kiss anybody and
      everybody kind of a girl. And that's not a bad
      thing.
Me: Even if you're right, that's not why I'm here.
Amanda: Maybe it should be. Stop trying to plan your life
      to death.

I didn't write her back. I sat in my chair, more confused than ever, when my phone jingled again. Another message.

Amanda: Sorry. What I meant was- you're there to LIVE,
      right? It sounds like you are.

Standing in the shower, I let the hot water run over me until it had gone almost cold. I hoped it would clear my head. It didn't.

Pulling my hair back into a ponytail, I put on a little mascara — my new habit. Falling into my arm chair, I covered my face with my hands but a tap on my rose door stopped my oncoming cry.

"I should have taken a bath." My voice muffled into my palms. *Don't be Victor. Don't be Victor. In fact, don't be any man.* "Cole," I said, pulling my door open.

"Hey, pretty lady." He leaned in and kissed my cheek. Not

exactly a friend greeting—unless you're Victor. "Do you want to go to Jack's? Mom tells me we both missed breakfast." He winked and I could feel my cheeks burning with the flush.

My head swooned—*crap*. Breakfast at Jack's with a side-dish of kissing sounded kind of... wonderful. *Focus!*

"Ahh—"

"Come on." He took my hand, guiding me out the door. "I'll buy."

I should have taken my hand away—I should have said something. *Our friendship is too valuable, or this isn't going to work, or I will be leaving for Wyoming in a little more than a month...* something... But I didn't. He drove and I sat, silent, staring at our fingers knotted together, resting between our bucket seats. I tried not to think about how nice his hand felt in mine.

*Focus.*

"Are you okay?" He turned off the ignition, his hand on the door handle. When I didn't answer, he got out of the car, meeting me around the front of it and held open Jack's entrance. "You're quiet."

"Yeah, I'm—" Words came slow, my head hurt. What was I going to say again?

"You two, again?" Maureen stood just inside the glass door. "Well, aren't you a sight!" Passing us, she set the plate of food in her hand in front of a man in a booth.

I scooched along the green and white striped booth seat. Cole sat across from me. Taking my hand again, he held it on the table top. He hadn't shaved.

*Focus.*

"Cole," I said, finding my voice. "I—"

"What can I get for you kids?" Maureen asked, pen and pad in hand.

"The special for me, with scrambled eggs," Cole smiled up at her, and I couldn't remember his smile ever being that big before.

He made it really difficult to *focus*. But she waited, so I answered. "Ah, make that two."

"Coming right up." Maureen tapped her tablet, and left us.

"Samantha, what's wrong?" He squeezed my fingers, his

head dipping until he met my eyes. "Unless you're angry with me—you're never this quiet." He gave a small laugh.

Couldn't I be though... last night I'd been livid... with good reason...why was that again?

"Hey," he said at my silence. "What is it? Let me help."

My eyes swelled with tears. Why did this have to be so hard? Why did he have to be so—

"Are you crying?" His thumb rubbed back forth over my hand.

Shaking my head no, I only made a tear fall. I wiped it away, brushing it off like it hadn't even been there. "I'm fine."

"No, you're not." His forehead wrinkled.

Saying nothing meant I lied to both of us—saying nothing wouldn't save our friendship.

"It's..." My voice cracked and my stupid eyes filled. "It's you." I couldn't talk. I couldn't breathe. I needed air. Standing, I sped for the door, pushing it open and sucking in the humidity. I heard Cole stand and follow after me. *Walk. Just walk.* Staring at the sidewalk in front of me, that's what I did—walk.

Snatching my hand, Cole's jerk stopped me before I'd made it far. "Hey, what's going on? What did I do?"

Staring up at him, my tears spilled over. I'd gone crazy. "You didn't shave." I started to walk again.

"Hey, hey," he said, both hands on my upper arms, he stopped me again. "I thought you liked me unshaven." He gave a light laugh. How could he keep up with my emotional melt downs? Wrapping his arms around me, he hugged me. His face buried in my neck, scratching where his whiskers touched. "What's going on, Sam?"

Sliding both of my hands into his, I stepped back, so I could see him. "I've been stagnate. I've been on pause. I was letting my Nana look for a husband, without trying to find my life, my happy, my soul."

He nodded, he knew all this. I'd already bared my embarrassing truth to him—and yet he still stood there with me, wanting me.

But I couldn't stop now. "And then you came along, with your whiskers and lips and—"

"Is that a bad thing?"

Grateful he'd interrupted me, I couldn't quite remember where I'd been going with that list. "No. You are a wonderful friend. It's just I'm here —"

"To find your life?"

"Yes. And I'm doing that now, finding my life." The tears rained down, but I kept talking. "I didn't realize I wasn't worthy of anyone—not the way I'd been living. And being here, it's made me realize the person I want to be worthy for is *myself*. I can't lose that. I can't give that up. Not when I just found it."

"You don't think you could be here for yourself and for me?" He pierced me with his stare, his eyes so earnest they tempted me to concede.

I bit my lip, not trusting my words. Hoping my silence would send the right answer.

Minutes passed and then he nodded, the rest of his body rigid. "Okay, then."

"Okay?" I said, taken aback. I had given myself away. He had to know I had feelings for him and his whiskers. But it didn't look as if he'd fight me on this—and for that I should feel grateful—I did feel grateful and yet I hung my head. My eyes filled up and my heart pinched with pain at a simple "okay."

In the quest to find myself, I'd learned how very insane I'd become over the years.

"You know why you're here. If this is what you need, okay." His mouth moved in a fast, stiff motion, his body still unmoving.

Walking back to Jack's we kept our hands to ourselves. Mine felt ridiculous and empty. I hoped all the progress I'd made hadn't flown out the window with my mutiny.

"I was wondering," Cole said, back in our booth. "If we could go over the ads you got yesterday?"

Thankful for a change in subject, I smiled ignoring the raw pain in my chest. "Oh, yes, I would love to go through them with you."

"Great," he said, truly seeming all right.

$S$tanding there, my door unlocked, I ran my fingers over the words Cole's father had etched into it. Roses don't have to be red. "*Roses don't have to be red*," I said out loud, wanting to hear the words.

"Samantha," Victor's voice came from behind me. "Am I allowed to speak? Have you forgiven me yet?"

Facing him, I rolled my eyes. "Are you kidding me?"

"Please," he said, holding his palms together. "It would sadden me greatly to lose your friendship. I am sorry for my moment of weakness. Can you forgive me?"

Stopping the massive urge to smack him, my arms fell to my sides. Inside my head I saw Cole's face, his kindness, his patience. How understanding he'd been with me. I didn't understand Vic's feelings or rash actions, but I did understand my own weakness. Taking his hand, I squeezed it. "Sure, Vic," I said, my tone completely changed, "I forgive you."

Victor would be gone soon. Tall, dark, eccentric Victor would be leaving—that part of my vacation adventure would be over. Grateful I'd met my Canadian friend, it saddened me—just a bit, to see him go. He was different than anyone I'd known. I wanted to end on a positive note. And strange enough, it seemed to serve my self-finding, self-loving quest to have an attractive successful man want me. I'd made the choice. I knew what I wanted and what I didn't, and found the strength to say no.

Meandering into my room, I made a list of what I wanted to do with the last half of my vacation. Reading down the tallies I'd made, I stopped on Cole's name. I wanted to help him. I needed to help him.

Sitting on the edge of my tub, I listened to the drumming of water rushing out. I should have been leaping for joy with Cole's contentment with our relationship. But I wasn't. I hadn't wanted him to fight me. I hadn't wanted to lose him. Or myself. Or my focus. So, why did I feel so—blah?

Cole. "Cole." His name on my lips made me smile. *My friend, Cole.* My eyes filled with moisture and I let the tears fall. They spilled over into the tub, hiding my remorse in the basin.

# Chapter 21

Seven days. Seven days of touring, working, busyness. Seven days of keeping our hands to ourselves. I'd made appointments for Cole and I to visit the houses I'd found information on. We checked things off his list faster than I thought possible. Cole had his duel-loan application filled out, waiting for Grace to agree to it—the only thing left on his list—finding a prospective house. Then he'd talk to Grace.

"You ready?" Cole stood in the corner of my room watching me gather my things.

"Yep." I shoved my cell into my purse. Checking my watch, I reminded him. "Our appointment's at 9:30."

"Don't worry. It only takes twenty minutes to get to Oakland. Luckily for you, I know Oakland as well as my home town." Smiling, he left me with wobbly knees.

Stopping at the kitchen on our way out, Cole brought out a small cooler. Carrying it out to the car, he set it in the back seat and opened the passenger door for me.

"What's that?" I jerked my thumb toward the back.

"Lunch." He stood in front of my door, his body holding it open. I squeezed by him, feeling warmer as I did so. Walking around, he climbed inside. "I may not be a chef like you, but I make a mean sandwich."

Holding my stomach, I begged it to stop fluttering. "I'm not a chef," I said, forcing the permanent grin from my face.

"I don't think anyone at The Redwood would agree with you on that."

Sitting on the dash, Cole's phone started to jingle. We hadn't been gone long—if Grace needed something we could easily turn around. I reached for his phone, just as he did. I got the phone, he got me. Glancing at me, he pulled back his hand in slow motion.

"You're driving, so I—"

"Yeah," he said, his eyes on the road.

The call had since gone to voicemail, but my hand still tingled at his touch. It had been seven long days since he'd held that hand. Why did that feel like such a long time? Hadn't I gone years without anyone holding on to me? Why did I have to meet him now—when I was so determined not to meet anyone!

Our short ride to Oakland was quiet and Cole's eyes were on the road. I gazed at sights all new to me. We pulled up to the first house and Cole pointed. "Look, there's the realtor."

Following Cole's finger, I saw the woman. She seemed to disappear though with the large home behind her. Trim ran around the house like Victorian Lace. The porch wrapped around the side of the house—how far, I couldn't see. Tilting my head to see the two-story home better, I blinked in the sunlight. The ugly, muddy, brown paint chipped away in spots, but I hardly saw it. I saw in this house, the beauty it *could* be—and we weren't even inside yet.

Sitting inside the car, I studied the house. I hadn't noticed Cole get out or walk around to open my door. Holding out his hand, he helped me from the car.

"Thank you," I said, too quiet for him to hear, I'm sure. My eyes were on the double door entrance.

When I stood there—still staring, he grabbed my hand, pulling me along behind him. One little touch in the car, one, and permission had been granted, we were back to normal.

Her wrist bent, the woman pointed to me, her eyes squinting to see me in the sun. "I'm Maddie Hale. We spoke on the phone the other day."

"I remember." I shook her hand with my free one.

We followed the middle-aged woman inside. Maddie wasted no time spouting facts for us. "The manor was built in 1911. Most of the architecture is original."

Walking into a small sitting room, I inhaled and dust filled my nostrils. The place had been vacant a while. There wasn't any furniture and an inch of dirt had settled onto every surface. The bay window sat sweetly, viewing the dead front yard. From the sitting room, we went into a large living room. And it seemed to me that Jane Austen characters should grace us with their presence. Yes, it was dirty and in some places falling apart—but it was also amazing. The flooring, the arches separating each room—it took me back to a different time. The baseboards were chipped and worn in some places, missing in others. They would all need to be replaced.

"And through here is the kitchen." Maddie pointed to a door within the living space. I almost ran into Cole getting to the door. The large room wasn't as big as The Redwood kitchen, but it had a great feel to it, lots of cupboards and wide countertops that would be perfect for making dinner and baking bread. Like everything else, it needed work. But I liked it. Already I wanted to cook a meal there.

"The owners have had this place up for sale a couple of times. It's been on the market over a year now. I'm sure they'd be willing to negotiate a price," Maddie said, watching Cole examined every corner of the kitchen.

A couple small bathrooms and a good-sized master bedroom later, we went upstairs. The wide antique staircase placed near the front door turned out to be my favorite feature in the house. The iron balusters spiraled and twisted, curving into a beautiful knot at the center of each. The wood railing needed sanding and stain, but it stayed in place, secure and sturdy.

Gliding my hand along the wide railing, we walked up the stairs, a few creaking under our feet. A small "bonus room" as Maddie put it, sat at the top of the landing. From the bonus room were three closed doors making an equilateral triangle. Behind each door, a spacious bedroom.

The backyard didn't have the space factor like The Redwood, but there'd be enough room for outdoor furnishings and a good size flower garden. The wooden fence ran around the entire enclosure, but the wood had been damaged in the back, some pieces missing all together.

"If you need more time we can always come back to this one, it's vacant. We do need to be on time for our other appointments though." Maddie looked at her watch.

Walking back through the house to the front yard, the three of us went to our cars. Cole opened the passenger door for me, but I didn't get inside. Stopping, I turned, wanting one more glance at the beautiful house. I saw it all in my mind, the off-white Victorian trim around the peaked edges of the large house, painted a cranberry red. The porch would match the trim in color, with large marble pots posted out in front, filled with purple pansies. The now dead grass would be green, the walkway edged with wildflowers. *Perfection.*

"What is it?" Cole turned his head back toward the manor.

"Nothing." Shaking my head, I lost the image.

He raised his eyebrows — not believing me.

Then clearing my throat, something possessed me to answer. "I was just picturing this place all fixed up." I hoped he wouldn't ask me anything further, it embarrassed me how much I'd invested in someone else's dream. Help could turn into *invading*.

The remainder of the morning and early into the afternoon Maddie showed houses to us. She had as much information on the others as the first we visited. They were all older vintage homes, but none were quite like *Redwood Manor*. I'd started calling the first house by a made-up name, but only in my head. I couldn't fathom the amount of work it would take. Still, the manor could be an Inn — The Redwood's little sister. The Redwood in San Francisco and Redwood Manor in Oakland — I liked it.

Driving away from house number five, Cole glanced over at me. "So, tell me about your picture."

"My what?"

"You said you could picture the first house. You didn't say that about the others. What did you see?"

I'd sort of counted on him forgetting all about that. "You don't want to know. It's silly and not my house. What do I know?"

"Sam, you're here, aren't you?" Peeking over at me, he said, "You're the reason I'm here. Tell me."

I couldn't stop smiling, I loved the vision my head created.

Still, I hadn't planned on sharing my silly romanticized moment. His eyes were on the road—thank goodness, so he didn't see my giddiness. "Okay." I told him every detail, down to the purple pansies. I let myself look ridiculous in front of him—why shouldn't I?

He nodded and listened. And maybe my imagination ran wild, but the corners of his lips seemed to turn up when I mentioned the purple pansies.

"It sounds perfect." He turned a corner.

"Well, that's just the outside of the house." I babbled on, feeling nervous. "You'll have to take care of the interior." I laughed—like he might consider going along with my picture. "I can't imagine the cost. *Everything* needed repair." How would he afford it all?

"I know." He breathed in deep. He'd already thought about that stress. "But that's why we've applied for loans. I'll supply the labor myself. That'll help some."

"Will you really be able to do all of it?" It seemed so daunting.

"I've been repairing and working on The Redwood since I was a boy. I've learned a lot over the years. I'll have to hire out a plumber, but yeah, the rest I should be able to do myself."

"Huh." I pressed my hands together between my legs and kept my eyes looking out the windshield.

"You're surprised?" he said, pulling the car over to the curb and parking.

"No." I pressed my lips together and faced him. "Not surprised, impressed."

The car now stopped, he looked at me too, smiling. "Are you ready to break for lunch?"

"Yes." Opening my door, I realized our surroundings. The familiar skinny sidewalk, the yard with more dirt than grass and the massive building behind them both—we were back at Redwood Manor. "What are we doing here?"

"I wanted one more look. And since only one place gave you a mental picture, I thought you wouldn't mind seeing it again, too." Getting out of the car, he pulled the cooler from the back seat.

"No, of course I don't mind. You wanted another look, huh?" I said, more excited than I had reason to be. He liked it too, though. "Does this mean Redwood Manor's your favorite too?"

"Redwood Manor? You've given the house a name?" He blinked, cocking his head and laughing.

"No, pshh, that would be—I mean…" I bit my lip. "It sounds kind of nice though… doesn't it?"

Stepping onto the porch, he peered up at the manor. "It does." Spreading a blanket onto the wooden deck, we sat. Cole pulled item after item from the cooler. "It's not much," he said, handing me a sub sandwich.

"It's wonderful."

Opening my mouth, I tried to force the tall sandwich inside, but the layers of meat and cheese were too much for my opened jaw.

Laughing at my attempts to take a bite, Cole took it from my hands. "Here," he said, removing a few of the toppings.

"Thanks." My lips twitched, watching him. "It's looks delicious by the way." I'd never had a man cook for me before. Even assemble a sandwich—somehow it tasted better knowing he'd made it.

His legs stretched out, his back rested against the house. "So, *Redwood Manor* must be your favorite of the few we've seen."

"As a matter of fact, it is. What about you? I know this old place would mean much more work for you. I wouldn't blame you at all if you kept looking."

"Actually," he said, "Redwood Manor is my favorite so far. It has that timeless quality that I want. The location is perfect. The price would have to come down a bit. But… yeah, I can see it. And with all the work it needs—it isn't impractical to think they would negotiate."

"We still have two more homes to see," I said. A quick trip to Sacramento was next on our agenda… lunch and then more real-estate.

"Yes, we do." He popped a grape into his mouth.

"Isn't Victor from Sacramento?" I asked, thinking out loud.

"That's right," Cole said, his smile gone. "Maybe I don't want to look in Sacramento."

176

Ignoring his comment, I wondered aloud once more. "It's funny to me that he'd vacation so close to his home. I guess it wasn't a vacation though, it was business."

"He has the means to vacation wherever he wants," Cole said. And I could see it wasn't the best conversation topic. "His *business* was finished a while ago. He just—"

"What do you mean?"

"Mom said he'd been done with his work for a couple of weeks." Cole shoved a bite into his mouth. Motioning at me with his sandwich, he said, "He hung around for you."

"That makes no sense," I said, but the expression on Cole's face told me we were both remembering Vic's unwanted kiss.

"Yeah, well maybe it's time to call it a day." He slapped the crumbs from his hands. "Who wants to go to Sacramento, anyway?"

"Now that makes no sense! You aren't going to let one eccentric man intrude on your business, are you?" I sat up straight, twirling a grape between my fingers. "Relax, have a grape." Throwing the fruit at him, it hit him right between the eyes.

"Hey!" He rubbed his forehead.

Laughing, I tossed another one his way, this time hitting his cheek. "You're supposed to open your mouth. You're supposed to catch it."

Reaching for my hand holding the bag of grapes, Cole jutted toward me. Scooting myself backward on instinct, I tumbled down half the porch steps.

Laughing, I lay against the steps, holding my pounding chest. Opening my eyes, Cole stood over me. His forehead wrinkled in worry and his hair flopped over into his eyes. Still, he grinned. "You all right?"

"Yep." Maybe a little humbled, but my body stayed intact. Delirious, I laughed again.

Holding out a hand for me, he helped me to my feet. Bumping into Cole, I steadied myself, holding onto his shoulder. Closing my eyes, I let go of him and held my head, my body swaying.

"Hey, hey, hey." He grabbed hold of my elbows. "Do you need to sit?"

"Yeah." I opened my eyes. Still holding me, he bent his face toward mine, his smile gone. Shaking my head, I smiled, trying to reassure him. "Really, I'm fine. I think I stood up too fast is all." My heart beat faster, feeling the warmth of his breath on my skin.

"Sit." His face still next to mine, his hands still clutched to my arms, he guided me downward. "And breathe."

Breathing in through my nose and out through my mouth, I studied him—his eyes, his nose, his mouth. "You didn't shave today."

Shaking his head, he smiled small. "No, I didn't."

The day flew by. We made our Sacramento appointments. We laughed and talked—I successfully didn't bring up whiskers again. But I thought about them—I couldn't stop.

Sitting in the car, I waited for Cole who'd gone inside the gas station. We had the car ride back and I needed someone sensible in my head.

Me: Liza, remind me why I'm here…please!
Liza: Uhh, for the longest vacation anyone on the planet
    has ever taken?
Me: Come on Liza. It's Cole. I can't think straight. I need
    you to tell me not to lose myself.
Liza: Okay… don't lose yourself. Do you need a map?
Me: Ha. Ha. You're hilarious. In case it doesn't translate
    through text—I'm being sarcastic.
Liza: Fine. You want advice. I'll give it. Stop being such a
    coward. You're afraid. This isn't about losing yourself.
Me: Not true.

Defensive, I knew where I'd been—where my happiness status currently stood. I knew what it felt like not to live, not to love myself. And I thought Liza would get that.

Liza: You won't lose yourself, Sam.
Me: How do you know?
Liza: It's not about losing yourself to someone else. It's
    about choosing.

I didn't write back. She hadn't said what I thought she would.

She hadn't been my reasonable, sensible, take-a-chill-pill rock. And I couldn't decide if she'd gone crazy or made complete sense.

"What did you think?" Cole handed me a fountain drink for the drive back.

I didn't look at his face — I kept his whiskers from my mind — they didn't allow me to think straight. Houses... houses... "I think you were right, we could have called it a day in Oakland."

"Me, right?" He shrugged. "It happens," he said, pulling out onto the road. "Every once in a while.

"Good to know." Laughing, I tapped his leg. I'm not sure why — I knew it was flirtatious. I just wanted to touch him. I crossed my arms in attempt to keep my hands to myself. "We'll make it home in time for dinner." Cole's lips creased into a smile at my words. "What?"

"Nothing," he said. But I raised my eyebrows when he didn't lose his smirk. "I just like hearing you call The Redwood *home*."

It wasn't the first time I'd done it — The Redwood felt like home to me, and it would be my home for the next few weeks. "You probably shouldn't get used to that."

Stopping at a light, he glanced over to me. "I know." Sighing, he blew out a puff of air. His knuckles turned white on the steering wheel. "So, do you want to go home for dinner or would you like to go out here?"

"Let's go out," I said, not allowing my mind to stress or worry, or think too much. I just *felt*, I just *chose* — and going out with my friend Cole felt like the perfect way to end this day.

"I think you ate more than me," Cole said when we left the restaurant.

"Ooooh." I moaned, holding my stomach. "I think I did. But it was so good."

We had not been on a date. We'd paid our bills separately. We told stories and talked about family and friends and life. It reminded me of sharing a meal with my best friend — granted, I don't get butterflies from Eve's lips or facial hair.

The setting sun blazed so different than our sunsets back home. There weren't hills and trees for the sun to disappear

179

beneath—at least not here in the city. Next to our restaurant the walls of buildings, different shapes and sizes had turned to silhouettes in front of the disappearing sun.

Another day, from morning to night spent with Cole. Exhausted from the long day, I yawned, climbing into the passenger seat. Exhaustion may have settled in, but it only helped mask my foolish, senseless happiness.

The speeding car, the lulling music—it all made my yawning increase. "Lay back," Cole said. And I listened without argument. Closing my eyes, I let myself drift while he drove, feeling for the moment content.

I couldn't say how long we'd been driving, but sleep hadn't completely come, when I heard Cole say, "You're asleep. Of course you are. And I'm left to think. And these days I hate thinking, because I always end up thinking about you."

Trying to keep my breathing steady, I didn't move. What a cowardly, terrible thing to do.

"You dismiss your feelings so easily." I heard him sigh and I pictured his hand running through his hair, agitated. "Maybe you should teach me how."

But he already knew how—or his feelings were easy enough to brush away—or so I thought. He gave in so easily, conceded to my stupid demand. Part of me wanted to sit up and tell him he couldn't be more wrong. How I hadn't stopped thinking about his kiss, his hands, his voice, his—all of him. But I couldn't—I *shouldn't*. My heart raced, listening to him.

I stayed quiet. I stayed still, thinking, until the car came to a stop. Blinking, I opened my eyes.

"We're home," he said, and I could see the sadness in his eyes. Had it been there all day?

"I see that." Sitting up, I didn't get out of the car. My feelings so conflicted. The exercise and strength fighting their incompatibility exhausted me. Liza made it sound so easy. A choice—not losing myself, but choosing. "Can I ask you something?"

"Sure." Staring at me, he waited. He turned off the ignition and we sat in the silence of the car.

"When I told you that this…" I pointed from myself to him.

"Couldn't happen…" I bit my lip. I'd never been so forward. This had to be too much. Still, I continued, exhaustion from fighting myself fueling me on. "You said okay."

Cole nodded, his lips pressed together.

"*Okay*, like you were fine with it."

He stayed quiet.

"Are you?"

Rubbing the back of his neck, he didn't answer. "Ahh…"

"It's not a trick question. It's just a question that I'd like an honest answer to."

Clearing his throat, he stared at me like we were in a competition. Who would turn away first? "Honest?"

"Honest." My heart fluttered and I hoped I looked calmer than I felt.

"No, I'm not." His eyes narrowed.

"But you know I'm leaving soon." I took his hand in my own, lacing my fingers through his.

His head fell, gazing down at our hands. "I do."

"Okay, then. You know. And I know. You aren't content just being friends." Placing my hand on his rough cheek, I brought his eyes up to my own. My stomach fluttering, I unbuckled my seatbelt, giving myself room to reach him. Leaning in, I kissed the corner of his mouth. "Neither am I."

Burying his head into my neck, he looped his arms around my back. His warm breath tickled the skin at my collar. "Samantha." He pulled me closer.

# Chapter 22

"You won't lose yourself. I promise." Holding my hand, Cole walked me to the front doors of the house.

"I know," I said, and I did. I had said no to Victor. Liza was right—my life, my choice, and I wouldn't lose myself again. Besides, in a short time I would be back in Wyoming and Cole would still be here—in California, at The Redwood.

"What do we do now?" He waited for me to make the next move.

"Now, you kiss me goodnight and tell me to go to bed. I'm exhausted."

The light from the porch illuminated his face. Raising his eyebrows, his lips twitched with my answer. Forcing away the shadows, he closed the gap between us. Wrapping his arms around my back, he drew me to him, kissing me like I might change my mind at any moment.

Waking after a full seven hours of glorious sleep, I stare at my rose ceiling. Even the pattern on the ceiling seemed a beautiful artistic vision—swirls and turns with carpentry mud. My heart swelled—like it could burst, but a good burst—a blissful burst. Getting up, I stretched and dressed, not bothering to shower. *I'm late.* Pulling my hair up into a tight bun, I studied myself in the mirror. I didn't look different—and yet I did. I looked… *alive.*

I knew the small tap on my door was him. Cole. Skipping over to the door, I opened it to see him beaming back at me.

"Hey," he said, a silly grin on his face.

"Hi." Pressing my lips together, I tried to repress my own silly grin.

"You look beautiful."

Glancing down at my jean shorts and my non-Amanda-approved Star Valley High T-shirt, I laughed. I hadn't even put on my mascara. "Ready to go?" I knew Grace would be downstairs, shelter food supplies in hand, waiting on us.

"Almost." Taking my hand, he pulled me toward him. Hugging me, his face nestled in my neck, he sighed. "Mom's in the parlor."

Pushing back, I peered at him. "Ah, have you told Grace about us?"

Cole quirked his eyebrow. "No, but it's not like I've had a chance. She was in bed when we got home last night. Why?"

I didn't mean for my sigh of relief to be quite so audible. "I don't think we should."

Dropping his hold on me, he furrowed his brow. "Why?"

Picking up his hand, I squeezed it. "Because—I mean, why would we? We both know I'm leaving in a few weeks."

"And once you're gone—you're gone?" He shook his head, his shrug exaggerated. "Forever? That doesn't seem extreme to you?"

"Not forever—forever. But I can't go home and go back to the old me just because I don't have you or The Redwood, or California."

"You don't give yourself any credit." He ran his hands through his hair—Cole's tell sign.

"You didn't know me before."

Cole stared at me and I stared back, not knowing what else to say.

"Are you two coming?" Grace called up the stairway. "We're going to be late."

"Yeah, Mom, we're coming," Cole said, his eyes on me. He picked up my hand and refused to let go. We trotted down the stairs.

Grace stood at the bottom of the stairs, waiting for us. She saw us. She saw us in the kitchen that night—she's an intelligent woman. I'm sure she'd put things together. But I still didn't want to come out and say the words to her. Then it would be like leaving Cole and Grace. I couldn't handle that.

We worked for three hours straight. Grace scanned the refrigerator content with how well we'd stocked it.

Cole left for the apartment he spent so little time at and I went upstairs to lay down. A long Sunday nap called out to me. I slept, I read—I waited for Cole to come back. What would I wait for once back home? I didn't want to think about that. I wanted to be strong—to be me—the me with a life. The tap on my door had me on my feet. Our morning had been awkward, but not terrible, I needed to see Cole again—to talk to him.

But it wasn't Cole. "Grace." I held the door open.

"Hi, Sam," she said, her smile sweet. "I wanted to ask you a favor."

"Sure, anything." I couldn't think of anything I wouldn't do for Grace at this point.

Folding her hands together, she lay them in front of her. "Would you mind helping me with dinner?"

"Of course." That would be easy. "I would love to."

"Great." Her grin widened. "I'll see you downstairs in a half hour."

This would be good, just what I needed. Cooking helped me, it cleared my head, helped me think—my creative outlet. Just thirty minutes...

"Thanks again, Sam." Grace handed me an apron, the same apron Cole had given me. I could see it had been washed clean, but the chocolate stains remained.

Trying to sound casual, just conversational, I said, "Is Cole still *home*?" The word didn't sound right. Home—Cole belonged with The Redwood.

"No, he's here, he's sleeping."

Passing me her plan and recipes, I scanned over dinner for the night. None of it was complicated. I didn't know why Grace had asked for my help, but I needed the distraction.

"Samantha," Grace said, staying busy. "I wanted to tell you

185

something."

"Yes?" I paused my chopping and waited for her to continue.

"I'm so thankful you've come here." She pushed down on her bread dough, not stopping her kneading motion.

Smiling, I went back to work. "I am too."

"I've appreciated your help." Her breath labored with her work.

"It's not a big deal, I enjoy helping in the kitchen." Sighing, I looked around the room. "Besides, I feel like I'm the one who owes you. I know you gave Eve a killer deal to allow me to stay this long."

Pinching off perfectly rounded balls of dough, she placed them in a pan. Setting the dozen rolls to the side, she brushed off her floury hands. "I do appreciate your help in the kitchen. But Samantha, I'm trying to thank you for your help with Cole. I haven't seen him this happy in a very long time."

Surprised, I choked on nothing. Turning my head to the side, I coughed in my elbow and then bolted to the sink to wash my hands. "I'm not—I mean—no, that's not because of *me*. His job. Other stuff—yeah, stuff."

Walking to the sink, she put her doughy hands on each of my shoulders, turning me to face her. "No, my dear, it's because of you." Tears welled in my eyes at her words and at her own streaked face. Wrapping her arms around me, she hugged me close.

"Grace, please, it can't be *me*." I couldn't be responsible for two broken hearts when I left here. I would be nursing my own — as well as proving I could be home and be the real me—the right me.

"Honey, it's you." She smiled as if she told me the best news ever—Grace knew I had an exit date too. How could everyone but me forget that small fact?

Pulling back, I wiped at my eyes, spilling my guts as if she were my mother—my confidant, instead of Cole's. "But Grace, I leave soon. My dad and my job and—" I hiccupped and covered my mouth—stifling my cry. *And me*, I'd wanted to say. I need to be home and be me.

"Sam, he knows you're leaving soon. We both do, honey. But

you're here now and he's happy. Aren't you?"

I nodded, not trusting my words to come out whole and without sobs.

"There you go," she said, holding my face in her hands. "Take advantage of the time you have."

"How did you know?" So, she didn't have blinders. No, Grace had good intuition. "How did you know I was struggling with this?"

Smiling an apologetic smile, she pulled me in for another hug. "I didn't." She brushed her hand over my hair—like a mother would. "I just wanted to thank you."

With both of us cooking, the room filled with savory aroma in no time. Grace began to plate a couple of dishes. I stood beside her, helping. "Here," she said, handing me a tray with both plates, though we still had fifteen minutes before the guests would arrive to eat. "For you and Cole," she said. "I can take it from here."

With my hands full, Grace walked me to the door of her home quarters. "Thank you, Grace." I closed the door and then walked into Grace's personal miniscule kitchen, where I set the tray onto her table for two.

The quiet place had a feel all its own—separate from the massive beauty of The Redwood, smaller, simpler, but content. No sign of Cole yet, I opened one kitchen drawer, I didn't find any silverware, but I did find a few lace tablecloths. Taking one out, I shook it open. Moving the tray to the counter, I positioned the cloth onto the table. Digging into another drawer, I found the forks I'd been searching for. Above Grace's sink was a ledge with knick knacks and a small vase with three little white daisies. I set the small table with the flowers in the middle and a plate on each end.

Feeling like an intruder, I kept my feet quiet, walking into Grace's living room. Cole lay asleep on the couch, his arms folded over his chest. He had changed into sweats and a T-shirt. He looked so peaceful. Biting my lip, I watched him, his even breaths up and down. I shouldn't wake him. It had been a long Sunday—a long work-filled, awkward Sunday. Would I ever get anything right? I didn't have the heart to wake him. Sighing, I turned away, I would eat alone, I supposed...

"Wait." Cole cleared his groggy throat. "Don't go."

Turning back to him, my hands flared about. "I didn't mean to wake you," I said, trying not to feel uncomfortable. But I had asked him to keep something from Grace, and my guilt wouldn't allow me any peace.

Still, he gave me a small, kind grin. My hands knotted together in front of me, I walked over to him, sitting on the edge of the couch beside him.

Sitting up, he met me at eye level. "It's all right. Is Mom with you?"

"No, she's serving dinner." I looked down at my hands still folded tight in my lap.

"I thought I heard her in the kitchen."

"That was me," Peering at him, I forced a smile. "I brought you dinner."

"Yeah?" A natural smile crept to his lips and his eyes roved over my face.

What had Grace said? *No time to waste.* Standing, I held my hand out to him. "Come on, before it gets cold." His hand warmed mine and the warmth spread throughout my body.

"Smells great." Cole gestured to the table. "Did you cook?"

"I chopped." I bounced my eyebrows once. "Your mom cooked."

"Well, thanks for chopping." Leaning over, he pecked my cheek. And the rightness of it seemed insane to me. Here we sat at a little table, sharing a meal, just the two of us. No fancy kitchen, no Sausalito—just me, just Cole, and a table for two.

Grabbing a fistful of his T-shirt, I stare at the logo on the front, not letting him pull back too far. "I'm sorry about earlier today."

His face hovered, close to mine. "It's okay." His eyes darted from my eyes to my mouth and back again.

I pulled the handful of T-shirt closer to me. "Thank you." I whispered the words, my mouth inches from his. Closing the gap, I kissed him like I'd been waiting to my whole life.

Letting go of his shirt, I stood straight, smoothing his front with my hand. Biting my lip, I flopped back in my seat.

"You…" He nodded, sitting opposite of me. "You apologize really well."

Laughing, I covered my face. Dragging my hands down, I saw him grinning at me. I shook my head and he laughed at me. "It was ridiculous of me to ask you to keep something from Grace." I picked up my fork, stirring my vegetables and pasta together. "Besides, she isn't blind—she knows. It's just I'm leaving, you know? And leaving you and her, I just—"

"Are you sure you have to leave?" He hadn't touched his food yet.

Tilting my head, I stared at him—wondering myself for a moment if I did…. "Cole, you know I do." Of course I had to go home.

"I know." Cutting into his meat, he took a bite of the steak Grace had grilled.

"Grace says we need to just enjoy the time we have." I peeked at him from under my lashes. "It's not like we won't ever see each other again." Reaching across the table he took my hand, tangling my fingers with his. My throat constricted and I suddenly didn't want to talk about this anymore. "When are you going to talk to Grace?" Changing the subject, I blinked back my tears.

His thumb brushed over my knuckles. "Tomorrow night."

"Are you sure? Tomorrow she's going out."

"She is?" He set down his fork.

I took a drink of my water and nodded. "Yeah, I told her I'd cook. She's going out with her friend again."

"Oh, okay. Do you want help?"

"Uh-yes. I sort of volunteered both of us." My stomach filled with butterflies. "So, talk to her tonight."

"Tonight? I don't know."

"Just do it," I said, feeling like my niece when she didn't get her three-year-old-way. My heals pumped up and down beneath the table, running a marathon. This would work. It had to. We'd put too much effort into for it not to work. It would make Cole happy. When I left, he'd still have this.

"Maybe." Scooting his chair along the tiled floor, he stood up.

"You have a cute impatient face."

I did not have a cute impatient face, and it wasn't cute—he only avoided the subject.

Turning on Grace's old AM portable radio, Cole twisted the dial knob until a slow jazz instrumental strummed through the air. "I think," he said, walking around to me, "we should dance."

"Dance?" I glanced around the small kitchen. The space didn't exactly allow for dancing. "There's no room." I laughed, my heartbeat running a race.

"There is." Taking my hand, he pulled me to my feet. Placing a hand at the small of my back and holding the other, he held me tight. We swayed to the music. "In fact," he said in my ear. "This might be the perfect place for dancing."

"Oh?" The warmth of his breath made my skin tingle.

"See, the smaller the space, the closer I get to hold you."

My skin pricked with goose bumps. Holding his cheek close to mine, the bristles on his chin rubbed against me. I closed my eyes, wishing I could stay there in that kitchen for the rest of my life.

# Chapter 23

"Ready to talk to Mom?" Cole handed me the last of the clean dishes in Grace's tiny kitchen.

"Whoa." I stepped back, my eyes wide on him. "Why do I need to be there when you talk to Grace?"

"I thought you'd want to be there, mastermind." His eyebrows bounced up and down.

Nowhere near the *mastermind* behind this project, I shook my head. He had the ideas. I just argued to get him to act. "I—I... I don't think so." He may have been teasing me, but I couldn't be more serious. "This is a family affair. I'd be intruding."

"You won't be. Besides, you convinced me." Drying his hands on a dishrag, he picked up mine. "Use your persuasion powers on Mom."

This was a lot less nerve racking when I didn't feel like it was my business deal. I had no power—I had no ideas—I had nothing, but nerves and blunt honesty at all the wrong moments.

Walking into the Redwood kitchen, Grace plated up the last of the dessert. "I was just about to bring these to you two."

"Thanks." I took the plates from her. "We're cleaning up. Go rest."

"Are you sure?" She gazed around the messy Redwood kitchen. "I am tired."

"Go on," Cole said, guiding her to the door. "We've got it." Closing the door behind her, he raised his eyebrows, staring at me. "You're good."

"Ah—"

"Get her rested, in a good mood—good thinking."

I laughed. Stalling more than strategy had been my motivation—that and being a decent human being.

Running my rag over the last of the countertop, we finished cleaning up. "You ready?"

"Sit. Eat," he said, pushing the plate of cherry pie toward me.

Sitting next to him, I took a small bite. I would need to ask Grace for her pie crust recipe. "What do you think she'll say?"

"I don't know." He dug into his piece, lifting a bite twice as big as mine to his mouth.

How could he not. He belonged to her. Didn't he have some idea? Ahh—how could I be more nervous than Cole? It wasn't my life being turned upside down. Maybe that's why—someone else would be affected by my convictions. But this needed to happen—I knew it. "This is awful," I said, the nerves in my stomach acrobating. "Let's get this over with. Rip off the band aid."

"Are you sure? We could dance again?" Cole held a teasing hand out to me.

Standing, I grabbed his hand. "Later. Let's go."

"Sam." He stopped my movement, his behind still planted on the stool. Resting his hands on my hips, we peered eye level. "Thank you, for everything."

Shaking my head, my cheeks burned. He spoke as if she'd already agreed to our designs. He spoke as if I deserved credit for any of it. "It was all you. I was just here."

"We both know that isn't true," he said, his hands pinching at my sides. "So, say *you're welcome* and accept the praise."

Biting my lip, I studied the blue flecks in his eyes. "You're welcome." I bit my lip, trying to hold back my silly smile.

Pecking my mouth, Cole led me to Grace's living room, where she sat on the couch reading. "Hello you two," she said, her eyes roving over our hands tangled together.

Leaving me standing there, he went to the closet and pulled out his briefcase. "Mom, could we talk?"

"Sure." Grace set her book down. "What's up, honey?"

Cole and I sat on the couch opposite of her. Setting the briefcase atop Grace's coffee table, Cole opened it up. "Samantha and I have been working on something the past few weeks." Grace crossed her legs, listening. Her eyes switched from Cole to me and I warmed at her glance, feeling anxious at Cole mentioning my involvement. Cole didn't mind, but maybe Grace wouldn't appreciate some outsider telling her how to run her successful, long standing business better.

"I don't want to sit at a desk managing other people for this company I'm with. I never have."

Grace nodded as if this wasn't a shock to her.

"I want to be your partner, Mom." He leaned toward her with each word.

Sitting on the edge of my seat, I waited for Grace's reaction. She just sat though—listening while Cole explained himself. She read the paperwork he handed her—but she didn't speak. She studied. Her brows rose at the mention of another Redwood, but they returned to normal when she took more paperwork from him.

"Mom, I love this place. I know we can do this. Together."

Grace glanced at me at the word *together*. Why was I here again? I hadn't said one persuasive word since we arrived. And I wouldn't be here to help to them make it happen.

Standing, Grace stretched her legs. Bending down, she put a hand on Cole's cheek. "Let me keep these," she said, pointing to the papers spread across the table top. "Let me think tonight. Okay?"

Cole nodded. "Yeah, take your time." He took her hand in his.

"Let's talk, tomorrow—before you work. Eight?" Grace shuffled the papers on the table together and held them to her chest.

"Sure." He stood, kissing her cheek before she walked back to her bedroom.

Letting out a breath I hadn't realized I'd been holding, I held my chest. "I love your mom Cole, but I couldn't read her at all. Was she happy? Was she upset? I shouldn't have been here. This is private and I just sat there—staring."

Cole laughed. "Private? Sam, you've been involved since stage one."

"Puh—" I squeaked unable to dispute what he'd said.

"And I'm glad." He laced his fingers with mine.

Closing my eyes, I shook my head. "Still, you should meet with Grace alone tomorrow morning. She may not feel comfortable talking about this with me there."

He rolled his eyes. It looked so ridiculous on him I had to stifle a laugh. "You'll be there," he said, pulling my hand up to his lips. "If I have to drag you downstairs in that short furry robe you're so fond of—you'll be there."

"Can I help?" I asked Grace, walking into the kitchen Monday morning.

"It's done." She brushed her hands together.

"Grace." I laughed, nervous, but needing to say this before Cole came in. "I will leave you and Cole to speak alone. This is family—and business—and…" I laughed again, but it wasn't natural. "I don't really belong in either of those categories."

"Don't be silly, Samantha," she said, patting my hand. "Cole wants you here."

Walking in, clean shaven, briefcase in hand, Cole pecked his mother's cheek and then my own. "Good morning," he said and my nervous stomach did somersaults.

Sitting side by side on the bar stools, Grace stood at our front. It was like we'd been sent to the principal's office. Grace set a plate of muffins and strawberries in front of us. I took a muffin, picking at its crust.

"You two have been busy," she said, setting a pile of Cole's research onto the counter.

"Mom, I know this is different. I know it's new and a little scary. But I really believe we can make this work." He rubbed his hands together, not inhaling his food like normal. Maybe his stomach somersaulted like mine.

"It seems as though we can." She smiled, her head bouncing from Cole to me.

"That's it?" Cole said, standing. He held his hands out to her. "You're sure? You're serious?"

Grace laughed. "Yes, I am sure. I have faith in you, and I'm

194

not the only one," she said, beaming at me. Taking Cole's hand, her dainty fingers wrapped around his. "You will do what Daniel always wanted to."

"What did Maddie say?" I glanced at Cole while still working on dinner. The day had started out with a yes from Grace and ended with Cole's two-week notice and a bid to Maddie on the manor.

"She said she'd call as soon as she heard something." Throwing off his suit coat, he grabbed an apron.

"You look good." I stirred my concoction.

"Yeah, thanks," he said, bouncing his eyebrows.

"No." I giggled. "I mean, you look happy, really happy."

"I am." Picking up a knife, he started chopping the potatoes on the counter with precision.

"Quite the day." I peeked at him again. His face lit like a fresh light bulb, his eyes brighter than I'd ever seen before. "And those need to be sliced, not chopped." I handed him his written instructions.

Smiling, he took his list of to do's. "Are you sure you don't want to come be my chef at Redwood Manor?"

Laughing at his joke, I taunted back. "You couldn't afford me."

"I could," he said, his voice serious and his slicing paused.

I didn't respond and I tried not to smile—but the thought, well, it made me smile. My phone jingled inside my pocket, distracting us both—thank goodness. I brushed off my hands before picking it up to see the text.

> Liza: Hey sis. I haven't heard from you in a while.
> Me: Sorry! I've been busy. I'll text you later. Making
>    dinner with Cole.
> Liza: Amanda says you've been kissing Cole. Feeling
>    a bit like a silly love struck teenage girl,

I giggled as my thumbs went to work, writing her back.

> Me: Later!!

"Who are you texting?" Cole asked, smiling at my expression.

"Liza." I didn't look up from my smart screen.

"What's so funny?"

"Nothing, nothings funny. Liza isn't exactly funny. Well, she can be, but—" I mumbled on, unable to stop my cheeks from swelling with my upturned lips.

"What are you grinning about?" He leaned to peek at my phone.

I held it to my chest. "Oh, gosh. It's nothing, she just asked about you—and the way she said it was—"

"Your sister is asking about me?" He pulled at my wrist holding the phone screen securely to my abdomen. "You've been talking about me?"

"Stop!" I laughed, pulling away from him. "I've mentioned you once—twice maybe." I pushed against his chest until he stood in front of his station again. "Something like that." I bit my lip to keep from smiling—it didn't work. "Stop looking at me like that. It's not a big deal."

"Sure, okay." He didn't sound believable. Why should he believe me? I didn't believe myself.

*Chapter 24*

Taking care of the breakfast menu for Grace, I thought about Cole—again. I always thought about Cole. The busyness of the previous two weeks had to be Mother Nature's way of weaning me from him. I still had him... I hadn't left yet. But with Grace's approval on his plans, Cole's days and nights went into a whole new swing of workload. His offer on the manor had been accepted more than two weeks ago. The owners wanted a rushed closing—which Cole agreed to happily. Though, it meant I hadn't seen him much—with everything that needed done. The days exhausted him. He had what seemed to be an endless to-do list, and for part of that time he still had a job. In the end for me that meant no midnight or even evening rendezvous' with Cole. I couldn't be upset with him. I couldn't be that selfish. I knew his workload. I'd helped him get into it.

I stared into space, holding Grace's homemade loaf of bread in my hands. Sure, I missed him, all too much I missed him. An insane amount, I missed him. Yep, Mother Nature—fate— some cosmic power tried these last weeks to prepare me for my inevitable departure. In two week's time I wouldn't be seeing him at all. I would be home. I needed to be home.

Circling Grace's kitchen, I continued to try and convince myself. I *wanted* to go. I wanted to go home happy. I wanted Dad to see the difference in me, to be proud. I wanted Nana to realize I'd made the right choice in coming here. I wanted the approving looks from my sisters and the *it's about time* expression from Eve. But mostly I wanted to be *me* for me—still, and always after. If

197

I went home nursing a broken heart—I wasn't sure my spirit would be able to shine.

Taking the French Toast, I'd made for the only two guests staying for breakfast, I tried to smile. Annoyed at how difficult a simple smile proved to be. But I missed him. "Did you need anything else?"

I had confused all of Grace's visitors. None of them knew whether I worked at The Redwood or not.

Turning on the hot water in the sink, I filled the basin with suds and the room with noise. The space too quiet with Cole and Grace both at the bank. I washed the dishes and scrubbed the counters. Keeping my mind busy, I made dessert for the evening meal—a simple custard that could stay in the fridge until dinner. Then, I followed the same steps over again—clean up, dishes, wipe down. Maybe I should give the floors a good scrub—

"We've got a house!" Cole bounded into the room, a key dangling from his fist.

I set the bucket I'd pulled from the cleaning cabinet down just in time for Cole to pick me up. He spun me around in a bear hug.

Grace laughed, shaking her head at him.

Setting me down, he pecked my lips. "The lease on my apartment is up at the end of this month," he slapped his hands together, "so, I need to start packing." Another to-do on his endless list.

"You're moving?" I ran my hands through my hair and steadied myself on the bar, my head still spinning.

"Well, yeah, into the manor. We'll be paying a mortgage on it and I'll be working there every day. It only makes sense." He shrugged, his face still like a lighthouse beaming at me.

"Right," I said, feeling excited and envious all at once.

"I'm going over now. Want to come?" He asked, sounding giddy.

"Yeah, I'd love to." An afternoon with Cole and the manor—perfect! I turned to my bucket. "I was going to—"

"I've got it." Grace patted my shoulder and gave me a push toward the door.

"Mom, you're coming too, right?"

198

"Not now. You two go on over. I don't have to make dinner tonight. Why don't we eat there and then you two can show me your house?"

Coughing at the word "your" — like it belonged to both of us, I covered my mouth. How did Cole not even flinch?

"Sounds great," he said, grabbing my hand and pulling me from the kitchen.

Peeking my head back into kitchen, I wanted to say something. Remind Grace I'd be leaving. She knew! But I needed to say something. I needed to keep things in check. This house didn't belong to me. I hadn't been sitting around the past few weeks pouting and waiting for a man to come home — well, except for today. I was strong and changed and — and I *would* be going home. "Grace?"

"Yes, honey?" Her long hair swung with her turn to look at me. Her smile so soft and kind and —

"There's custard in the fridge — for dessert tonight. Sorry, I didn't know —"

"It's fine, Sam. Go. I know you're as anxious as Cole for this."

I pressed my lips together. Yep, strong, happy, changed, but anxious. I couldn't wait to get into the manor I felt so ridiculously connected to.

Walking out to the car, our entwined hands swung between us. Standing next to the passenger side door, Cole pulled me close. Wrapping his arms around me, he closed any gap between us. "I've missed you."

"I've missed you, too." Our trial run had weighed on him too.

"Now that we'll be in the house and I'm done with the desk job, I can make my own work schedule. Things are calming down and —"

"Cole, I'm going home in two weeks." I pulled back, looking at his face. Had he forgotten? "When you get on a schedule, when things calm down, I won't be here." I turned my stare to the ground, not wanting to meet his eyes.

"Right." He ran his hand down the length of my hair, resting it on my back. He opened my passenger door and I climbed inside.

The almost thirty-minute drive was filled with only music

from the radio.

Pulling up to the house, Cole sighed, his excitement gone. With his arms draped across the steering wheel, he looked up at his new investment, his new life.

"I didn't mean to ruin your celebration." I ran my hand down his arm. "My going home is just a fact. Can we still enjoy today?"

"Sure." He grinned, but it didn't convince me.

Stepping onto the porch where we'd shared lunch just a few weeks earlier, I thought about us then. So different from now — better and worse all at the same time.

Standing on the porch, I reached up on my tip toes. I could just touch the tip of the wooden lace trim, where it turned down into a peak. This place belonged to Cole — somehow that made it even more beautiful.

We walked through the entire house again, this time just us, this time without the facts and chatter of the realtor. No wondering, *is this it*? Now we knew. Cole would make this place amazing.

Coming back downstairs, we returned to the kitchen. Tugging on my hand, Cole stare at me. "So, do you still love it?"

I loved listening to Cole's ideas for each room, the things he would do, the changes he'd make. I hoped to come back and see it one day. Nodding, my voice caught in my throat. Clearing away the ache, I said, "More importantly, do you?"

Leaning against the kitchen counters, he crossed his arms over his chest, his gaze almost studying me. "I think I love it a little more every day."

Scooping my hair behind my ear, my throat swelled again. I couldn't explain why. I loved the manor too — I didn't know why that would make my throat and eyes act up.

"Hellooo." Grace called from the front door.

My throat and eye sockets seemed to relax with the distraction. Following her voice to the front of the house, we hurried over, taking the grocery bags filling her arms.

"Mom, you didn't make dinner, did you? No guests eating in — that means it's your night off."

"No. I brought groceries. You're going to be spending most of your time here. I don't want you starving yourself on chips and Pop-tarts."

"So, dinner, take out?" Cole set the grocery bags on the counter.

Keeping myself busy, I went through the bags, filling Cole's empty cupboards.

Grace clapped her hands at Cole's suggestion. "Yes, what about that little Chinese place your father loved?"

"Sounds great." Cole pulled out his phone, already looking up the number. "Is that okay with you, Sam?"

"Yeah, I'll order." I took his phone. "You show Grace the house."

"Okay." His smile reached every part of his face. This was what he must have looked like as a child on Christmas morning.

Grace took over finding a home for all the goods she'd brought. Leaving them, I started for the living room as the dialing on the phone stopped. "New Garden," the woman on the line said.

"Have you talked to her yet?" Grace's voice traveled over from behind me.

I turned back, my hand on the door, the woman on the phone still waiting for my response.

"No, Mom. Don't." Cole's tone hushed her. He glanced over at me and I jumped, facing the door once more.

"She should know, before she leaves," Grace said.

In slow motion, I walked through the doorway and into the living room.

"Hello? You want to order?" The voice in the phone startled me. My guilty eavesdropping conscience had me running to the living room window—far away from where Grace and Cole shared a private conversation. Private, but about me.

Staring out the large front window, I placed our order. Beef and broccoli, sesame shrimp, and lemon chicken with egg rolls and ham fried rice would arrive at the manor in half an hour. Ending the call, I stared at the front of Cole's phone screen—a picture of the two of us on our last trip to Oakland. I roved over Cole's face, but I had it memorized by now—the curve of his nose, the blue flecks in his eyes, his full lips, the way the dark whiskers from his chin contrasted his light hair. His face I knew. But mine—that stuck out to me. I didn't remember my smile looking like that. I'd never thought of it as pretty before—and my eyes… It had to be Amanda's mascara, but they reminded me of Mom's. I'd always loved Mom's eyes. They seemed to speak their joy.

Shoving Cole's phone into my pocket, before my vain head grew too big to fit through the door, I headed upstairs.

"Samantha!" Cole yelled my name as I entered the room.

Startled, I scanned the room. What had I missed? "Yeah?"

Turning to face me, Grace's eyes roved over the spare room. "I can see why you fell in love with this place, Samantha. It'll be marvelous once Cole's done with it."

Flushing until the heat burned my cheeks, I pressed my lips together. Why Grace acknowledging my small part in this embarrassed me, I didn't know. "It will be."

Winking at me, Cole led Grace into the last bedroom. Standing next to the elongated window, alone in the room, I peered outside. The backyard would be beautiful one day. I pictured it, again, hoping one day I *would* see it.

Cole's hands on my shoulders made me jump inside. "Hey." He squeezed. "What are you doing?"

"I was just thinking." I kept my eyes outside. I couldn't look at him, but I needed to say it aloud—maybe then it would happen. "I hope I get to come back and see you running this place one day."

"You're kidding, right? You better be back—soon." Letting go of my shoulders he moved beside me, looking out the window too. "So," he picked up my hand and laced his fingers with mine, "can I take you out tomorrow night, on a date?"

"A real date, huh?" Squeezing his fingers, I licked my lips.

"Yeah." His hair fell into his eyes. "You can dress up and I won't shave. I'll take you some place you've never been, and spend way too much money. What do you think?"

I laughed. It sounded perfect. "Hmm…aren't you trying to save money? I mean you have a few—"

"You're the one who reminded me you're leaving soon. So,

let me worry about saving money. I want to take my girl out."

"Okay." I bit my lip through a grin.

*Cole's girl.* I liked the sound of that. And it's who I wanted to be—at least for two more weeks.

# Chapter 25

Standing in front of the mirror, I spun around for the third time. My new dress flared at the bottom like a bell. Laughing, I smoothed the skirt. My dark hair and eyes stood out against the pale yellow of the dress. I was being vain again, but it didn't feel vain, just happy. I spun once more, knowing this probably wasn't appropriate behavior for an almost thirty-year-old, but here I stood, almost thirty and spinning.

Stopping with a tap on my rose door, I hurried over. Cole stood there in a black dress shirt and khaki's—unshaven, as promised.

"You look wonderful." He scanned over my dress. "Is it new?"

I twirled for the "bell" effect. "It is."

"I like it," he said, watching me.

"Let me get my—"

Grabbing my wrist, he stopped me, and pulled                    me into the hall. "One minute." Holding my face in his hands, he leaned his head to mine, but stopped before our lips met. "You're beautiful." He inched forward kissing my lips.

Had anyone ever told me that? Besides Dad, I mean. Holding onto his waist, my insides fluttered. "Aren't you supposed to wait until the end of the date to kiss me?" I whispered.

"Am I?" His lips brushed mine again and again.

I tried to nod, but I stood frozen—afraid of moving away from him.

"Ahem."

Up-righting at the noise of someone else in hall, I ducked back into my room, not wanting to see which guest had caught us. "Let me grab my bag!"

*I* couldn't help but think of the irony as Cole pulled into an Italian bistro downtown. The old, beautiful, brick building could have come from Venice itself. Had I really attempted a trip to Italy? I couldn't imagine it being any better than California. Italy didn't have The Redwood—Italy didn't have Cole.

Following the hostess to a table for two, we sat down. Scanning over our menu, Cole tapped his thumbs on the edge of the embossed booklet. The table wiggled with the shake of his knee. Where had his sudden nerves come from? It wasn't exactly our first date.

Reaching across the table, I took his hand and his body settled.

The server left with our orders and Cole exhaled a sigh of relief.

"What's with you?" A small laugh escaped my lips. I couldn't help it—he acted funny.

"I've been waiting." He looked in the direction the waiter had gone. "I don't want to be interrupted."

"Ah, okay." Laughing again, I shook my head, not knowing what he babbled about. "Cole, are you sweating?"

With the back of his hand he rubbed perspiration from his forehead. "No." He brought his arm down quick, his hand hiding under the table. "I'm thinking. You aren't making it easy."

Biting my lip, I tried not to laugh again. "Sorry. I'll be quiet."

"That would be great." His hands shot up from under the table, jostling our water glasses. "Sorry. I just need a minute."

Nodding, I kept quiet. So odd. Funny, but odd.

He took a deep breath and I almost started giggling again. He wasn't this nervous when he interviewed for a job or when he talked to Grace about the business. Reaching over, he took both my hands in his. "Sam," he said through a staggered breath. "You are wonderful."

Taken by surprise, I blinked back my tears and squeezed his hand, staying quiet without trouble now.

"You're beautiful, and intelligent, so kind...You make me crazy and happy—usually at the same time. I want to be with you, and when I'm not, I'm thinking about the next time I will be with you."

This wasn't what I expected. He held tight to my hands, and I couldn't brush away the few tears spilling over. Grateful for the dimness of the restaurant, I blinked, letting them fall. My throat tightened with emotion.

"Samantha, I know you're leaving. And I know I can't stop you. But I need to tell you—"

The obnoxious singing of a ring tone I hadn't heard in weeks filled the air, disrupting the entire bistro.

"Ahh—" I moaned, toppling Cole's water over to reach for my purse. I rifled through until I found the stupid thing, ignoring the call to quiet the device.

Cole sopped up the water with his linen napkin.

Staring at the number that had called and gone to voicemail, I met Cole's eyes. "It was Liza."

"I thought you were only texting."

"Yeah, we are." Standing, I flung my purse over my shoulder. I walked for the exit, my phone singing again before I'd left the building. Cole followed behind me. "Liza," I said, my heart fluttering at the thought of hearing my sister's voice.

"Sam, thank goodness."

"Liza, what's—what is it—I'll be home in two weeks—" I stumbled over my words through a nervous laugh, afraid of why she would have called me.

"I know, honey," she said, sounding too much like a big sister. "It's Nana. She's had a heart attack."

"No, no, no..." I said, my no's trailing off. I paced and listened to the details Liza gave me. No, this couldn't be happening. Not my Nana.

"Sam," she said, crying into the phone. "I'm sorry, but the doctors say the damage is excessive. They're keeping her comfortable, but—"

"No!" A sob heaved from my chest. I stopped my pace and Cole's hand rested on my back, his face contorted with worry.

"She's been asking for you, Sam."

I had nothing else to say. I told my sister I would see her the next day and hung up the phone. Dropping my cell to the ground, I buried my face in Cole's chest and cried. He wrapped his arms around me and we stood there—who knows how long.

My Nana, my grandmother, the woman I looked to almost as

my mother... *Oh Mom*, it felt like losing her all over again. It had been more than ten years, but once that heartache surfaced, so fresh, so raw, it was like we had just barely lost her, all over again.

Back at The Redwood my body went into speed mode. Pulling my bags from under the bed, I flung them open and in no order, threw things inside.

Cole left to talk with Grace. He hadn't been gone long when my door opened. He carried a platter with two dishes. Setting it down on my tall dresser, he came to me. "You need to eat something."

"I need to pack." I gathered my belongings, annoyed at the moment that my Redwood room appeared as if I'd lived there for years.

"I will help you—as soon as you've eaten. You're going to make yourself sick. That won't help her." His fingers like a feather, swept at my neck. He was worried.

But I was angry.

"I can't help her!" I yelled at him, throwing another shirt into my luggage. My anger hadn't exploded because of Cole. Why would it—because he's wonderful? No, it all came back to me, he just happened to be there. "I've been off selfishly playing the last few months of her life. I haven't done anything but leave and disappoint her."

"Sam." He attempted to wrap an arm around me but I pushed it away. "That isn't true."

"How would you know?" I held my hand out against his chest, distancing him from me. I stared at him, like maybe he could be to blame. "You don't know her. You barely know me."

The words tasted bitter on my tongue, so mean—and untruthful—and awful.

Still, he didn't look angry. His brow wrinkled with worry. I could insult him all day long and he would stay with me. I didn't deserve him. But I wanted him.

"I'm sorry." I held my face in my hands—his silent forgiveness knocking some sense into me.

Taking a hand from my face, he held it in his, guiding me to the bed. Caressing my cheek, he leaned over, pressing his mouth to my head. "Eat and I will help."

My eyes pooled with tears at his kindness—at my relief to have him there. In my vulnerable state, I wanted to tell him that I needed him, that I loved him, but I didn't know what those words would do. They scared me. They weren't the words of someone about to abandon him. Sitting there on my bed, his much too kind arms around me, I realized how dumb I'd been. That's what he'd been trying to tell me at the restaurant—he loved me.

Cole loved me.

Man, how that sweetness complicated things.

I needed to get home. Now.

"Thank you." I took a bite of the food he'd brought, Grace's skills wasted on my panicked pallet. It could have been cardboard—I tasted nothing but guilt and urgency. Setting the fork down, I licked my lips. "I have to pack, Cole. I have to go."

"Whoa—you can't leave tonight."

"Yes, I—"

"Sam, it's almost nine o'clock at night. You aren't even packed—no, no. You aren't going. Not tonight."

"Cole—"

"No, you can sleep and then leave at dawn, but you aren't going now." Handing me my fork and plate, he stood, and started tossing my things into my suitcases.

Too tired to fight, I picked at the food he gave me. Cole's mind thought straight at least. My body and mind had become a jumble of exhaustions—physical, mental, emotional—driving now wouldn't be a good idea, but sleep seemed impossible.

With my things packed, Cole took them, bag by bag, down to the car. I sat in my rose room, empty of me, except for clothes for tomorrow's journey and a few toiletries. Searching around my room, my eyes filled with tears. I loved this room. It had been a haven for me for the last two and a half months. *Home.*

"Everything's in the car." Cole stood in the doorway. "Ah… well, almost everything…" He motioned toward me.

I still wore my new dress. "Oh… yeah." Shaking my head, tears spilled over again. Wiping them away, I couldn't look at him. "I'll go change." Picking up my sweats, I headed into the bathroom.

Changing, I washed my face and brushed my teeth, taking my

time. This wasn't how things were suppose to end here. *This isn't how Nana's supposed to go — without me there.* Fully dressed, I got into my tub, laying my head against the porcelain. It had been hell for Nana watching her daughter suffer and die. And now, she had so many concerns — her hopes and dreams and worries for me. Things she would never see reconciled, things she would never see happen — just more that I wouldn't be able to give her. My brain ran a marathon while I sat in the empty tub, my tears spilling over. I wiped them away, hoping and praying I'd make it home in time to see her.

I'm not sure when my mind's course changed directions, but somewhere along the way, I took a detour. I found myself hoping and praying for *Cole*, for his success and happiness, for all the goodness he deserved.

A rap on the bathroom door jolted me upright, waking me from my conscious dreams.

"Sam? Are you okay? You've been in there a while."

"Yeah, I'm okay." I cleared my throat, trying to make my voice stronger. "I'm coming." But I didn't move.

"Sam?"

My legs wouldn't move. Closing my eyes, I called to him. "Come in."

"Ah —"

"It's okay. Come in."

Peeking into the bathroom, he walked in — slow, wary. "You're in your tub…"

"Yeah." I forced a smile to reassure him I wasn't crazy.

Smirking, he gave me a small smile. "You'll miss it, won't you?"

"I will." It wasn't the only thing I'd be missing. Cole leaned against bathroom vanity, talking to me — probably waiting for me to crack at any moment. Yet somehow, somewhere inside of me came peace. I was miserable — utterly and totally miserable, but someone cared enough to sit in a bathroom and talk to me all night long about it.

# *Chapter 26*

Still dark outside, I dressed in my driving clothes. I hadn't
decided if I'd wake Cole or not—despite him making me
promise to. I half expected to find him asleep outside my
door. He'd offered to sleep in my chair, but I wouldn't let him.
Hitting my speed dial, I called my sister. "Amanda, did I wake
you?"

"Sam, oh, Sammy." Amanda's sobs blubbered through the
receiver. "I've missed you so much."

"How are you?" I asked—I was the big sister now.

"Okay. Tired. Yesterday lasted forever, I stayed at the hospital
until they kicked me out."

"How is she?" I bit down my thumbnail, stripping away at
the short nail.

"She misses you. She's been trying to set Eve up on dates
these last two months."

Laughter came out through my tears. "How's that worked
out for her?"

"Not so well. Eve isn't nearly as willing as you were."

"She's much smarter than I am." I laughed again, but had to
wipe the tears off my cheeks. "I need to go," I said. "I just wanted
to let someone know I'd be leaving soon." Sighing, I glanced over
my room. "I'll see you in around fifteen hours."

Heading downstairs, I'd decided to wake Cole. I had to. I
couldn't leave without a *goodbye*. He'd hate me. I'd hate myself.
Breathing in through my nose, I summoned courage. But just the
word goodbye made me cower.

A light beneath the swinging kitchen door shone bright in the dark parlor. Opening the door, I saw Grace, packing a box full of food.

"Good morning, dear." Setting down the Tupperware in her hands, she walked over to me. Wrapping her arms around me, she hugged me tight. "I'm so sorry."

"Thank you," I said, holding on to her. "Grace, why are you up?"

"I'm packing up your breakfast, lunch, and dinner." Her tone sounded like a normal, everyday occurrence.

"Grace." I smiled, my throat aching. *Two* goodbyes. "You didn't have to do that." She'd already done so much for me. She turned the switch to my tears back on. And I'd been trying so hard to be strong.

"I wanted to." Patting my shoulder, she went back to work, filling the cardboard box with mystery containers.

Holding up a hand, I stopped her. "Whoa, really, that's too much food for just me."

"It's not just for you," Cole said, behind me.

"What are you doing?" I turned to face him.

He'd showered… I hadn't bothered to shower. He'd dressed, shaved, and held a pack on his back. "I'm going with you."

"No you're not." And I meant it. *What was he thinking?* He didn't—he couldn't—

Clearing her throat, Grace set the last of the food containers into the box. "I'm going to my room. Let me know when you take off." Closing the box, she left us.

"I'm not letting you drive almost fifteen hours tired, miserable, and alone." Opening the box, he squeezed in a package of cookies.

Blinking, I stared at him—unsure what to say.

"You're not the only one who can be stubborn, Samantha Blake."

"Cole, you can't—" My voice cracked, betraying me. He had too much to do here—so much he'd been working for. He couldn't abandon that for me.

"I can." He picked up the box of food.

"How will you get home?"

"I'll fly."

"What about the manor? You can't just leave it... I mean... Cole..."

With the food box in one hand, he opened the door to Grace's place with the other. "Mom!" he called to her. "We're heading out."

Without further arguments, we both hugged Grace goodbye and climbed into my car—Cole behind the wheel. I had never seen the streets of San Francisco this quiet. Four in the morning must have been quiet time.

"Will you pass me a Pop-Tart?" Cole glanced at me.

Reaching into the back seat, I opened the box Grace had packed. Chuckling, I said, "You really thought your mom would pack Pop-Tarts? What time did she get up anyway?"

"I don't know, before me. Why, what's in there?"

"It looks like crumb cake." Covered in aluminum and still warm, I took a slice from the box and handed it to Cole.

Hours passed—though the sun hadn't been up long when my phone rang. Cole still sat in the driver's seat. Free to be distracted, I answered the call. "Hi, Dad." I smiled at the sound of his voice. I'd never been away from him this long, not in my almost twenty-nine years.

"Hello, sweetie. I've missed you."

My eyes swelled again at his endearment and the love and concern there. He continued on and I swallowed, trying not to be too emotional. "I miss you, too."

"Are you on the road yet?"

"Yes, we left a few of hours ago," I said, looking at the clock. "We should be there around seven."

"We?"

"Oh?" I glanced at Cole, who glanced back. "Ah, yes, *we*. Did Amanda happen tell you about my friend, Cole?" Looking at Cole again, he smiled.

Staring out at the greenery and weeds hurrying by my window, I finished my conversation with Dad.

"Well, that was interesting." Cole's crooked grin pursed, trying not to laugh.

Rolling my eyes, I turned the volume on the radio up.

Driving until noon, we stopped to stretch, eat, and walk around for a minute. I dug out Grace's gourmet lunch, and we sat on the grass outside a rest area somewhere in Nevada to eat.

"So, you never said, did Amanda tell your dad about me?"

Choking on the strawberry I'd just stuck into my mouth, I tried to gain my composure. "Nope, I didn't say — you eavesdropper."

"You were sitting two inches from me," he said, his eyes wide and innocent. "It's kind of hard not to."

"I know." I covered my face with my hands. "It's just embarrassing."

"Why?"

"My dad asking about you — and you sitting there listening — ugh."

"So," he smiled, "what did Amanda tell him?"

Resting my forearms on the grass, I leaned back, my head tilting up to the sky. I squinted in the sunshine. "Honestly, I don't know. He never said." How would Amanda know what to tell Dad? I didn't even know.

Finishing our meal, we stood, stretching our legs for a few minutes. Cole put his arm around me, and we walked back to the car. "How are you?"

I didn't know how to answer that question though. Cole's arm rested around me, he stood there with me — so I could answer that question with an honest good. Nana lay ill in a hospital bed — so *awful* could be just as accurate. He'd be leaving in just days, so — *miserable*. I leaned into his hold. "I'm ready to drive — that's how I am."

My fifteen hours home was much more entertaining with Cole there. My drive to California had seemed twice as long — even with my urgency to get home. We stopped once more before climbing back into the car for our last leg. With Cole behind the wheel, we pulled into Dad's driveway, and nervous energy filled my body. In minutes Cole would meet my family. That fact hadn't really occurred to me. I rushed home for Nana. But with Cole by my side —I'd be making introductions I hadn't even thought to panic over.

Sitting in the car, Cole turned off the ignition. "You okay?"

"Yes." I said, hit with another dose of the honesty disease, "you're going to meet my family." I peeked over at him. "Are you nervous?"

"No. Should I be? Does your dad greet strange men with a shotgun?" He smirked at his joke.

"No, but if Nana were healthy, she might. She'd lock you in the basement until you agreed to stay." I laughed, but the sound came out sad. Sighing, I shook my head. "Don't be nervous. There's nothing to feel nervous about." It wasn't as if he'd *come* to meet my family, but that didn't diminish the fact that he would — and soon. With all that happened to Nana, I tremored inside, completely unprepared for it.

"Were you nervous when you met my mom?" He teased.

"No!" I smacked his arm. "But I didn't even know you. I fell in love with Grace long before I — I mean before you — before we — " I groaned. "Let's go."

Smiling at me, he opened the car door.

Standing in front of my parent's two-story home, I hadn't realized just how much I'd missed it. I missed our Sunday dinners. I missed Nana demanding my age as I walked through the door. I missed my sisters, my nieces and nephews. My dad.

Blowing out a nervous puff of air, I pushed through the front door. This would be interesting.

Cole followed after me, his backpack in his hand.

"Sam!" Amanda squealed, rushing toward us. Wrapping me in a hug, her head tilted up — at Cole. Amanda giggled and pulled away to gawk at me. "Sam, you didn't mention you were bringing someone home."

"Dad didn't tell you? This is Cole. Cole this is my baby sister, Amanda."

Amanda giggled again, as if I introduced my ten-year-old sister, instead of my twenty-six year old sister. She held her hand out. "It's nice to meet you."

"You too."

Hugging and introducing my way through my sisters, nieces and nephews, and brothers-in-law, my jitters calmed. My family. And Cole my... my — something. And they should meet — right? The stupidity of wanting to keep Cole all to myself where only I could ache for him after all this ended, sunk in.

"Where's Dad?" I looked past the crowd for my father—his graying head should be at the end of this line somewhere.

"He's at the hospital." The circles under Liza's eyes told me she'd been there all day too. "Visiting hours end at eight. He should be home any minute."

"Oh no." My arms flapped at my sides. "I was hoping to see her tonight." We shouldn't have spent so much time at that rest area in Nevada. We wasted precious time. Time Nana didn't have.

Liza put her arm through mine, but I didn't miss her quick second glance at Cole. "I'm sure she's sleeping. She sleeps a lot."

But I still wanted to see her. Who knew how much time we had left?

With my brothers-in-law getting Cole's opinion on the San Francisco 49ers, I headed upstairs to see my baby niece. She'd been so tiny when I left for California. Sarah, still small, but so much bigger than when I left lay on Dad's bed. Sitting down, I tried not to jostle her. I rubbed her back and she squawked. As the aunt I didn't have to let her cry—or in this case—think about crying. Picking her up, I held her up to my chest and her breathing became heavy again. I stroked the silky blonde fuzz Liza called her hair. "What do you think, Sarah? Does heaven really need her just yet?"

"What does she think?" Cole stood in the doorway.

I shrugged. I wished she could tell me.

"Can I come in?"

"Yeah." I whispered, my mouth so close to sleeping Sarah.

Standing next to me in the dim room, he followed my hushed tone. "She's beautiful."

"She is." Grinning at him, I moved my hand under her bottom, adjusting her weight in my arms.

His eyes roved over my face. He'd never had a niece or a nephew, and loving my sister's children had been such a gift. With the back of his finger, Cole rubbed little Sarah's cheek. His lips broke into a grin with her purr at the affection. The room warmed with Sarah in my arms and Cole so close.

Down the stairs, we heard the front door open and my sisters chatter to Dad. *Dad!* "It's my dad," I said. "Here."

"Whoa, are you sure?" His brows knit together, panicked over an infant.

Smiling at his sweet insecurity, I placed Sarah in Cole's hands.

She squawked again, flipping her head to rest on the other side and then hummed herself back to sleep. She lay on his chest, his big hands covering her backside.

"We're good." Cole smiled down at her. "Go."

Nodding, I flew from the room. "Daddy!" I took the stairs two at a time.

"Oh, I'm glad to have you home." He hugged me close, whispering in my ear. Pulling away, his gaze ran up the stairway.

Cole walked down each stair with care, Sarah in his arms. My sisters' chatter came to a halt, and I wanted to smack them both. *Make noise!* Their silence only made the awkward moment more so.

Clearing my throat, I had no idea what to do with my hands—put them in the pockets—hold them together—at my back... "Ahh, Dad, this is my friend, Cole. Cole, this is my dad, Jack."

"Cole." Dad stared past me to Cole. "Thank you for bringing Samantha home."

Nodding, he seemed nervous, despite what he'd said earlier. "I was happy to help."

"I see you've met Sarah." Dad gestured to his granddaughter.

"Here," Liza said when Cole reached the landing. "I'll take her." Taking the baby, Liza shooed the rest of the crowd into the family room basement.

"How's Nana?" I asked Dad.

"About the same. I wanted to speak with her doctor, but he was never available." He sighed and the wear on his face aged him a decade.

"I'll go in the morning." I pinched my sides, where my hands had decided to land. "I can talk to him. Ask him whatever you need. You look so tired, Dad. Why don't you go to bed?"

"I think I will." He held onto the stair railing. Blowing out a puff of air, he patted my shoulder and started up the stairs.

My chest heavy, I sighed, trying to release some of the pressure.

"Are you alright?" Cole's worry wrinkles made waves across his forehead.

"Yeah." But I shook my head. "He's just so tired. He looks older than ever—and I haven't been gone *that* long. This is hard on him. He promised Mom he'd take care of her. But he isn't a miracle worker."

Rubbing my back, like he had Sarah's, Cole didn't say anything. I didn't need someone telling me what I already knew. I just needed a hand in mine—*his* hand in mine. "Come on." I ran my hand down his arm until I could tangle my fingers with his. "I'll show you to your room."

"Does it have a giant tub?" He winked.

"No." I led him back upstairs. "But it does have blue walls and a comfortable bed. There's a shower with a mediocre tub down the hallway. I'll sleep in here," I pointed to a closed door. "Right next to your room." Opening his door, I showed him inside.

"You don't want to sleep back at your place?"

I shook my head. "Nah." Not tonight anyway, not with him here, just a bedroom away.

Cole ran down to the car to grab one of my many bags—my toiletry bag. We'd bring the rest of my things over to my house in the morning. Changing the sheets on his bed, I waited for him to return. Back upstairs, he set my bag next to his backpack on the ground.

Staring at his pack, I bit my lip. Being strong wasn't going to be easy. "How long are you staying?"

"As long as you need me." He nodded, his eyes never wavering from mine.

Crossing my arms, I protected my chest—my stupid, heavy chest. "Well, that's a pretty small bag." I tried to laugh. "I know you need to get back to work. It's—"

"I'm here as long as you need..." He stressed each word. "Clothes wash."

Shaking my head, my eyes filled. I wrapped my arms around his waist. My emotions mixed together as if inside a blender, grateful and sad all at the same time.

Venturing to the basement, we faced my family again. Cole

played with my nephews and talked with my brothers-in-law. I sat with my sisters, visiting and trying not to be too obvious watching the "Cole Show." For an *hour* I wasn't single Samantha. I'd transformed this summer into Samantha and Cole. And I hated how much I loved that. How could I go back to real life? Me, happy and living—without him? How would they see that I'd done it, I'd put away my unhappiness, my ingratitude, all on my own?

Yawning, Amanda got up. She held to my hand, giving it a squeeze. "We need to get going. Max, will you get Jill's shoes on her? Sam, come help me pack up." She pulled me up and I followed her up the stairs and into the kitchen. But she didn't start packing Jillian's things. "Sam," she held onto my shoulders, pulling me in to face her, "he is wonderful."

"What?" I held Jill's baby spoon in the sink under the running water, my body twisted and uncomfortable in her hold.

Grabbing both my wrists, she stopped my work, forcing me to face her. "Cole."

I couldn't help the smile that came with his name. I pulled my arms from her grasp, returning to the sink. "Yes. He is great." The weight in my chest grew.

Sighing, Amanda slapped the countertop with her hand. "What are you doing?"

"I—" Stopping with footsteps on the stairs, we both turned to see Liza.

Amanda stomped over to our sister. Taking her by the hand she dragged her over to me. "Talk to her," she said to Liza.

Liza's brows rose in question.

I held up my hands, I didn't want to be lumped in with my crazy sister at the moment. "Don't ask me."

Amanda gasped, exasperated. "She needs to do something about Cole. Ask her Liza, ask her what she's doing."

Turning to me, Liza's eyebrows were still high on her head, this time waiting for my answer.

Rolling my eyes, I busied myself with more dirty dishes. "I don't know what you mean."

"She means, what are you waiting for?" Liza—my supposed-

221

to-be-the-logical sister asked. "You have a good guy downstairs who is crazy about you."

"Yep," Amanda said, popping her "p," and every time you look at him. Ugh, it's obvious."

"What's obvious? What am I supposed to do?" I cleared my throat, trying to keep my voice without tremors. "He has a life. A career. He has to go home. As do I. I'm better now — I'm not so... old Sam. I'm happy. And I — "

"Sam." Liza's hand on my back stopped my scrubbing. "We don't doubt you. We've seen the change in you — even without being around you. But — "

"But you can't let him get away!" Amanda jumped in the air, both of her feet coming down in a stomp. Instantly, I knew where Jill had learned to tantrum. "You need a plan. How will you see him again?"

I stared at them. Were they really asking these questions — now? "I can't think about that now. None of us can. I can worry about that later. Right now, Nana — "

Footsteps on the stairs interrupted me. I stopped, grateful for the intrusion. The rest of the family piled into the kitchen, ready to head for home.

Amanda hugged me on her way out the door. She pressed her mouth to ear. "Worry now!" She forced the whisper.

I must have hidden it well, because I hadn't stopped worrying — not since we crossed the Wyoming border.

# *Chapter 27*

*A* gleam of sunshine found its way in through the small hole in my curtains and right into my eyes. Blinking, I found the clock in Dad's spare room where I slept—almost seven o'clock—already. Dad had been so exhausted and Cole and I drove all those hours, I didn't want to wake them. Just because I couldn't sleep didn't mean they should have to wake up. I could make them a big breakfast—let them wake to the smell of sausage. Every man loves that, right? And maybe waking to sausage would make Dad and Cole's morning greeting a little less awkward than last nights.

Pulling on my robe, I started down the stairs, stopping on the last. I listened. Voices drifted in from my Dad's kitchen—two voices. Oh, no! I had more than one reason to stay at Dad's—monitoring being number one. I hadn't had a "boyfriend" in years. I didn't know how Dad would feel about it, and with the extra stress from Nana...

Stepping into the open entrance, like a spy trying not to be seen, I hovered in the doorway. Maybe they wouldn't see me and I could scope out the situation. But nothing frightening or horrible, or even awkward appeared to be brewing.

Dad sat at the table—a tired smile on his face.

Cole stood at the stove, flipping French toast in a skillet.

"It's early," I said, making them both turn to see me. "What are you two doing up?"

"Breakfast." Cole waved his spatula. "I was just telling Jack that he shares the name of my favorite café back in San Francisco."

"Then we both started craving French toast." Dad winked at me.

"I see." I rubbed my hands together. Dad and Cole getting along so well almost made me more nervous than the awkwardness.

"So, Cole, your parents run the Inn where Samantha stayed?"

And just like that they'd forgotten all about me again. Cole chattered on, telling Dad about The Redwood and Redwood Manor.

Listening to their conversation for a solid four minutes, I bit my lip. I didn't know how to explain it... maybe, fascinating, but... "Okay," I said, interrupting them. "I'm going to shower. I want to get to the hospital as soon as I can."

"Yeah, okay," Cole said. "I'm just going to finish these."

"Sure, okay." I repressed the urge to kiss him goodbye — father in the room and all.

Silly, but I chose to wear my hair down, give it a little style — it would please Nana. My face inches from the bathroom mirror, I applied my ritual mascara.

Cole peeked his head in through the open door. "Are you ready?"

"Yeah." I spun the lid back onto my tube of eye makeup. "You don't have to come. I mean, I understand hanging out at a hospital isn't much fun."

"I want to come." He tugged on my shirt sleeve. "Let's go."

Walking into Nana's hospital room terrified me. The bleach clean smell, the blank white walls, the dimness with the drawn curtains — it couldn't be real. And Nana — my strong-willed, independent, get-it-done grandmother lie in that room, in that bed, frail and breakable. Stopping, I wiped at my cheeks, the tears already falling. My throat choked up and I turned to face Cole. "I don't want to do this." My words muffled as I spoke into his chest. I *did* want to be home — but not like this. This isn't how she should see me after three months — this isn't how I should see her.

"She's missed you." He held my shoulders like I might make a run for it. "You're the one she wants to see."

224

I had always been stronger than this. But somehow his presence gave me permission to be weak.

"You can do it." He sounded so confident, I believed him.

Nodding, I held his hands. I had to do this—whether I walked into that room strong, weak, married or single. I had to. I didn't have the gift of time to avoid it any longer. "Don't leave," I said. "But here. . ." I pushed him against the hospital room wall. "Stay here."

"I'm not going anywhere." Leaning down, he brushed his lips to mine, his touch so soft I almost didn't feel it.

The machines and tubes at her bed left a small space to greet her. Her eyes stayed shut, and her chest moved up and down with steady breaths. I crossed my arms, not wanting to touch and wake her. And then my weakling tears came again. I couldn't stop them. I loved this woman, almost as I loved my own mother.

Nana's eyes fluttered. "Please don't cry, Samantha." Her strong my-way-or-the-highway voice cracked with strain.

Wiping at my cheeks, I rubbed them dry. "Oh, Nana, I'm sorry. I didn't mean to wake you."

"You didn't, dear." She licked her lips. "It would seem my body doesn't always want to obey anymore."

Taking her hand, I leaned down, looking into her beautiful face. "Nana, I'm so sorry. I was gone. You needed me and I wasn't here—"

"Oh hush. Don't be sorry." Her head bobbled trying to shake off my nonsense. "You couldn't have stopped it, my dear. And you're here now."

Giving her hand a gentle squeeze, I nodded. Not too late.

"Besides, you were right." She closed her eyes, cocking her right eyebrow. "That isn't something I say easily." That I knew, Nana was *always* right. "I am thankful my granddaughter is smart enough to listen to her heart, rather than everyone around her, even if that includes her Nana." She gave me her best glare, but it held little merit. Giving up on the reprimand, she asked, "Did you have a good trip?"

Choking on my tears, I laughed. Bending down, I kissed her cheek. "Yes, Nana, I did. I had a wonderful trip."

Her mouth creased into a small smile. "I'm glad." Switching her gaze from me to the back of the wall—where I knew Cole hid in the shadows, she said, "And who are you? Yes, you, the burly boy, smooching my granddaughter?"

My eyes widened, but Nana hadn't turned back to me.

Moving beside me, Cole smiled down at Nana. Putting his hands on my shoulders, he said, "I'm the man in love with you granddaughter."

Bolting around, I stare at him, my eyes wide, wide and warning. Did he really just say that—to my Nana? Not to me—ever, but to her?

Nana's blue eyes twinkled. Reaching out, she took Cole's hand. Her eyes darted to me, glistening and happy. "He's a hunk, Samantha," she said, sounding bubbly. "I guess you didn't need your Nana's help after all."

I spun back around to her. "Oh—well—ah—"

Laughing, Cole interrupted the jumbles of nothing bubbling from my lips.

"Well, then, when is the big day?" She studied Cole, waiting for an answer. "I've never cared for long engagements." And just like that my old strong-headed Nana returned, lecturing us—on an engagement that didn't exist.

Wrapping his arm around me, Cole peeked down at her over my shoulder. "I don't know yet," he said. "But hopefully sooner, then later."

# Chapter 28

My hands on his chest, I pushed him from the hospital room. "What are you doing?"

Peering down at me, like it should be obvious, Cole said, "I told the truth. I love you, Sam. When Nana asked, it only seemed right to tell her."

"She didn't ask if you loved me!" I slugged his shoulder. Was he crazy? "She asked who you were!"

Picking up my hands, his gaze didn't waver from my eyes. "That is who I am, to her that's all that matters."

Shaking my head, I ripped my hands from his and started pacing in front of him. "And you couldn't clue me in first? You thought mentioning it to my dying grandmother was the right way to go?"

"Samantha." Grabbing my arm, he brought my pace to a halt. "That's exactly why I told her. That's what she's been worried about all this time. I just—"

Squeezing his cheeks with my hand, his lips puckered and stopped their nonsense. I covered my face with my hands, reeling. That didn't just happen. He didn't just do that—to Nana of all people. My face burned with frustration.

"She's happy. I hoped you would be too. I tried to tell you— that night, at the restaurant, but Liza called." He reached out a hand to touch me, but thought better of it. "We've made her happy."

Jerking my head, I looked at him. "We've lied to her." Really, he'd lied to my her. "She thinks we're getting married." Crossing my arms into a tight fold I dropped my head, staring at our feet.

227

"Yeah, but I thought we—"

"You thought!" My head shot up at his words. Glaring at him, I didn't care if I lost control—or if everyone in the Valley heard me. "Were you even thinking at all?"

His face lost its confidence. My words pierced right where I needed them to. They cut him, bleeding. His eyes moist, he stared at me.

In my fury, I went on. "You lied to her." Losing my adrenaline rushed rage, my eyes welled with tears. "She's dying. And now I'm letting her go with lies."

He wiped a tear from my cheek, holding my face in his hands. "It doesn't have to be a lie."

Shoving away from him, I didn't care if people stared. "We are not engaged." Walking away, I kept talking, knowing he'd follow. "I told you I was coming home. I told you I needed to be here on my own—"

"You came to The Redwood to live, to find yourself, to start again." His long legs kept pace with me easily. "You did it. You think you're the only one who needed fixing? We fixed each other, Sam." Grabbing onto my hand, we stopped again.

My eyes blurred with tears.

"We should be together," Cole whispered.

Shaking my head, the tears fell. "I can't—I need to—"

"We should be together."

"I have to know," I whispered through my cry. "I have to stay."

"Then I'll stay."

Shaking my head, I started walking again. He couldn't stay. I couldn't be the reason every dream he'd ever had didn't come true. How was that proving myself. No. Turning to him, I held up my hands, stopping him. "Go."

"Sam—"

Making my voice strong—trying to make us both believe I meant it. I kept my eyes on his. "Go."

# Chapter 29

*P*ulling my hair back, I stare in my bathroom mirror.

He'd gone. He left.

Why wouldn't he? I yelled at him. I told him to go. I didn't deserve him. He'd committed the horrid crime of saying he *loved* me. Yep... What. A. Jerk.

I didn't bother to grab my mascara—I'd only cry it off anyway. Besides Nana was waiting.

Walking into her hospital room, she sat propped up against a pillow, eating red Jell-o. Setting it aside, she rubbed her hands together, her let's-get-going expression all over her face. "Where is he?" She moved her head from side to side, trying to see past me. "Where did your handsome friend go?" She had more color in her face today. She still sounded quiet and weak... but she looked more like herself. Maybe the doctors had it wrong. Maybe it wasn't "just a matter of time" — *this is my Nana after all.*

"He left."

"I'm not going to make it to your wedding, Samantha." She shook her head and shrugged her shoulders—not sad, just offering the facts.

"Nana, please..." I held her hands, my eyes welling up again.

"Well, I'm not," she said and though her voice wasn't strong like normal, it didn't sound weak either—again, just the facts. "Where did you say he went?"

"I—uh—I didn't. He left. I told him to leave. He went home." Clearing my throat, I adjusted in my seat. "Nana, the thing is... Cole and I... we... see we aren't engaged."

Crossing her arms across her tiny chest, she lay her head

back against the upright bed. Sighing, she said, "Do you love him?"

"Wha—"

"Do-you-love-him?"

Wringing my hands in my lap, I closed my eyes. *Sausalito, pansies, midnight talks, Redwood Manor.* Opening my eyes, I blew out a breath of air. "Yes. I do."

"Well, then." She waved her hand, brushing away the technicality. "It's only a matter of time, isn't it?"

I smiled at her logic—she'd always been brilliant. Too bad I would never be as smart as she thought I was. Did she not hear me when I said I sent him home? I sent the man packing—without even a goodbye.

"So, business," she said, her small voice a little louder than it had been before, "I want you to have my ring. Your grandfather gave it to me sixty-one years ago. Such a proud man—in the best way. He saved for months to buy it. He knelt on one knee and asked if he could love me all the days of his life." Grinning, she bounced her eyebrows. "He knew how to do it."

Laughing, I gripped my hands at my chest. "Nana, I can't take Grandpa's ring, his gift to you." Though the thought left me swooning.

"Samantha, I have several granddaughters. Many of whom are married. Do you know why I haven't offered this ring to anyone else?"

I shook my head. My sisters had married, a few of my cousins too… I didn't know why. It belonged on her finger, so I'd never thought about it.

"It's because I knew that one day, I would give this ring to you."

"Me?" I blinked back my tears. "Why?"

"Because you, my dear, remind me very much of myself."

I almost laughed out loud. Me, like Nana? "Nana, you are brilliant! And by my, age you had two kids."

"Oh, my dear, my children and my husband completed me, filled me, and made me exceptionally happy, but they did not define me." Reaching for my hand, I gave it to her—hoping after all this time she would tell me the secret of life. The one thing I'd been missing all these years. *Tell me Nana.* "I am still my own person. You work hard—with your hands and your body—hard mill-work. And you cook—your passion, your creativity. Samantha, you *are* brilliant. You are passionate and kind and funny. I knew from the time you were twelve years old that *you* would wear this ring one day." Letting out a small wheeze, she held her chest. "Why, dear, do you think I worked so hard to make sure you would? I hoped to give it to you myself, rather than through my will."

Her frail fingers fumbled at her chest. Right then, right there, she took the white gold diamond band from her left hand and laid it on my palm. She held my hand, the ring between us—quiet and worn out after her grand speech.

Sitting there, I thought about all she'd said, holding her hand until she fell asleep. Pinching the ring between my fingers, I stared at the tiny diamonds circling the band. I couldn't imagine any physical object meaning more to me than this tiny ring did. It had sat on my Nana's hand for more than sixty years. I knew right then, I wanted it on mine just as long. And I knew with whom I wanted to share those years.

$T$hree days later my Nana died.

The day after Nana's funeral, I knew what I had to do, for me, for her, for him.

Pounding on Eve's door all too early in the morning, I waited for my friend to answer.

"Sam," she said through a yawn, her blonde hair in disarray and still in her jammies. She moved aside, letting me in. "How are you?" She'd been there beside me as we buried my Nana. She would do anything for me—which was one reason I pummeled *her* door.

"Evie," I said getting down to business. "I'm in love with your cousin."

"Oh." She rubbed her eyes. It wasn't exactly what she'd expected. Cole hadn't been here long enough for her to even see him.

"I'm going back. But I need your help."

"Ah—okay."

"The shop, Mr. Bell said we could go in—I've used up all my savings—I—"

"Wait—the shop? What are we doing?"

Dragging Eve into the mill, I explained about Redwood Manor along the way—Cole's house in Oakland. The manor that we'd found and loved together—his plans, our plans, all of it, an edited version.

"So… you want to make the base boards for the manor?"

"Yes, but not just a base board. Molding that fits the manor—remember the wide butterfly board we made for the Marshall's?"

"Yeah…"

"I want to make that, only out of poplar."

Drumming her fingers against her cheek, I could see her thinking. "Hmm…" I'd piqued her interest. Eve liked her work. She'd worked hard to become good at it. Years together had made us a great a team. I would miss that. If Cole would take me, then I would miss it—happily.

Four long days later, we finished. We had a mound of poplar butterfly molding—that would create an amazing finish in Cole's Manor. I hadn't returned a call or replied to a text to my sisters or Dad, not in four days, too busy.

But now, I needed Dad.

"My truck?" Dad sat at his kitchen table.

"Yeah. I know it's a lot to ask, but—"

"Honey, if it's the truck you need, it's the truck you've got." Holding a hand to my face, he rubbed my cheek. "I'd do anything for you, my girl."

A small sob fell from my chest. "Thanks, Dad. You know if this works I'll be leaving. I can't ask him to leave behind Grace, the manor, all he's worked for."

"Sounds like you've put quite a bit of effort into that yourself."

Nodding, I stare at my hands, pink from wringing them together. "I have." Peeking at him from under my lashes, I said, "Dad, I kind of love it all."

Laughing, he stopped my clinging hands and held them in his own. "I would hope so."

Pressing my lips together, my throat constricted. I loved him. "I couldn't leave you — for anything — anything less."

"Sweetheart, you aren't leaving me. You're living. That's all I've ever wanted."

# Chapter 30

Driving through the night with a truck and a trailer bed of baseboards nearly doubled my drive time. I stopped as little as possible. Planning a speech out in my mind, I knew what I'd say to Cole, I practiced out loud the last leg of my drive, many... *many* times.

Pulling into The Redwood, it was dinner time. I could picture Grace bustling around, taking care of everything and everyone. And I could picture myself bustling next to her.

Walking into the house, like I had just a week and a half ago, I sauntered into the parlor. My joints were stiff and sore from sitting in the same spot for so long, but I didn't care.

"Sam?" Grace's voice echoed through the entry.

"Hi, Grace." I hadn't planned a speech for Grace... *Hi there, sorry I busted up your son's heart. Maybe you were wrong about me...* Yeah... that wasn't right, but no time to practice now.

Smiling, she walked to me, folding me into a hug. "What are you doing here?"

Maybe I didn't need a speech for Grace. She didn't run from me or look at me with disgust. "I came to see Cole. Where is he?" Our absence from one another left me feeling as if it had been forever since I'd seen him.

"Did you come here with that truck and a trailer?" Tilting her head, she stared out the open door behind me, her brows knit together.

"Oh, well, yes. I brought something..." Biting my lip, I took one of her hands. "Cole?"

"What time did you leave, dear? You couldn't have driven that load very fast."

"I left... twenty—um, twenty-something hours ago. I don't know. I couldn't sleep anyway," I said, still waiting for her to answer my question. "So, Cole..."

"He's working—at Redwood Manor."

Shaking my head, I blew out a sigh. Why didn't I go there first? Of course he would be there. Kissing her cheek, I started for the door. "Please don't call him." I needed to see his face—his unprepared face, when he saw me.

Nodding, she seemed to understand.

Thirty-five long minutes later, I pulled my load in front of the manor. He'd been busy. Part of the house still wore its original mucky brown, but most of it had been painted red, the cranberry red I'd pictured in my mind. The top of the house still needed painting, including the trim, but it brought my 2D, day dreamed image to life. For once, my head got it right.

Running my fingers through my tousled hair, I checked my mascara in the side view mirror. *Okay... this is it!* Taking a deep breath, I walked up the porch steps and knocked on the front door.

Tapping my foot, I waited but held very little patience within me—and no one approached the door. I knocked again, but walked to the end of the porch and scanned down the driveway, looking for Cole's car. There it sat. Maybe Grace had called him. Maybe he'd gone running for the hills when he heard I'd come back. Sanity hadn't been my forte the last time we talked.

Giving the door one last tap, I tried the knob, it unfastened. Loud rock music flooded the space when I opened up the barrier. The blaring music came from upstairs. No wonder he hadn't hear me. Walking in, like an intruder, I tiptoed into the living area and kitchen. The house appeared the same indoors, except for bits and pieces of Cole here and there, and a few tools strewn around.

Starting up the staircase the music grew louder. Shaking, I held to the banister and followed the sound into the first bedroom at the top of the stairs. And there he knelt, his back facing me. My heart pounded in my chest. I'd never been so afraid of rejection before. Because no blind date from my Nana could compare. No high school boyfriend could equal in importance. Not to *Cole*— he was mine. What if I'd offended and hurt him too much, too deep? What if he'd changed his mind?

I sucked in a breath and brushed my hair behind my ears, letting go of the thought. I didn't have an answer to finish it. Watching his back, he moved with the music, crouched and sanding the window ledge. Bending down, I paused his iPod and the stereo died to silence. The house went from noise splitting loud to the hum of the sander. My pounding heart could have produced more noise.

Switching off the sander, he turned to investigate his small stereo. I stood next to it. He followed my feet up to my face. He ran his hand through his hair, pulling off his plastic safety glasses in the process. A cloud of sawdust rained down with his movements. His face speckled in brown dust and the dry woodsy air gave me a sense of the mill. He whispered my name. "Sam?"

My breath came out staggered, and no words followed.

Standing, his shoulders slumped. He stared at me. "Sam, what are you doing here?"

"Was that Aerosmith?" I spouted the question out of nervousness. He gave no signs, no signals whether he welcomed my presence or not. Like the night we talked to Grace about the manor, about Cole's ideas, I couldn't tell then how she felt. Now Cole gave no indication at how this visit might end.

Furrowing his brows, he rubbed his whiskered chin. "Uh, yeah."

Forcing a laugh, my hands found my hips—not knowing where else to go. I tried to move, but my feet were nailed to the floor. "I thought so."

"Why are you here?" He rubbed his dusty hands onto his jeans, his eyes never leaving mine.

"Well," I said, my prepared speech completely forgotten. I had a plan, dang it, and all I could utter was *Aerosmith*? "I—I am here." Shrugging my shoulders, I tried to remember why I'd come… the perfect words that I'd rehearsed so many times

237

disappeared. "I have something for you." Yep, sure, that would do—I had something for him.

Un-nailing my feet, I backed out of the doorway, afraid he wouldn't follow after me. Down the stairs and through the living room, I opened the front door. I walked out to Dad's truck, Cole just a yard behind.

"You came in this?" He eyed the trailer bed, and maybe my brain made things up but he sounded concerned, as if I'd risked my life to come in such a contraption.

"This is what I brought for you." Unlatching the door to the trailer I opened the back, and waited for him to come close enough to see.

"You brought me wood?" He didn't sound like he was about to fall into my arms—he sounded confused.

At once this seemed like an outrageous, stupid idea. When would he see through my awkwardness and forgive me? When would he drop the wary expression and kiss me? Maybe he wouldn't.

Shaking my head, I swallowed my tears. "Not wood. I mean it is—they're baseboards. Eve and I thought we'd—well, it's nothing."

His eyes narrowed again as he stare at me.

Crossing my arms across my chest, I bowed my head and smeared the ground with my feet. "Nana died."

Hanging his own head, he sighed. "I'm really sorry, Sam." His brows pressed together and his face flushed. He looked miserable.

I had driven more than twenty hours. I had dozens upon dozens of poplar base boards in a trailer I had no business driving. I had a ring in my pocket. I hadn't come to leave with my pride. It wasn't pride I wanted. And maybe I wouldn't leave with Cole either—but I had to try. I had to live. So, I would at least leave with honesty.

"She left something for you." I closed the trailer and stepped toward him, making the physical gap between us smaller.

Jutting his head back, his eyes narrowed, confused again. "Really?"

Feeling peace for the first time since I'd arrived, I smiled and nodded, closing the gap a little more. Standing there in the street, I picked up his hand. Turning it over, I ran my hand over his fingers, opening them up to lay his palm flat. Reaching into my pocket, I pulled out Nana's ring and lay it in his cupped hand.

Beaming up at him, I gave it all I had. If I had to, I'd leave with nothing—nothing unsaid—nothing in my trailer—nothing left to give. "I love you, Cole. And she wanted the man I love to give this to me."

Tightening his fist around Nana's ring, his fingers turned a bright unforgiving white. Narrowing his eyes, he shook his head at the ground.

I would leave with nothing.

Lifting his head, he wiped at the tears falling down his cheeks. Letting out a breath I couldn't tell he'd been holding, he depleted the space between us. Wrapping his arms around my back, he scooped me up and held me against him.

Standing on tiptoes, I wrapped my arms around him and buried my face in his neck. "I'm sorry. I'm so—"

Shutting me up with a kiss, his arms tightened around me. Tears fell down both of our cheeks and I laughed, so thankful I had tried. I hadn't hidden or cowered or stood stagnant. I'd *lived*—and Cole loved me for it.

Pulling back, he opened his hand. Nana's ring glistened with the setting sun raining down on it. Spinning it onto my left ring finger, he kissed me. "You're not allowed to take this off. Ever."

Laughing, I gazed at Nana's band on my finger. "Never."

# *Epilogue*

*L*ying in bed, I turned to my husband. Somehow, he'd been mine for more than a year. Nana had been right about long engagements being overrated. Cole lay with his eyes closed from sleep, his breathing still and steady. Dad's guest bed didn't hold the same lumps or comfort as ours at the manor. My back hurt. Rolling over, I laid on my side, still looking at Cole. My stomach growled and I held onto my protruding belly. It wasn't enormous, but then I still had three months to go. Another thing I tried wrapping my brain around.

Rolling my whaleness over, I attempted to get out of bed, but Cole draped an arm over me, stopping my effort. Scooting toward me, I eased into the comfort of being next to him.

Holding me close, he rubbed my belly. "Don't go."

"Why not?"

"Because I need to make your birthday breakfast." He yawned, moving just an inch to kiss my temple.

"Ah, in that case, I will stay in bed."

Snuggling down, he gave me little hope for breakfast. "What would you two like this morning?"

"Hmm…" I ran my fingers over his arm. "I think Daniel Michelson would love some of his daddy's scrambled eggs," I said, trying out Cole's dad's name with Nana's last name and Mom's maiden name.

Sitting up onto his elbow, Cole grinned. "You're right. Daniel Michelson. It sounds good."

"I think so, too."

Daniel and Grace gave Cole to the world, and had it not been for Nana, I wouldn't have run away to California. It seemed fitting — it seemed perfect. Their combined efforts brought this child's parents together.

Cole left and I adjusted myself upright with three pillows behind my back.

Bringing in a tray with eggs, orange juice and a card, Cole sat next to me. "I wanted to give you a gift before the party — if that's okay."

Sitting up, I took the envelope from the tray. "Of course." My dumb pregnant eyes filled with tears at the message he wrote.

Grinning, he pointed to the envelope. "There's more."

Unfolding the catalog page inside, I started to giggle. "You're kidding — right?"

"It's already at the manor." He pointed to the jets on the picture of a big whirlpool tub. "It's from Mom and your dad, too."

"I love it." Holding his whiskered cheek, he leaned down so I could kiss him.

"So, thirty," he said, his face inches from mine. "How does it feel?"

Breathing in, I looked at my life, at what I'd done — at what I still planned to do. I gazed at Cole, seeing my present and future in his eyes. "Never better."